What People Are

The Unbroken

The Unbroken has a firm place in the great traditions of spiritual adventure and of enduring love. And it is a rattling good read. Yet far more than this, it is a book that encompasses many cultures and traditions in its narrative whilst offering the reader an entirely original understanding of human consciousness. This is at the same time challenging and joyful, disturbing and life-affirming. Even the book's unique structure intrigues as it resonates with our innate recognition of the beauty of nature. The author has devoted his life to the study of spirituality and this astonishing, beautifully written novel is his gift to us all.
Clifford White, composer of the much-loved *Ascension* and many other albums, and Creative Director of The Spiritual Arts Foundation, spiritualarts.org.uk

I love fiction that delves into spirituality, and Nigel has written an immensely readable novel brimming with wisdom. A brave and timely work which clearly demonstrates the author's knowledge of the great mysteries. Warmly recommended.
Malcolm Stern, psychotherapist, co-founder of Alternatives and author of the bestselling *Slay Your Dragons With Compassion*

The stories of Roy and Eva, independently, take the reader on an uplifting spiritual journey as, cleverly aided by the book's geometric pattern, the writer merges their different worlds. Truly, a novel that makes us wonder more deeply about the nature of things we take for granted, including religious and moral teachings and that indefinable entity... time. Definitely a "must read".
Oliver Eade, doctor and inaugural winner of the national Spiritual Writing Competition for *A Single Petal*

This is an important and intriguing novel, written beautifully. It deals with our concepts of consciousness and of reality, delving deep into the multiple layers of our perceptions and experiences. **Peter Walker**, author of the national prize-winning collection of spiritual verse, *The House of Being*

The Unbroken

A Novel

Other spiritual books by this author

Spirit Revelations (978-1-907203-14-5)
Signs of Life (978-1-907203-20-6)
Lighting the Path (978-1-907203-26-8)
Broken Sea (978-1-910027-23-3)
Blood (978-1-910027-45-5)

spiritrevelations.com

The Unbroken

A Novel

Nigel Peace

ROUNDFIRE
BOOKS

London, UK
Washington, DC, USA

CollectiveInk

First published by Roundfire Books, 2024
Roundfire Books is an imprint of Collective Ink Ltd.,
Unit 11, Shepperton House, 89 Shepperton Road, London, N1 3DF
office@collectiveink.com
www.collectiveink.com
www.roundfire-books.com

For distributor details and how to order please visit the 'Ordering' section on our website.

Text copyright: Nigel Peace 2023

ISBN: 978 1 80341 576 5
978 1 80341 592 5 (ebook)
Library of Congress Control Number: 2023909176

A CIP catalogue record for this book is available from the British Library.

Design: Lapiz Digital Services

UK: Printed and bound by CPI Group (UK) Ltd, Croydon, CR0 4YY
Printed in North America by CPI GPS partners

We operate a distinctive and ethical publishing philosophy in
all areas of our business, from our global network of authors to
production and worldwide distribution.

The light shines in the darkness,
and the darkness does not comprehend it.
John 1.5

And by the way, I didn't write my part of this story.
Apparently, everything is recorded... somewhere.
Eva x

Written with true gratitude to

Peter,
Vaishali,
Ash and John,
Hana, Jamie and Rubeo,
José Carlos, Mollie, Ron, Freddie and Nina

NOUGHT

ONE : ONE

In the beginning, there was nothing. It is the strangest thing imaginable, being aware of nothing. There was no ground, no surrounding, neither ceiling nor sky. Nothing above, beside or below. Even I was not there. No, the philosophers were wrong. Though I was aware of nothing, I was not. Can you conceive this? I am doing my best to tell you because you may experience this yourself someday and, when you think about it, you may be afraid. But I can tell you that there will be no fear, nor pain, because you will... you will not be.

I cannot say how long this lasted because there was nothing to measure time by, of course. Oh, it occurs to me now why it's foolish to speak of the origin of the universe, for in timelessness, in nothing, there is no first moment. This was somewhere else, beyond universes, or in some alternative one that none but the greatest mystics have known. Even so, they struggle, as do I, to describe it.

Yet I suppose I can say that it was... beautiful. Yes, nothing has real beauty.

Very, very gradually, I moved from nothing into something. And I remember feeling a sense of loss, of sadness, at having to leave nothing behind. Even though, there, I was not, and then I was beginning to be, to become, it had been the most beautiful place. Peace is not the right word, because that's a state of mind and there was no mind yet, but it's the best I can say. Anyway, by little increments I began to be aware of me.

I still had no form, no body as far as I could tell, and there was still total darkness and silence. I once visited a friend in Liberec, on the old Bohemian trade route, and spent a day hiking across the Ještěd-Kozákov Ridge. Towards evening — we had come prepared with warm clothes, food and strong torches — we came upon a large cave and excitedly explored it, going ever

3

deeper until we found a grotto. Water ran very quietly down the ancient rock walls before disappearing below. The air was fresh. Our torches picked out traces of copper, cobalt and perhaps silver in the rocks. And when we had poured hot drinks and turned off the torches, there was utter darkness and peace. That had been beautiful, and we had stayed as long as we dared, yet it was a poor imitation of what I now became aware of.

As if I were gradually becoming accustomed to the place, a kind of outline of my body emerged and, with it, I felt a dull, faraway pain where my head would be. There were, too, numerous to count, incredibly thin filaments like strands of a spider web streaming out from this body, sparkling in places along their length like our torches picking out the minute seams of silver. I can't say that I looked at them curiously, for I still had neither sight nor hearing nor touch, yet I sensed them and I sensed surprise, especially as a few began to detach themselves and float away to be lost beyond me, dissipating. 'Where have they gone?' I felt myself asking, rather than the more obvious 'What are they?'

And with that thought, probably my first thought in this new world, my surroundings were created as the darkness began to lift, like the vague shadows of trees and beasts in a valley below a mountain beyond which the morning sun has yet to rise. The silence, too, gave way to the soft murmurings of a gentle, cool breeze that carried on it moments of far distant sounds... the faint lowing of cattle, perhaps, the cry of a lapwing held back in its throat, a crack, a shout...

There was an impulse now, beyond my control, to move forward and so I drifted. No legs were involved, no muscles, no intention. Whatever I was becoming began to move and so did the shadows around me. Some of them faded away whilst others floated towards me, even looming up before me like great beasts inspecting this interloper to their kingdom. Yes, a few of them even seemed to have intelligence of a kind, if not faces or limbs, as though peering intently and moving around me, breaking off a few more of my light filaments. But there was no threat, I felt no fear, and one by one they drifted away into the twilight apparently satisfied.

Sounds began to grow, some deep rumbling disturbance like the depths of a volcano stirring into life, the rustling of a growing wind through the Bulovka as their birds take off at dawn with cries of greeting, the hooves of a running horse and — what was that? — the faint echo of Zelenka's *Missa Votiva*?

I missed the darkness and the silence, the nothing, as I now became part of this new landscape. I even tried to turn around and go back, but the gossamer filaments that held me there had all but disappeared. The dull ache in my head became more pronounced, too, so that I had little control of myself. My self. I had a self now, even a body of sorts, although it was ill-formed and shifting, almost transparent to my growing sight, just a kind of luminous energy I didn't recognise.

I moved faster. There were more shifting shadows that took on the vaguely recognisable shapes of people and animals, approaching one by one from all sides... a censorious-looking monk, a down-at-heel dog with straggly hair sniffing where my feet should be, a Templar knight with only one arm, a young woman in a dirty, ragged smock who seemed to leer scornfully close up to my face... Her laughter encircled me. The monk boomed something that seemed to make them all scatter. Yet I moved through them ever faster, untouched and unafraid, because now I was myself and I could see an end of the beginning.

Φ

When I was a child, perhaps seven years old, I became fascinated by the blind. There had been an old woman — she seemed old to me then — who would often walk in Mestsky Park near where we lived; she always wore dark glasses and carried a white stick. She seemed to have no trouble finding her way around. Yet what awful world is this, unable to see the blue sky, the trees and flowers, others' faces… unable to watch television or read a book? I couldn't imagine it. One of our teachers at school, I think it was Pan Černý, appropriately, told us that the brain receives ninety per cent of its information visually. So this old woman must have been really stupid, I thought, she must know almost nothing.

As I thought more about this, at first I became really sad for her and then really terrified that it might happen to me one day. So I began to practise finding my way around our house with my eyes closed and arms outstretched, bumping into furniture (and my mother), until I knew every part. I even progressed to pouring myself a glass of juice and dressing myself in the morning, although that didn't always go quite to plan.

What I didn't know, because no one ever told me, was that we have other senses besides the physical ones.

I mention this because, as the beginning ended, I left the monk and the dog and the ragged young woman behind to find myself once more in darkness and silence as though passing through a stage play into a new scene where the set hasn't yet been assembled, the rigs are unconnected and the players not yet called.

This place did not have the peace, the beauty, of the nothing.

I felt enclosed, though there were no walls, and I was still moving forward, though there was nothing beneath me. I had become myself but I could neither see nor feel my body except for that faraway dull pain that was getting more intrusive. For the first time, I began to feel a little fear, a loss of control that hadn't mattered before because it seemed meaningless. It was important now because I had become myself.

With fear comes heightened sense, of whatever kind, so gradually my body appeared as a soft, almost translucent glow with faint and minute luminescent flashes along my limbs. With these came more pain, beginning to grip and release in a musical rhythm, a fiendish dance.

And like that seven-year-old girl, instinctively I reached in front of me to feel the way, afraid of stumbling over nothing now, wishing above all else to touch something, but without an amused mother to give me clues. Did the old woman in Mestsky Park feel this aching loneliness too?

'Hold yourself together,' I heard myself tell myself. 'You're not a child anymore and you've been through scary times before — tanks in the streets, missing friends, police interviews. Remember being in love, and deciding to leave? You were strong then and got stronger, defied them all, the liars and the betrayers and bullies...'

These thoughts were rewarded by the sense that fingers were finding something in front of me, a spidery gossamer film that dissolved to the touch only to reform and envelop me in a gentle, moist embrace as I continued to move. And with my new senses and thoughts came the idea that perhaps after all I wasn't moving forward at all, since I had not willed it, but was entirely still and this strange new world was coming to meet me. It was intelligent, then, it had a purpose. Whether that might be benign or not, I couldn't tell.

And to be honest, I didn't really care. The fear simply lifted because there was nothing I could do about it. I would often stay on late at school, playing games with friends or kept in for extra work, and would have to walk home in the dark across the park and along our narrow avenue lined with trees and large bushes overhanging the pavement. The streetlamps didn't come on until later. There was always the terror lurking at the back of my mind of who, or what, monstrous beast might be lurking behind one of those bushes, intent on evil. Nothing ever happened, of course, but that's no consolation to naïvety. Then one day I said to myself, 'Look, you're a kid, you wouldn't be able to do anything about it anyway.' The fear instantly vanished and I was never afraid of the dark again.

The darkness and silence of this world was altogether different, yet still there was nothing I could have done. So I moved through the silky webs uncaring, though becoming ever more tired with the effort of parting the strands. Dimly, I began to see now that this was indeed a mist enfolding me, a mořská mlha drifting in on all sides, tangible yet vaporous and becoming ever more dense. Whatever sense I might have had of where I was, my place in nothing, disappeared. I gave myself up to it.

Far, far ahead, there must have been a light, I reasoned, because some kind of sight was returning and the mist was beginning to glow with the pure white of newly fallen snow. In fact, it was becoming more and more like the softest snow, gently moist and decidedly colder until it billowed into cumulus passing before a morning sun.

I wanted that light, I had to reach it, but now I was exhausted by everything, by the nothing, by not being and becoming, by the increasing pain and the effort of thought.

I gave up and simply allowed myself to fall into the cloud. Oh, that moment, if it was a moment, was beautful beyond description, like settling back into the softest imaginable mattress at the end of a hard day, and continuing to fall and to fall and to fall...

TWO

Suppose you went hiking one day and found yourself, after a huge effort, at the highest peak of the Krkonoše mountains or, say, on Snowdonia's Yr Wyddfa... heavens, how do I remember that name? Anyway, you're exhausted by the climb but also exhilarated and the thin air makes you feel light-headed. Strangely, all the other walkers you'd seen along the way have disappeared back home and you're now alone in this majestic nature. You take in the snow-covered volcanic rocks below, the late afternoon sunlight gleaming off the crystals as far as you can see. You open your arms and turn around with a new and numinous sense of what it means to be alive quietly growing within. And you know that life will never be the same again. You close your eyes to sense your inner being more fully and turn again, unconscious of your body, forgetting that you are standing right at the edge...

You fall and fall... If you are lucky, and your sense of being is true, your mind may let go of reason and your self may let go of its body, so that you feel nothing but the unutterable joy of freedom from everything you had cared about before, all the challenges that had weighed you down for so long and now seem utterly unimportant.

I fell slowly and peacefully through the cumulus until very gradually it began to thin out. I can't say that I enjoyed it because that would involve emotion, which hadn't returned yet, but the other side of that immaterial coin is that I could observe what was happening to me dispassionately, somehow knowing that on the other side there would be no harsh and abrupt rocky landing. And yes, I knew that I was free.

In fact, I simply emerged onto relatively solid ground — I mean, I now had some feeling in my lower body and a sense of beginning to learn how to walk again. There was no awareness of the majesty of nature as I could barely see my own hand in front of me, enveloped as I was in that soft and moist white mist that I had entered before. At least, it was not so cold and there ahead of me was that light, brighter now and clawing its way through the swirls of vapour as though parting one net curtain after another.

Sometimes, when you're on a train in a station, you may glance out of the window as another train glides in. For a few moments, everything is still and other faces look back at you and smile. Then there's a silent movement, but you can't tell which train has resumed its journey… Was I walking towards that light or was it coming forward to embrace me? It didn't matter, I just wanted it. So I put one hesitant foot in front of the other and tried to get a feeling of what this place was and of my part in it.

'My part'? Yes, I was beginning to know that I was someone I could call 'me' even though my body was still translucent, the mist gently passing through it, and my head still light except for that persistent dull pain that had never moved. A few of those gossamer threads still clung to my outline with a faint drag as I moved, but one by one they detached and dissolved as I inspected my form — and formlessness — with great curiosity. Hmm, this was new: or had I somehow always been this?

I began to pick up the pace, feeling something swirl around my feet like long grasses or perhaps small animals playing with this strange, lumbering invader of their territory, all the while the mist thinning out and the light becoming warmer. My senses, of whatever kind I couldn't say, were beginning to return yet still remaining just out of reach, like the garden birds that are wary of you even though you put food out for them every day. They didn't know what I might do with them here and couldn't take the risk of getting too close. To be fair, I couldn't be sure that I could trust myself either, so better just to let things take their course.

The beach was a surprise.

Having walked ever more assuredly for timeless ages, sometimes stumbling over stones and hillocks, my eyes adjusting to the greens and greys around my feet, I suddenly found myself apparently on soft sand. It glistened, silvery, and yielded to my steps leaving traces of water in their prints. And not far away, though still shrouded to my eyes, was the faint but unmistakable sound of gently lapping waves.

For the first time since the beginning, I asked myself, 'Where am I?' This was no longer the dreamlike journey; I had arrived in a real place. And with that arrival, as though I had been using every milligram of strength I possessed to get here, I suddenly felt incredibly tired. Literally. Any shred of comprehension that I had carefully nurtured during the long walk now disappeared and exhaustion flooded through me as though the dam of human resilience had been breached by some great and terrible storm.

Yet a small candle flame of energy deep inside told me I must keep going, I could still escape the onslaught, there was somewhere I needed to get to. One foot in front of the other. One arm forward then the other. Head held high scanning the way as some primaeval instinct moved me along that beach, neither knowing nor caring if this were the right direction. Stumbling, sinking in, pausing to check that candle, trying again, and fighting off the pain that was now throbbing in my head.

It was the right direction. And at last I was not alone.

A small, strange-looking craft with stubby wings sat on the beach a little way ahead, waves of light reflected from the water flowing over its silvery body so that it was almost indistinguishable from the sand. And next to it, so it seemed to my dull mind, stood an angel in a white trouser suit and incongruous red high-heeled shoes. 'Hardly appropriate for the seaside,' I thought briefly, but then what did I know about anything anymore. She was very tall, with long blonde hair that flowed around her shoulders and a slim, boyish figure. As I approached, ever more slowly, she smiled a beautiful welcome and her eyes opened wide. One was blue, the other green, or perhaps I'm making that up.

"Well, you took your time." Her lips didn't move but I heard the quiet, teasing words anyway. "I've been waiting ages, or so it seems."

By now, my flame was fluttering weakly, almost burnt out, and I could barely stand. And even if I'd had the energy to speak, I wouldn't have known what to say. A door opened silently in the side of the craft and she helped me inside, wrapped a blanket around me and settled me in a seat at the back, locking a belt in place across my lap.

"There'll be a bit of turbulence," I heard her say as I finally gave in to the tiredness and closed my eyes, "but nothing to worry about. You just rest and we'll be there before you know it."

Worry? I simply didn't have any choice in the matter. Not for the first time, I gave up and allowed it all to happen.

With the faintest sense of movement, the door closed, my new friend went forward to sit up front and the craft silently lifted off the beach. Was she controlling this thing? And in those shoes? The last thing I remember for a while was her eyes smiling at me in the rear view mirror.

I slept deeply, disturbed only by fragmentary scenes from dark, thankfully fleeting, dreams of walking among friends across Karlův Most towards grey-coated soldiers levelling Kalashnikovs at us. One boy got up defiantly next to the statue of the saint Johánek z Pomuka but they shot him. As his body fell to the Vlatava, the craft lurched and dropped, shaking me awake.

"Kam jdeme?" I mumbled, not at all sure which language was suitable for this situation, but it didn't matter because the answer came back clearly.

"We're going to the island. They'll look after you there in the hospital. You'll soon be on your way."

I wasn't aware of being on my way anywhere but that didn't seem important just now. Being looked after sounded good, though. I looked out of the window to see through the persistent fine mist a great expanse of calming pale blue all around us, below and above, so I couldn't tell if it was sea or sky or both at the same time. There was that light again, much brighter now and shining from... somewhere... glinting on patches of powder blue and dancing from one misty edge to another, the only clue that we were indeed moving through it all.

"Where is this island? What's it called?"

"It's just the island. Doesn't need to have a name. But it seems to remind people of places they think they know so I've heard it called everything from Maui to Okinawa to Zakynthos. The last chap I picked up said everything is blue so that's what he was going to call it. It isn't, of course."

I didn't really need a rhetorical conversation at this point but my mind was beginning to wake up and never did like loose ends.

"It isn't what?"

"Blue."

That didn't really help. But whatever it was, the nameless island was now coming into view, at first a small, darker anomaly on the featureless scene outside like a coffee stain on favourite curtains, then rapidly revealing itself to have a rocky shoreline edging yellow sandy bays and an interior mountain covered in dark green forest. As we circled, I could make out a patchwork of paths around the perimeter.

But before I could get a proper sense of the place we were down, landing silently on a grassy strip and almost immediately coming to a stop near a low and unprepossessing wooden building. There were no steel fences, no gates, no name (of course) and no signs — not even the ubiquitous Coca Cola advertisement — and no guards.

My pilot stood up and was by my side, releasing the seatbelt and helping me to shrug off the blanket as I got up unsteadily. I was now aware of my own body at last, a bit fragile but everything seemed to be in the right place and doing its best to cooperate. I was wearing a soft, fawn leather jacket over a thin green blouse, and pale blue jeans with black ankle boots. The woman smiled again and took my arm, helping me to the door and out into the fresh air, warm and salty on my face.

I stood for a moment, bewildered, then turned to thank her. But she and her craft were nowhere to be seen. Instead, there was another figure now standing beside me, again tall and fair, dressed in white chinos and a loose, short-sleeved white shirt with some kind of colourful badge on the breast pocket that I couldn't make out. A snake, perhaps? I reasoned that this person was male, since he had a short beard of fine white hair, but he spoke in the same gentle musical tones as my pilot.

"Hello, Eva. Please follow me. Are you okay to walk?"

I nodded, too surprised to answer because I was trying to compute the fact that apparently I had a name. And that I was expected.

We walked slowly towards the — what, terminal? — and foolishly I found myself searching my pockets for a passport. I only found some tissues, a packet of chocolate peanuts and a small bunch of keys. So at least it wouldn't take long to get through Customs.

THREE

The young man shuffles slowly along Oxford Road, the Lancashire night wind whipping up newspaper and discarded takeaway packages around his feet. Black jeans are tucked into thick woollen socks at the ankle, the pockets of a blue Air Force surplus greatcoat bulge, one with a bottle, and a black woolly hat is pulled down low over his ears and long, tangled brown hair. His arms are folded, hands thrust into opposite sleeves. He's a shambles. His eyes are downcast, the rest of his face lost beneath an unkempt, straggling beard.

A few minutes from the university, traditions end and relics begin: relics of the industrial revolution and of community, relics a hundred yards long with thirty doors, row upon row of relics. And, as the casual observer may think, smelly relics with arms and legs.

He pauses beneath the halo of a streetlamp to pull out his left hand and squint at a silver watch reflecting in the light. Realising he's late, he sets off at a lope until at last he meets the glare of the precinct lights.

"Hurry yourself, mate. There'll be none left."

The duty constable's greeting is rough but friendly. He wishes he were almost anywhere else, preferably warm at home with a hot chocolate in front of the TV, but then everyone at the station has to take their turn on this shift. It's just in case. Nothing much ever happens, of course, maybe an argument or two and some choice language before finally everyone gets moved on to someone else's patch. But the constable is a bit surprised tonight to have been joined by a tall, fair-haired man in a dark suit and grey raincoat who flashed a warrant card and introduced himself as Inspector Peter Jones.

"Just keeping an eye open, Constable," he'd said as he melted back into the shadows of a doorway. He stands there silently and has said nothing more. Still, it's not a constable's job, or inclination, to question his superior officers.

There's a battered white Transit van parked half on the pavement and the air is full of steam and quiet chatter around the short queue formed by its open rear doors. A nearby church has begun to spill out its sparse Vespers congregation and a few on their way to warm homes pause to stare at the shabby creatures with their bowls and bottles. But not for long.

The young man settles himself slowly, as though in pain, onto a wooden bench and waits, refusing to join the queue. Jonno watches him arrive with quick, curious glances from the corners of his guarded gimlet eyes. Nothing about Jonno is ever still. His eyebrows arch and his thin lips curl as he edges along the pavement like a sparrow after crumbs and sits at the other end of the bench, chewing on his soup with yellowed teeth before taking a piece of dry crust from his pocket to scrape the bowl.

"You's 'ere agin, then," he observes, eyes switching back and forth between the bowl and the new arrival. There's no response. "Thought you wasn't goin' to mek it tonight."

Jonno doesn't have what you'd call friends. Nor does he have any family, not that he knows about anyway. The streets have been his life for as long as he can remember, which admittedly isn't far since his mind is generally clouded by rough cider. Yes, there had been Tom, they'd been on sort-of speaking terms. But Tom never said much and anyway he was dead now. Still, Jonno is not unfriendly and he is observant, which is why he tries again with the young man.

"You's new 'ere, then? An' you's a stoodent, 'int you?" There's no response, perhaps because everything he's said so far is obvious. The young man's greatcoat looks almost new with several fresh streaks of dirt on it and he's wearing good sound shoes rather than the cloth and string-bound reject boots that are the common uniform in these parts.

A couple of innocent-faced young men are moving around the precinct collecting up the bowls and exchanging a few words with each pile of rags. Jonno obediently holds out his bowl to one of them, whose brow furrows as he looks across at the other before returning to the van and having an urgent whispered conversation with a raven-haired girl who has bright blue eyes and large breasts struggling to stay within an inappropriate dress that's far too thin for an early October evening in Manchester. She scrapes the last of the congealed green soup from the tureen, ladles it into a plastic bowl and brings it over to the bench.

"Sorry, that's all there's left," she says, watching the young man closely as he takes it without a word, head still bowed. "Um... aren't you Roy?" There's no response. She walks back slowly, shaking her head and whispering again to the others.

"'Ere," says Jonno when his companion has finished, offering him a whole cigarette. This is gold dust and a true act of friendship, because he recognises that there is something strange and dark about this young man. "Look as what I found. Tek it, goo on. I got more."

He takes out another one and inspects it ritually, holding it up to the light of the Chemist's window and sniffing it as though it's a glass of Bordeaux '58. Roy nods his thanks and they light up, Jonno nearly bending double wheezing before inspecting the cigarette again with obvious appreciation. He's clearly going to have to make the running with this conversation.

"Bloody youniversiplace stoodents, eh?" he spits, watching with distaste as the Transit belches blue smoke and shakes away. "Does this outta conscience, innit." He rocks forward with a hissing laugh like a deflating balloon and doesn't notice that his new friend has got up and walked away.

The constable pads around the benches and raised redbrick flowerbeds now, urging the homeless bundles to move on — anywhere as long as it's not here — and wishing with all his heart that he wasn't police. Bums and students, wastes of space. But at least he can soon head off back to the station for the day's final paperwork. Within a few minutes everyone is merging back into the heavy black void from which they've come. It's a darkness that somehow clings like fog and gets into your pores. And Inspector Jones seems to have disappeared too.

Roy shuffles slowly back along Rusholme's curry mile, retreating into doorways to avoid the noisy knots of students, then waits quietly outside Alan's Plaice for the kind Asian owner to bring him out a bag of chips and a couple of old newspapers. He nods his thanks and is on his way again, coat collar pulled up tight against the wind, before carefully climbing through the gap in the railings of Platt Fields.

He sits on the bench at the far side of the lake beneath the overhanging oaks and silently watches darkness fall for the next hour, his thoughts many hundreds of miles away yet still fighting on the frontline of memory. Eventually, exhausted by the conflict, his brain shuts down. The newspapers are wrapped around him inside the coat and he lies along the bench, instantly asleep.

"Summer's gone, then, mister."

He opens one bleary eye to see the young girl standing a couple of feet away and observing him closely. It's morning, although if the sun has risen it's yet to make much progress through the heavy grey clouds. Still, the park is waking up and on the other side of the lake the lights of the café are shining a bright welcome. A couple of dog walkers and mothers with pushchairs are doing the rounds.

The girl is about eight or nine, thin and short for her age, wearing a torn grey anorak over a colourful but streaked floral dress, short white socks and black trainers with red flashes on the side. The toe cap of the left one is flapping loose. Curly black hair peeps from the edges of her hood.

A fine drizzle from the leafy canopy above drips onto the young man's face and he eases himself up to a sitting position, rubbing his eyes. Somehow, this girl is demanding attention.

"Totally," he agrees. "A while ago."

She tries again, gesturing to the water.

"Do you think there's any fish in there?"

"I doubt anything could survive long in that. Even the ducks spend all their time on the pavement, walking round like people."

"I had one once."

"What, you had a pet duck?"

"You're daft, a goldfish."

"Doesn't every kid?"

"Maybe. Blackie were special."

"You called your goldfish Blackie?" This is the longest conversation he's had for many days and he's not quite prepared for it to be turning surreal.

"You can call a fish what you like. It can't hear you. Anyway, Blackie were my friend. I won her at the fair. I spent hours watching her go round and round and I'm sure she smiled at us every time she came past."

"That's nice." He stretches his arms and shoulders as a long yawn takes over his face.

"Am I boring you? Well, I saved up the money from my paper round and bought her some plastic shells and snails and things. Everything her little fishy heart could want. Do fish have hearts?"

"I guess so."

"Funny thing, mister, she always swam the same way round. Like, left to right round the back then right to left at the front."

"Clockwise."

"So I tried sprinkling the ants' eggs a few at a time the other way. To see if she'd swim unclockwise."

"Interesting. What happened?"

"Oh, she died."

"Sorry about that."

"Why? It weren't your fault. Budge up, then."

He shifts himself, limbs and back aching, to one side and she settles down at the other end of the bench, her feet barely reaching the ground. A young mother pauses nearby to smile at them as her toddler excitedly tosses small pieces of bread to the half dozen ducks gathered at the water's edge.

"You shouldn't do that, missus," says the girl. "It's bad for 'em. They need seed. Or corn." The woman glares at her and gathers up her child, moving on quickly. "Grown-ups don't like the truth, do they, mister?" the girl observes, looking straight at him with wide, pale brown eyes shaded with a touch of sadness.

"Mmm, maybe not. You seem to know a lot. Where did you read that?"

"Can't read. I just listen."

He stands up to move his arms and legs for a minute but catches a worried look on the girl's face so sits back down. Some company seems the most important thing at the moment. The ducks have tried to follow the mother and her child along the paving for a while, wondering why their breakfast, however unhealthy, has been interrupted but have given up now and are nosing about in an overgrown, dying flowerbed for whatever can be found. Across the lake, Mary, the café owner, can be seen closing the door behind her and walking purposefully around the perimeter. She is middle-aged and her hair is tied back in a net and she wears a full-length apron over jeans and a red sweater. She looks at the girl quizzically but says nothing, nodding to Roy and handing him a carton of coffee and two rounds of cheese and tomato sandwiches wrapped in paper. He nods too as he takes them and she strides back the way she came. The girl's eyes open wide.

"Wow, you're lucky, mister. Summun's looking after you."
The same thought had begun to occur to him. "Does she know you, then?"

"Used to," he mumbles, his mouth full of sandwich.

"Gi'us some, then."

She's looking at him expectantly and holds out a hand. He hesitates, but only for a moment. When you're hungry, you recognise others' hunger. She takes it without a word, peels back the bread to check the filling and carefully picks out the pieces of tomato, tossing them towards the ducks. He opens his mouth to object but thinks better of it. Nobody's perfect. They lapse into silence as they eat, the girl taking tiny bites and chewing thoroughly to make it last as long as possible.

Slowly, their bodies begin to warm up. He finishes the sandwich and notices that the girl is still eking hers out until it's barely crumbs. Without thinking, he delves deep into an inside pocket of the greatcoat for the packet of Bourbons he was given yesterday and passes it over to her. She immediately puts it in an anorak pocket and her lopsided smile briefly lights up the shadows beneath the oaks.

He checks his watch.

"Shouldn't you be in school?"

"Shouldn't you be in college?"

It's a fair point. But events have gone far beyond shoulds and shouldn'ts, that curious collective morality by which we all live and that makes us believe we're at least as good as the next man.

When the storm hits there are basically two ways of responding. There are those who belong to what they like to call a community, and they rally round to cry on one another's shoulders and set up a food bank in the local primary school and clear the pews of the church to make space for sleeping bags. For the independent others it's every man for himself, taking what you need and avoiding the cloying crowd of victim emotion.

Eventually, as the food runs out and the insurance companies claim acts of God and refuse to pay out, most of the first group begin to drift away too. Collective decisions are often disastrous, as people prefer to cling onto their status as members of the group rather than heed their own minds. A group of friends drove out to a cabin in the woods for a weekend one winter, only to find themselves snowed in next morning with the phone lines down. They made a committee decision to try and hike back home but none of them made it alive. When rescuers reached the cabin they found notes left by the friends, nearly every one of them expressing personal disagreement with the decision to leave.

Roy has a family and some friends. But none of them know that he's snowed in.

"So won't your mother be worried about you?"

"Nope. She'll still be asleep. Too spaced out to notice. That's what they call it, i'n't it? Heroin."

"I'm sorry."

"'S not your fault."

"Wouldn't you be safer in school, then? You'd be warm there. And the teachers would look after you."

"You haven't met my teachers. Anyway, told you, I can't read. What about you, then, mister?"

"Yes, I can read."

"You're daft. I meant what're you doing here making the place untidy? That's what my Nana Dorothy would of said. You don't look like the others."

"Other what?"

"Bums."

"Is that what I am? Yeah, s'pose so. Didn't always do this, just made a bad decision."

The girl retreats into silence for a couple of minutes, apparently thinking this over carefully, then her face comes to life again as she seems to remember something.

"Not sure you can do that, mister. Like, whatever it was you decided was whatever you had to decide at the time. Can't be good or bad, just is."

"But decisions have conseq... I mean, things happen as a result."

"That's not down to you, though, is it? It's all made up in advance."

"Don't you think your mother's decision to do heroin was a bad decision? It hasn't been good for you, has it?"

The girl shrugs and spreads her hands.

"The state she were in — everything that were going on — maybe she didn't decide. It just happened. And she weren't interested in us before, anyway."

"I'm sor... I mean, that's sad." He frowns, fully awake now that this child has got the attention of his clouded mind more than anything else has lately. "And look, what do you mean 'It's all made up in advance'?"

She stands up now and faces him, adopting the mock pose of teacher with a serious expression.

"It's what my Nana Dorothy told me. In the war, she worked at that code place with computers. Do you know about them?"

"Yeah, I had to do some programming when I... last year. So your Nana was at Bletchley Park?"

"That's the place. There were this man there called Two Rings and he made a computer what could work out every possible Jerry code."

"Colossus."

"Yeah, it were big all right. Then he made another one, Nana said, that could play chess, with all the moves anyone could think of. So when you played it, everything were worked out ahead of you. You could of decided something else but it didn't matter what move you tried."

"So everything's planned out already for us?"

"Dur, don't be daft, mister. You still make your own mind up, don't you? You just don't know what's going to happen next. You just decide something what seems right at the time."

He smiles for the first time in weeks.

"Your Nana Dorothy sounds like a nice woman. She taught you well. Can't she look after you, I mean, if your mother—"

"She died. Driving too fast."

"I'm sor... that's bad."

The girl spreads her arms as though that's all she's got for today and turns on her heels to set off back towards the café.

"Anyway, got friends to meet now. 'Spect I'll see you again, Roy."

"'Bye... Hey, how do you know—"

But she's disappearing along the path so he turns back to the ducks and the pale northern sun now breaking through and reflecting on the dark water of the lake. His head hurting a little, he waits twenty minutes then sets off to walk the Manchester streets.

FIVE

There weren't any Customs. Nor were there any stern, cold-eyed officials demanding to know the purpose of my visit. We simply walked through the cool building to a sleek, silver vehicle waiting outside at the entrance with yet another blonde woman in a white suit at the wheel. The man with the musical voice, the one who named me, opened the rear door with a flourish and when I turned back to thank him had, of course, disappeared. (In time, I would remember the streets of Prague after the Russians came and how people kept disappearing, but this was altogether stranger.)

The vehicle moved off silently and there again was a smile in the rear-view mirror, but nothing was said. A little person inside me wanted to ask all sorts of questions but, like that toddler, I just allowed myself to be led. In any case, the tiredness was overtaking me again with the smooth motion. The narrow dirt road was fringed on both sides by tall overhanging trees that all but cut out the light along with any clue about my new surroundings.

The pain in my head was getting worse.

There were several sharp turns and steep inclines along this leafy tunnel until, with a blast of light that hurt my eyes and a rush of cool wind through my open window, we emerged. As far as I could tell, we seemed to be travelling over a well-worn track across common land, near a border of tall grasses dotted with brightly coloured flowers. I couldn't see much ahead until, out of the mist, loomed a tall wooden archway over double gates flanked on each side by broken down rustic fences. There were no signs anywhere to identify the place. Somehow it occurred to me that this was a decisive moment.

The gates opened.

We came to a stop beside the front doors of an incongruously modern-looking low building, long and whitewashed, beside which stood a woman in nurse's uniform. She wore a dark blue cotton shift tied with a simple fabric belt at the waist and it had that snake-like badge on one breast pocket. She looked middle-aged, with greying hair tied back beneath a small white cap; she was tall and upright with a fearsome expression, in stark contrast to the friendly faces I'd met so far. The door of the vehicle opened by itself and I levered myself out.

"I'm Sister Nora," she said curtly. "I'll show you to your room."

I recognised the Irish accent as a memory fragment surfaced in my brain of when I travelled to Liverpool to improve my English and worked in a hospital kitchen where I'd made friends with Nurse Mallory. (Yes, all right, I realised the irony of dealing with all those voices, once I had learned the special meaning of British irony.) As I entered the hospital — surely that's what this building was — her lilting voice came back to me calling from far away.

"Holy Mary, you can't go on like this, so you can't."

But I didn't have a choice, not being in charge of my feet that were tentatively following Sister Nora along a completely featureless white corridor. We turned once or twice and then were at the end. The room was light and airy and actually quite homely. In fact, it was more than that. With another rush of awareness — they were coming fast now — I saw with a comforting flush that it was almost identical to my own bedroom back home in Trutnov that looked out over the rooftops to the wooded foothills of the Krkonoše Mountains. I grew up in that room, my private place, and as a child spent hours sitting at the window watching the hook-beaked red kites circle lazily in the distance, looking for supper, as a few wispy clouds drifted across an otherwise clear sky. I had yearned for their freedom, knowing my place was not here.

This room had a large open window too. The building seemed to be high up on a promontory overlooking what I took to be the sea, pale blue and shimmering in the ever-present light. I strained my eyes for kites but the only movement I saw in the distance was the small craft with stubby wings and waves of light flowing over its silvery body as it flashed away from the island like a shooting star.

I turned back and looked carefully around the room. Yes, there's the wooden shelf my father had made, with some of the childhood books I could never bear to let go of. There's the oak chest of drawers and the glass display case above it showing off my collection of gymnastics medals. I was never going to be among the best and the club had dropped me anyway when my breasts started to grow, but I'd loved the training. It made me strong. Aaaah... I saw myself now doing a cartwheel on some beach as a young man walked towards me holding an ice cream and the image made the pain throb harder deep within my head.

Sister Nora had waited patiently as I looked around — perhaps she was kinder than she appeared — and then left, saying only, "Have a rest, Eva. And I suggest you get yourself cleaned up."

I watched her go and rubbed my eyes with incomprehension because, quite clearly, there was no door in this room. Just walls. I didn't have the energy to worry about that now. A lot of things could wait.

I hadn't thought that I needed to clean myself but when I went over to the mirror above the small wash basin in the corner I didn't recognise myself. Why had nobody else pointed out the streaks of dirt and congealed blood? I eased myself out of the fawn leather jacket, let it fall to the floor and kicked off the ankle boots, then washed myself with the large bar of coal tar soap put out for me next to a blue bath towel.

I sat down heavily on the bed, one hand touching with surprise my worn, patched-up, limp rabbit doll, Králi. I had a friend.

As sleep overcame me, I took another look around the room. There was my wardrobe and the small bedside table, its top drawer partly open. Within I could see a blue airmail envelope with a foreign postmark. It could wait. The light gradually dimmed and my eyes closed.

Dreaming is one of the great mysteries of being human and I think it's right to say that nobody is quite sure what it is and why we do it. But someone, a student I think, once told me with great confidence that there are four kinds of dream and we all go through that cycle every time we sleep. The first kind, reasonably enough, is when our brains revisit all the things that have happened recently, deciding how important they are and whether they're worth storing away. These dreams are usually chaotic compared with the review that comes next, looking back at old memory files, throwing some of them away and connecting others with more recent experiences.

This is all routine organisation that sounded way too logical to me because the only dreams I would ever remember were the ones that woke me up sweating and with heart pounding because my mind wanted to tell me something important that I needed to know. Naturally, I could never work out what it was. I suppose that's why I kept getting them. I can't remember what the fourth kind was except that this guy used a phrase that's always stuck in my head, 'a dip into the inner stream of consciousness.' Yes, he was that kind of guy.

I say all this because the dreams I had in that room were almost nothing like what he'd said. (By the way, a lot of these memories only came back to me much later; in the hospital I could barely think let alone do psychology.) No, they were just fragments snatched from another life — I don't even know if it was mine — that were unconnected and meant nothing to me then, although they stayed swimming around my inner stream like shoals of inquisitive fish long afterwards until someone else helped me put them together.

FIVE

There was one where I felt myself moving very slowly through darkness with numerous, incredibly thin filaments like strands of a spider's web streaming out from my body as huge shadows loomed up in front as though inspecting me. So yes, I think that was a recent experience yet somehow it wasn't a memory; I was actually reliving it in full. And it had nothing to do with me walking along a grassy bank beside the Úpa River and slowly opening a letter with a foreign postmark, or with watching a young woman sitting across an office desk to a large slug who was drinking vodka as she fingered a Tokarev TT-33 semi-automatic pistol on her lap.

Often I would wake briefly after one of these episodes to find the pillow damp beside my face and new pains running through all different parts of my body as though I'd swallowed large eels that were desperately searching every limb for a way out.

This sleeping was not what you'd call restful. And these dreams, rather than organising my brain, seemed to be breaking it into dozens of pieces each with an indecipherable label.

I cannot say how long this went on because night and day didn't mean much. When I was awake the light outside was bright and then it would dim when I felt tired. When I was awake I walked around the room trailing my patched-up rabbit doll and touching the familiar things with pleasure. In the wardrobe, I discovered a few of my old clothes, all thin and summery, along with my blue canvas shoes and small leather holdall.

Despite the pain, my body felt increasingly light and for all that had been happening I wasn't hungry. Yet each time I awoke, I found a tray had been left on the floor for me where the door should have been. It was usually something like toasted vánočka bread with cooked tomatoes and mushrooms and a tall glass of sparkling water. A few bites were usually enough for me although the water was delicious.

I was sitting on the edge of the window, scanning the water below for the pelican I'd seen drift past elegantly soon after

I arrived, when the door opened — it was back again — and Sister Nora came in. It was the first time I'd seen her since she brought me here. There was the faintest crease in her face that might perhaps have been a smile.

"You can go now, Eva."

I sat on the end of the bed staring at her. What place was this? She was unmoved.

"I don't understand, Sister. I haven't... I mean, no one's... not even a doctor."

"The doctor has seen you. You're free to be on your way, so you are."

"But... I don't know where I am. I haven't anywhere to go."

"There'll be a place for you, always is. You'll find it."

"My head still hurts."

"Well, it would, wouldn't it?"

And she turned on her heels and left. I didn't see her again or, indeed, anyone else as I put a few things in the holdall, slipped into my boots and jacket and wandered down the long white corridor and out of the front doors that closed behind me by themselves. Growing up in a communist regime, you're accustomed to calmly doing as you're told; the rebel within objects but it knows better than to raise its voice and it bides its time. The opportunity will always come eventually, because there will be others working together in underground shadows to create an escape route. You may not know them, you may never meet them, yet they will get you where you need to be.

One thing was certain, I was not going to go back the way I came. So I followed the broken down fence that surrounded the building, which seemed even longer now than when I first saw it, going on and on, white and windowless, along the cliff top until it stopped abruptly and a dirt path appeared heading into woodland.

I clambered over a stile and along the track before turning down a sharp incline beneath a rocky overhang. A hundred metres or so further on there was a rushing of water tumbling down along a deep gash in the hillside and crashing over nearby rocks that looked like carved faces. The path was muddy now and I picked my way ever so slowly, my body aching, over gnarled roots and piles of wet leaves, climbing again to emerge on a wide sandy-coloured bank in the heart of the wood. There was a huge white cedar with five trunks and branches outstretched, commanding the area, whilst smaller trees at the fringe of the clearing were all bending over to one side like stooping old men. Grateful for the penetrating tranquillity of this spot, I rested on a large grey rock to gather my thoughts until my feet told me it was time to move on.

It was all downhill from there. Leaving the treeline, I saw that I was at the coast skirting a little bay where the pelican was perched on a jetty, turning its head to watch me as I passed. Someone once told me that pelicans never die of old age because the continuous diving into saltwater for their food eventually damages their eyes so much that they can't hunt and then just starve. The very skill that makes them successful is also their greatest weakness. Now, much later, I can remember people like that. Anyway, there was certainly nothing wrong with this one's eyes, boring into me with questions I couldn't answer.

I was moving faster than I expected to be able to. It was as though as soon as I noticed something up ahead through the mist I was almost there. I didn't see anyone else, but occasionally vague people-shapes passed silently through my peripheral vision. So the young girl was a surprise.

Solid as me, she looked about eight or nine, thin and short for her age, wearing a colourful but streaked floral dress, short white socks and white trainers with red flashes on the side. The toe cap of the left one was flapping loose. She was dark-skinned with long black hair in braids falling around her shoulders and she sat on a wooden bench at the side of the path with her legs barely reaching the ground. Behind her was a tumbledown wooden shack with an assortment of long cotton dresses and blouses on rails outside under a canopy.

The girl was nibbling very slowly at a large apple, watching me approach with wide brown eyes unmistakably touched with sadness.

"Hello," I said, "I'm Eva. What's your name?" She carried on nibbling as she inspected me. "Um, is this your shop?"

"Don't be daft, Miss. It ent a shop, you can take what you want. Same as there." She jerked a finger over her shoulder towards another shack a little further on with piles of fruit laid out on a trestle in front. At the moment, I wasn't really up for a surreal conversation so I just tried to be friendly.

"Does your Mum know you're here on your own?"

"Mum's not around."

"Oh, I'm sorry."

"Not your fault, Miss. Looks like you'se new here, yeah?"

"Yes... and... and I don't really know where I am, to be honest."

"They all say that. 'S no sweat, you'll work it out."

"Right. Only I was told there's a place for me—"

"'S right."

"—and I have no idea where that is."

"There's always somewhere, Miss, ent there? Like my Granny says, it's all worked out ahead." She jumped down from the bench and walked slowly around me with arms folded, perhaps deciding whether I was worthy of her continuing. "Whatever you decide doesn't matter."

I was taken aback. People always knew me, even if they didn't like it, as someone who made up their own mind — leaving for Prague, my first lover, Liverpool and all that. Now this pint-sized, very self-assured and philosophical girl was telling me that none of it meant anything.

"So everything's planned out already?"

"Dur, don't be daft, Miss. You'se still making up yer own mind, ent you, what seems right at the time."

"I see." I didn't, of course. "Well, I'd better be on my way... see where I get to."

"Yeah. Got any biscuits?"

"Sorry, no."

With a sideways glance at the strange shacks, I headed on along the dusty track that was hugging the shoreline, hearing the girl's last exasperated words to herself drifting on the breeze from behind me.

"Grown-ups don't like the truth," she observed quietly. I turned to smile at her but there was no one there.

It didn't take long to find the path. Or maybe it found me. It was just there and I turned left onto it. Every so often there were some rough white stone steps then a hard earthen slope before more steps — always groups of seven — and so on, winding upwards and deeper into a forest of mainly mahogany that formed arches above my head until finally I came to a real arch. These were beginning to be a bit of a theme already in my new experience and would continue to do so, each signalling a new move. This one was two thick wooden upright branches with a simple rough timber crossbeam and it had probably once been painted dark green. It was now pretty dilapidated although the latch on the low gate below it still worked.

A tall neem stood just to one side like a sentinel, its branches spread widely and dark foliage drooping white, fragrant flowers. A pair of small orioles observed me from a low branch, their breasts ablaze with orange and yellow, discussing me in soft, fluty tones. Around its base were soft yellow buxifolia bushes interspersed with rondeletia, the vibrant pink, pentagonal flowers the brightest things I had seen since arriving on the island, lifting my heart. How did I know what all these things were? They were certainly not native to the Polish border region. Their names just came into my mind, as though they were introducing themselves to me.

They formed the welcome to a broad craggy rock on which I could just make out a wooden cabin up ahead, on low stilts for leveling. To either side, the rock dropped away sheer. This castle even had its own moat of sorts, with clear, fresh water rushing from the heights beyond along a channel beside the building before disappearing over the edge.

It had been relatively easy to make the climb up here, almost unconscious of my limbs, but as I approached the cabin along a gravel path the tiredness was starting to overtake me again and, sure enough, the light to dim. It was not locked. I pushed open the lower part of the stable door, hardly caring by now — and definitely not fearing — what, or who, I may find inside.

It was pleasantly cool and almost empty, as I could see by the low light that filtered through several small leaded windows, and hadn't been inhabited for quite a while to judge by the dust that covered almost every surface and floated in the narrow beams from outside.

I think it was at this moment that I realised the mist that had followed me inside was in my own eyes.

There was a small wooden table with one dining chair, another more comfortable but threadbare armchair in one corner, a familiar-looking oak chest of drawers and a bed, made up with sheets and enclosed by a canopy of transparent fine white netting. On the table sat a small, fresh writing pad and a sharpened pencil — an invitation if ever I saw one — and a bowl of fruit. I stood still, trying to take it all in, the whys and the wheres filling my head, until... there was a small wooden shelf halfway up one wall with three of my favourite childhood books lying there. I fingered *Brigáda v Mateřské Škole* by Olga Štruncová fondly.

So, yes, this place was mine.

I dropped the holdall, draped my jacket over the chair taking Králi out of the pocket and just made it to the bed before sleep overtook me again. More stupid dream bits. Sitting around a large soup tureen with my parents in Trutnov. Then outside a pub as a bright red MG sports car came screaming into the carpark straight at me. That sort of thing. At one point I woke myself crying aloud with the pain splitting my head in two and there didn't seem anything I could do about that except wait for it to subside.

In the morning, if that's what it was, the light outside was predictably as bright as ever when I wandered out to sit on the small veranda. From here I could look back over the long way I'd come, out over the tree canopy towards the sea, a blur of pale blue in the far distance. I had still never seen the sun itself, nor a moon when the light dimmed. And I still had no idea why I was here. But in a communist regime you get used to calmly accepting where you are and not expecting much, knowing that all things change eventually.

The tour of my new home didn't take long. It was basically just the one room with a tiny alcove off to one side that an estate agent would no doubt call a fully-fitted kitchen. In reality, there was a sink with a single tap above it from which gushed fresh and very cold water, and a hotplate with no obvious means of turning it on. Perhaps the free-standing cupboard would reveal interesting secrets... It was virtually bare except for a few plates and dishes and, in its top drawer, a spattering of cutlery with wooden handles.

But then I struck gold as my searching fingers closed on a small, dusty package hidden away at the back of the drawer, a pack of *Petra* cigarettes from Kutná Hora, the old silver mining town an hour east of Prague. We had gone there once on a university field trip — they called it a heritage tour — to dutifully marvel at the mediaeval frescoes. Of course, we had been far more interested in the tobacco factory and the ironically appropriate Sedlec Ossuary decorated with human skeletons.

Of all the bewildering numinous experiences I had been through on this island, how strange that this discovery should fill me, like Štruncová's book, with the joy of familiarity. Despite turning the place upside down I found no means of actually lighting a cigarette, but it didn't matter.

A door at the back of the cabin revealed an equally tiny bathroom with a shower but no toilet. There was a toothbrush and a folded blue bath towel next to the basin, on which sat a bar of creamy-coloured soap with definite teeth marks in it, and a small wall-mounted cabinet with a mirrored door. It was empty.

Until now, I hadn't changed my clothes since my arrival. It never felt important, and anyway, whenever tiredness enveloped me, I had simply lain down and been out like a light. Coming 'home' now, it seemed right to take a shower and freshen up. I dropped the green blouse, jeans and white pants onto the bed and stepped beneath the fresh and cool water, standing quite still with eyes closed and allowing it to find and renew every part of my body.

It felt so good... until I looked down at myself. Surely this was not me? This thought locking out all others, I walked ever so slowly out into the bright light of the veranda and stood to observe myself. I had never been very big but now I seemed to have lost a lot of weight, almost thin, and my breasts were disappointingly much smaller. I stretched out one arm, then the other, then each leg in disbelief, hoping to find at least one normal limb. How can I describe this? The simplest thing to say is that I didn't look very solid. My skin was wafer-thin so that I could see the vague outlines of bone and muscle. It wasn't this that bothered me, though, since having been a gymnast I had done anatomy classes as a child and felt a close relationship to everything that was packed inside, revelling in the feeling of their growing strength. And then later as a young woman, when I had met Josef, there had been the further joy of discovering what a trained and supple body could experience.

No, what shocked me now in my nakedness was that everything was moving. There were gentle ripples on my skin like white-foamed waves slowly spreading out across a stony beach and, beyond them, thin beams of light streaming through and around the shapes, pausing, blinking, travelling up and down as though in a restless search for a way out. These, then, were the eels I had felt painfully in my hospital room. Perhaps I had received some sort of treatment after all because now, as I focused on them in morbid fascination, there was just a dull ache throughout my body, not unpleasant, of the sort I would feel after a good training routine. The difference was that then it would be accompanied by a sense of achievement and vitality. Now... well, I suppose I was alive anyway.

I stood still for I don't know how long with waves of an altogether more violent sort battering the inside of my head, thoughts of all that had been happening tossed about, wrecked and sinking, replaced by those dark, lumbering shapes of the deep that opened grinning mouths and spewed out more fragments of ancient memory that swarmed to the front and begged for attention. The pain was intense and I held my head in my hands until a blessed involuntary scream brought everything to a stop.

Even the birds were watching me in silent pity now, their heads on one side. And below them, just beyond the latched gate of the wooden arch, stood a figure watching me. The mist was swirling more thickly there but I could make out the shape of a woman. She looked quite old, a little stooped though tall with dark hair, and there was something unusual about her left eye, perhaps a squint. With one arm she held a bundle — could it be a baby? — wrapped in a blanket and she slowly raised the other arm towards me. As though borne on the wind across a vast ocean, I dimly heard her call, "Evička..." The pet name that only very few knew. As I realised this, she was gone.

Suddenly, I felt rather too self-conscious and went back inside to wrap the bath towel around myself. Thankfully, it was big enough to cover most of the revelations. As I stood at the basin and stared unseeingly into the grubby oval mirror, there was the faintest pattering sound nearby and I looked down with resignation to see a large grey rat nibbling at the soap; it looked up at me briefly with tiny bright eyes, its mouth curving slightly into what could be taken for a smile, then scurried away through a hole I hadn't noticed before to one side of the cabinet.

It didn't bother me. Nothing else could at the moment.

Indeed, in a peculiar way I welcomed this sign of normal life and in the absence of other company, save for the ghostly old woman who reappeared from time to time outside my gate yet never came closer, I found myself looking forward to the appearances of wildlife. In particular, there was one animal that emerged with clockwork regularity from the forest at the back of the cabin to cross the rocky ground, pause to drink at the stream, then disappear on its slow and deliberate journey into the foliage.

Iggy was the nearest thing I had to a live friend. All right, not the most creative of names but then I hadn't made friends with an iguana before. He was almost as long including the tail as I am tall and looked reassuringly prehistoric with a modern twist of colour, rust and pale green scales, grey spines and a crazy paving black and white patchwork pattern around the cheek shield. When he first stopped to look at me, his wide open mouth with protruding pink tongue looked for all the world like he was silently laughing at me. Probably in a nice way, though, because his skin was also almost transparent and the eels had clearly taken up residence there too.

I put out fruit for him every day once I'd learned his routine and sat on the cool rock beside him while he obliged me by eating a little. Then his tail would lift in salute and he'd be away, with just a brief backward glance before he disappeared into the foliage. These meetings gave me pleasure — you have to take it where you can — and a structure to these early times. Then I would go back inside to sit at the table and record in the writing pad, as it seemed I was bid, everything I could remember so far. And every so often I would rerun the girl's conversation aloud to myself: "...whatever you decide doesn't matter... it's all worked out ahead... don't be daft, Miss..."

What did I decide? And who's working it out?

EIGHT

In the comfortable and warm detached house near Sandwell Park, beyond the carefully raked gravel driveway and heavy brocade curtains, Mrs Carter sits alone in the lounge by the light of the mahogany standard lamp. She turns off the television because there only seems to be disturbing news on it these days.

She would like to talk but Mr Carter has shut himself away in the dining room. This is a normal evening. The table is strewn with reports alongside the Hewlett-Packard electronic 9100 calculator borrowed from his office. He has a black fountain pen in hand and will almost certainly be here until midnight. It may be over twenty years since demob but his work ethic hasn't dimmed, the drive to provide security for his family, despite his evident success. And you have to keep ahead of the others.

His wife picks up her own pen and the pad of pale blue writing paper from the coffee table beside her chair, knowing that she really should write to her son. Things being hard, surely he would appreciate some news from home. Except there isn't any. Life follows just the same pattern it has done for years: she gets up and makes breakfast, kisses her husband goodbye on the cheek, does some unnecessary housework before an afternoon rest, reads a magazine and begins to think about what to make for dinner. Sometimes she thinks it would be nice to get a little job, but her husband wouldn't like it. She can't write this to Roy.

What she does want to write is that his father is proud of him, even though he's never said it and isn't likely to any time soon. It may not even be quite true lately, considering the worry he's put them through this last year. However hard she tries to forget upsets, most of them simply won't go away and pile up in her mind like a car crash that keeps happening over and over again. And her husband's reaction that time still haunts her like a soundtrack on a loop.

"How can he be so selfish?" he'd said, spitting the words out like a wounded animal. "Doesn't he think about other people?"

Her head falling to one side in a moment's despair, she knows that it has all been precisely because Roy was thinking of others. But that's not what Mr Carter meant.

She wants to write that there are reasons for his father being... less than tolerant, so conservative. There were things that happened in the war, and earlier, things he's never talked about to anyone else. He's certainly never tried to have a conversation about them with his son. There are reasons. But she can't write this either.

'My dear son,

We hope that you are enjoying university and eating well...' she begins, then immediately breaks off. What on Earth does he eat anyway, since he announced that he was vegetarian and grew his hair long? With every passing month she understands him less and feels more and more isolated herself.

He'd come home in the summer and barely said a word for days, shut away upstairs, going for long walks up the hill to the fields like he did as a child then spending his evenings at The Mermaid. Even that's changed. The old coaching inn has been modernised now — that's what they call it — with dim lights and draping fishnets. Why keep changing things when they're perfectly all right?

Then one morning he'd just come down with his bags packed and mumbled that he was going back to Manchester early. He hadn't even waited for the Albion's first home match of the season, against Arsenal. Perhaps it was just as well, since they'd lost.

Mrs Carter puts the writing pad back on the coffee table and stands up to go to the front window, parting the curtains slightly to check for headlights. She finds herself doing this every evening recently, even though they live in a cul-de-sac and nothing ever moves after about six-thirty when her husband comes home. Two weeks ago, though, he'd been watching the early news while she prepared the dinner when the bright lights of a large car had penetrated the room as it drove right up, crunching the gravel.

This was not a time for uninvited visitors and she had hovered just inside the kitchen as her husband went to the door and there was an exchange of low voices. The man had been shown into the lounge where the television was turned off and he'd sat in her chair by the standard lamp, his grey raincoat folded over his knees. When she went in he'd flashed some sort of card and called himself Inspector Peter Jones, but she never found out what sort of policeman he was.

He was sorry to disturb their evening but there was something they should know. The way he'd spoken, though, was as if he thought they should already know and in fact knew more than they were saying. Maybe that's how all policemen speak. When he'd narrowed his eyes and asked Mr Carter about his 'connections', her husband had given him very short shrift — he was good at that sort of thing — and shown him to the door.

As he stood for a moment beneath the porch light to put his raincoat on, Mrs Carter had managed to get a word in and ask him whether he'd seen Roy and was he all right. Jones said yes, a few days ago and he was fine. This wasn't entirely true, but that may be what all policemen do.

The fact was that he'd been waiting in the car outside Fallow Court for Roy to come out to his own ageing Ford, then carefully driven across his path to block the way.

"We need to talk, young man," he'd said, ushering him onto the brown leather back seat. Actually, he'd done all the talking because Roy just stared at him in total disbelief with evident pain etched across his face. In the end, he simply gave the boy his card and said, "I've got my eye on you." That was true at least.

For the last two weeks, Mrs Carter hasn't known what to think, her nerves constantly on edge. At breakfast the next day she had tried to suggest to her husband that perhaps one of them should go to Manchester to see — but that's as far as she got.

"The boy has to stand on his own two feet. He doesn't know he's born. Trouble is, we've made his life too easy. Comfortable home, good school, his own car, everything paid... Christ, we even gave him the money for... No, let it go, Wyn. He has to live in the real world."

She pulls the curtains back together tightly and goes back to her chair, picking up the notepad again. Something has to be said. And for all that her husband had been right about certain things — their children had had an unimaginably easier life than her own upbringing in a run-down cottage in rural Berkshire with an outside toilet and one log fire — there were things that they hadn't been given. Their father's company, for one, except at silent Sunday dinners.

And maybe she could have tried harder to accept, if never understand, the loud music and strange clothes they got so excited about. When she was a girl, she'd only had one change of clothes and had a smack if she got her school dress dirty. Roy had been unrecognisable when he came home last Christmas, beard and ponytail and thin as a rake. Now Helen is going the same way at sixteen, out in the evenings wearing almost nothing, dark make-up, school reports describing a girl she doesn't know.

"Make me a coffee, Wyn." She hasn't noticed her husband open the door and put his head round but as she looks up in surprise he sees the tear on her cheek and comes in to sit in his own chair nearby. It hurts him to see her upset. He has protected her all these years and that's exactly why he wants to keep troubles on the other side of the gravel driveway.

"I don't know what to write," she cries, throwing the pad and pen to the carpet and covering her face with her hands. He goes to pick them up then thinks better of it, reaching out a hand to touch hers instead. There is silence for a full minute until he begins, his voice low and unusually soft.

"You lost your mother. Cancer. Three operations and you nursed her for years. TB got my mother when I was five and I was farmed out to an aunt who didn't know what to do with me. My big brother was shot down. We went through six years of hell not knowing from one day to another if our names were on the next bomb. Ronnie was stillborn." He pauses and she lifts her head to look at him angrily.

"Is that supposed to make me feel better?"

"No, of course not. I'm just saying... we got through it all, didn't we? And we worked hard to pick up all the pieces and make something better." His other arm gestures to the comfortable furniture and everything beyond. "The thing is, Wyn, what I've learned, for what it's worth... is that we only find out what being human is really all about when we've been through great pain and come out the other side. Travelling through this life — and we've done a bit of that, haven't we? — you come across, well, suffering... all the time. It's inevitable. It comes with the job. And it's how we grow up, or at least how we deal with it—" he pauses, knowing this bit is a sore point and trying to put it as gently as possible, "—because the worst thing we can do is just carry on living and wanting things to be different. Easy. Painless. Life doesn't work like that. What was it Hemingway said in *Farewell to Arms*? 'The world breaks us and that's how we get stronger.' Something like that."

His wife looks at him with soft eyes and returns the grip of his hand.

"Surely the heart doesn't always have to get broken? Especially when you're young?"

"Yes, maybe especially then."

"I'll make your coffee, dear."

She gets up and wipes her eyes on a handkerchief before giving her husband a wan smile and heading to the kitchen. When she brings the coffee into the dining room, he is already engrossed again in his papers and she has to guess which one is least important so she can move it to put the cup down. She is about to leave when he suddenly looks up at her, the habitual coldness back in his eyes.

"Tell the boy to have a bit of gratitude for everything he's been given. And some humility wouldn't go amiss either. He's in the real world now and he'd better learn to get on with it. Fast. Tell you what, Wyn, you tell him to read Viktor Frankl's book — *Search for Meaning*, or something — about the concentration camps. And go to the bloody pictures and see *The Guns of Navarone*. Then maybe he'll start to grow up."

It ends up being a relatively short letter, saying they miss him and hope he's eating properly and not smoking too much. She says his father does care and she passes on some of the evening's conversation, only in what she hopes is a more gentle way. It finishes with hoping that he might come home for a weekend before long and maybe go to see that nice girl Kate at the factory when he does.

She wonders if that last bit may be wrong but anyway it is what she thinks so she licks the envelope and goes up to bed.

Φ

Roy walks with more purpose alongside Gartside Gardens then cuts through and up Sackville Street. The collar of the greatcoat is turned up against the cold night air and his arms are folded with hands thrust into opposite sleeves. His eyes are downcast against the wind that always seems to channel along here from the north.

"You here again, mate?" The constable's greeting is less friendly this evening. He's annoyed at drawing the short straw two nights running with the station men down sick, and that Inspector Jones here again, standing silently in the shadows and saying nothing, making him feel very uneasy.

Throughout the day, the conversation with the girl has been running through Roy's head like a cassette loop as he tries to make sense not only of what she said but why she turned up at all. He hasn't spoken a word to anyone since, only nodding his thanks to the couple of people who'd broken from the crowds outside Piccadilly Station to give him a hot drink and a Chelsea bun. He has refused to beg, yet others have pressed coins into his gloved hands before hurrying away, seeing his need but unable to engage. He doesn't mind that, having nothing to share. Yet it crosses his mind how extraordinary it is to be able to get by with nothing.

The battered white Transit van is parked half on the pavement and the air is full of steam and quiet chatter by its open rear doors. He settles on the wooden bench at the other end from Jonno and takes out the ten pack of Benson and Hedges, passing one across and lighting it for him. Debts must be paid. Jonno wheezes thanks but has learned that conversation is pointless.

After a few minutes, the girl with big breasts brings a bowl of hot vegetable soup and half a baguette, which Jonno regards with wide jealous eyes. The girl opens her mouth as though to try some questions but thinks better of it and returns to her whispered conversation with the young men at the back of the van. Roy dips the bread in the thick soup and eats slowly, head downcast, thoughts swirling in the gathering October mist and only increasing the headache he's had for some days. It's better when he doesn't think.

"You're a hard chap to find."

Professor Meeks takes out a handkerchief to give the bench a cursory wipe and sits gingerly between its two occupants. He is a short, tubby man with silvering hair and bright, round eyes. He wears a light grey French Vestra overcoat in Tyroler loden wool with a dark purple satin lining, considered by his colleagues a bit too modern for his status and age. And distinctly out of place here. Jonno recognises this immediately and stands up, hovering for a moment as though bowing to the new arrival, then edges away to sit on a nearby brick wall, all the while watching the unfolding scene with sharp eyes.

Roy sits bolt upright at the voice, nearly spilling his soup, and turns guiltily to Meeks. The Chair is this man's life and he cares for his students like a father. And, like a naughty child, Roy realises he has let him down. Another one for the list.

"Prof... um, hello, sir. What are you doing here?"

"You haven't forgotten how to think already, have you?"

The young man had arrived in the Department late after switching course last year but had taken to the challenge like a caged parakeet to an ash tree, his essays just as colourful and noisy and his effort huge. His mind had been free, despite personal challenges that most other students could never imagine. So his absence this term was a worry.

"Perhaps I have, sir. How did you find me?"

Meeks gestures towards the small knot of students by the Transit. They are all watching the pair with bated breath and one of them flashes a lopsided smile and a thumbs-up as though he has achieved a major peace treaty. Roy, needing above all to be invisible, makes a mental note to have a few words with him later.

The professor takes out a pack of Player's Navy Cut and lights up two of them, handing one to Roy. It's the sort of thing students do, so perhaps it's a gesture of empathy. They sit in silence for a few minutes, the younger man knowing what's coming and feeling uncomfortable, the other searching his considerable mind for appropriate words. He doesn't find them.

"Look..." he pauses, then gives up and carries on anyway. "I want you back. You had a great year and you mustn't throw that away."

Roy's eyebrows arch and he looks straight at the professor's eyes for the first time.

"A great year, was it? You do know what happened, I suppose?"

"You know what I mean. And yes, I was just told a few days ago. Like I said, you're not easy to find — or find out about. Sorry, that's not grammatical." Roy smiles despite himself, allowing one or two good tutorial memories to slip back into his mind.

"Then you'll know why I can't do it, sir. I can't deal with... books and conversations and the Union bar and..."

"Or eating, shaving and showering, by the look of you, and the smell," says Meeks, deciding on the direct approach after all.

"Sorry. Actually, it's been quite... enlightening, on the street. A lot of people are kind. Only a few swear at you and kick you as they go past. And you don't have to think much."

"Hmm, I think I can see that. Maybe that's something you can bring to the Ethics module."

"I told you, sir, I can't—"

"Yes, you can, and I won't hear otherwise. Look, I'm not here to give you a hard time. I'm no good at that sort of thing, as you know. And if I'd wanted to, I'd just get Nora to write a stiff letter to you. You remember my secretary? She's got a way with letters. So what we'll do is—"

"You don't get it, do you, Prof? My life isn't the same anymore, my head isn't—"

"Yes, all right, I'm sure. But you have to understand that what happened was not your fault. Not at all. You're not responsible for oth—"

"But I am. That's the whole point. I should have made a different decision, so then—"

"Lord, you're trying my patience, lad. Did you not read Moore's *Principia*? You were under no... obligation."

The word silences Roy. It trips a switch in his brain and dormant neurons begin to light up. It's a losing battle now for the darkness. He leans over to put the bowl carefully, almost decisively, on the paving and turns his body towards Meeks.

"Maybe." There's still a brief rear-guard action. "But anyway, I'll have lost my room at Fallow Court and I don't have any—"

"Leave all that to me, old chap. I do have, um, some influence. For tonight, you're going to Nora's house. There's a spare room and she's expecting you. Not the most sympathetic character, I agree, but she'll feed you and get you cleaned up. Then you can go back to your room in a day or so and start with Epistemology on Monday. All right?"

Roy gives up. The force of kindness is too great and he allows himself to be led like a toddler across the road where the professor's Wolseley 4/44 waits patiently for its next task. The constable jumps slightly as Inspector Peter Jones suddenly exhales loudly, swears to himself, and sets off back to his own car round the corner.

The steam and chatter around the open rear doors of the Transit fade away through the Wolseley's rear window, along with the sparse congregation that spills from the church, hardly pausing to stare at the shabby creatures across the road. Professor Meeks drives fast as though taking his chance and heading off any change of mind.

The three-bed terrace in Withington has slightly parted thick floral curtains to the front through which a bright light burns like a beacon in the dense mist that's falling. Such a sight brings joy to sailors after a long voyage, although there is always one who fears the homecoming and what he may find when he opens the door.

In her own way, Nora is quite fearsome.

"You did it, then, you ol' fool," she mutters, turning on her heels and leading them into the front room. She wears a dark blue cotton shift with a simple fabric belt at the waist. Mid-fifties, already greying hair tied back, quite tall and upright with a facial expression that could freeze a Capsaicin.

"Worth her weight in emeralds," Meeks whispers. "Don't be put off."

The room is furnished simply with a small screen television in one corner, a dark oak sideboard and a chest of drawers above which a glass display case holds a collection of ceramic animal figurines. Roy's eyes are drawn to the particularly impressive panther holding centre stage and commanding the room.

She gestures them to sit and they sink into the ancient settee, decorated with macramé antimacassars, as she leaves for the kitchen. All is silent except for the faint, regular tick of the carriage clock in the hallway counting down lives. After a few minutes Nora returns with a tray of coffees, using one foot with surprising dexterity to hook a small table out from beside the settee.

"Did you put extra sugar in mine, Nora?" Meeks asks.

"To be sure I did. An' if you're after wanting any biscuits you'll have to buy them yourself."

As Roy reaches forward for his cup, there's a quiet cough from the far corner of the room and he jerks upright again in surprise. Neither he nor the professor had noticed the old lady sitting there, shrunk into a deep armchair and almost completely covered in a thick blanket. She is fixing them with small, penetrating eyes behind heavy-rimmed glasses and they both feel judged.

"It's all right, mother," says Nora, "they're friends. Well, sort of."

They sit in awkward silence for a few minutes until at last the professor drains his cup with the faintest of grimaces and stands to leave. He smiles his thanks to Nora — their relationship is not a very vocal one — and winks surreptitiously towards Roy.

"Everything will be fine, old chap, you'll see." It's something he feels ought to be said at such a moment. "There's some good stuff coming up this term, you'll like it. And," he racks his memory, "I believe there's some famous, er, group coming to the Union in a few weeks. Pink Floors, or something like that."

As the door closes behind him, Nora considers the niceties done with and turns to her new house guest with a business-like expression. After all, organising fools is something she's good at.

"Your room is top of the stairs at the front of the house, young man. I suggest you get yourself cleaned up."

The room is spare in every sense of the word. There's a single bed and an old oak wardrobe, brown linoleum on the floor and no lampshade. But the bed is made up with clean sheets and two blankets, and sitting accusingly on top of it are a blue bath towel, toothbrush and new tube of paste, and an impressively large bar of coal tar soap.

Roy is suddenly too tired to think about what he's doing, or indeed what he's done or will do next. He washes his long hair thoroughly in the bath and then soaks unmoving for ten minutes until the water starts to chill. Having been brought up in suburban middle class where standards are important — and must be visible — he then cleans the bath carefully and picks out the hairs from the plug hole so that no trace of him is left behind.

He sleeps for fourteen hours.

He wakes in the late morning to find proper sunshine streaming through the thin curtains and every muscle in his body aching. Slipping the black jeans on he opens the bedroom door and almost falls over the breakfast tray left there. It's scrambled eggs on toast with fried mushrooms and tomatoes and a cup of coffee. Everything is stone cold by now but it still tastes very good.

He takes the tray down to the kitchen and washes up, acutely aware that the house is absolutely still and silent except for the clock.

This quiet feels good. It puts him in mind of the evenings he'd spent on Alderley Edge last year, sometimes with his friend Graham but often quite alone, an ancient woodland with a tangible peace all of its own. From the carpark they would clamber over a stile and along a dirt track, always muddy even in summer, before turning down a sharp incline beneath a rocky overhang. A hundred yards further on there's a trickle of water on the rock and the carved face of the wizard, then they'd pick their way over gnarled roots and damp earthy steps, kicking up piles of leaves as they climbed up towards the sandy-coloured bank in the hidden heart of the place. There's a huge birch with five trunks, motionless with branches outstretched as though controlling the land and the trees at the clearing's fringe, all bending over to one side like stooping old men with limbs outstretched in supplication. All of this walk would be in silent awe of nature and any problems they had brought with them to share and resolve would by now just not seem so important.

Nature heals, and Roy now makes a mental note of the fact. He slips on the greatcoat, stuffing his woolly hat in a pocket, and pops his head round the door of the sitting room to check that everything is as it should be before he leaves. Somehow he is not surprised to see the old lady still motionless in her armchair, tucked beneath a blanket. In a world in constant motion, some things never change. He mouths a 'thank you' to her and there is the faintest crease in her face that may perhaps be a smile.

It's not far to go. He gets his bearings then turns right onto Mauldeth Road before taking a left along Ladybarn Lane, walking slowly and still shrinking back into doorways when groups of people approach from the other direction. It's not going to be as easy as Alan Meeks thinks to rejoin humanity. All the same, he's at Fallow Court within twenty minutes.

Entering by the side gate, he suddenly freezes as a police car with blue light flashing and siren wailing races along Wilmslow Road. He has already begun to develop the instincts of the street. But then he notices with a pang of pleasure his own small green car parked in a shady corner and for the first time in weeks feels a pang of guilt that perhaps he hasn't been grateful enough for the advantages life has given him. Maybe he should write to his parents. Maybe. And he is only here because he is being paid by the company his father works for. So that is an obligation.

In a state of free will, is gratitude a Good? And showing it a Right Action? He can't remember.

It's early afternoon and the block is mostly empty. There are just one or two inquisitive but not unfriendly faces at the open kitchen door to negotiate before he reaches the top floor and pauses outside his own room, wondering what he'll find within. A sudden wrench of the heart causes an involuntary tear as he realises there won't be a blue airmail envelope pushed under the door.

Just get on with it. He fishes into the depths of the left coat pocket for his key and is almost surprised to find that it still works and that the place is almost exactly as he left it. Someone has made the bed, tidied up the dirty clothes on the floor and emptied the waste bin. The posters on the yellow walls have been removed but his guitar sits safely in one corner. Propped up against it is the oil painting.

John Cotton had surprised him. Ordinary and homely, in his late fifties and a cornerstone of the local Anglican church, John had been deferential in describing his psychic gifts. Apparently, it all began spontaneously, he'd never had any art training and hadn't even heard of Perugino before. He had taken Roy to a studio he'd felt moved to create in the large Victorian house, put some classical music on and then seemed to go into a kind of trance while muttering to himself in Italian. Paint and brushes had flown about and the portrait of a Franciscan monk had been finished in fifteen minutes. With John's eyes closed. It was signed 'PP' and it was impossible.

"This is your guide," the man had said. "Sorry, I didn't get his name." Then he had put a hand gently on the young man's arm as he'd left, given him a concerned look and said, "Take care."

Roy had been developing an interest in the paranormal ever since meeting a spiritualist medium, Marian, in his home town. He'd found her vitality and simple conviction very attractive, and she was sexy too despite being considerably older than him, her eyes and mouth bearing lines of experience. They'd developed a kind of unequal friendship, she always taking the lead with an unwavering authority, he too naïve to question her pronouncements or even know what questions to ask. And she had introduced him to John Cotton. All these new ideas had sat uneasily alongside academic philosophy and brought Roy a bit of a reputation among other students as possibly unhinged. And, among his own family, as downright ridiculous.

Nonetheless, the portrait somehow spoke to him. Right now, sitting on the floor in the corner, it glares at him and asks to be hung in its proper place above the bed.

The room has a simple wooden desk, chair and lamp. He is pretty sure he had left it bare but now there are two neat, high piles of freshly printed books beside a thick writing pad and two biros. Each pile of books has a small, neatly handwritten note sitting on it. 'Read these first' is on top of John Locke's *Essay Concerning Human Understanding*, David Hume's *Treatise on Human Nature* and other tomes by Leibniz and Kant. Roy's heart sinks at the sheer weight of intellect he is being expected to get to grips with.

The shorter pile declares, 'These come later. You'll like them.' First is Gilbert Ryle's *Concept of Mind* with its forbidding black cover in the centre of which is a human brain broken into more than forty pieces, each bearing an almost indecipherable image. Well, Roy can relate to that, anyway. He turns it over and glances at the blurb. "...expose the myth of Descartes' doctrine... the idea of a ghost in the machine... ordinary common sense..." That doesn't seem very likely. The next book, though equally thick, is far more attractive. Koestler's *Sleepwalkers* is apparently written "...tensely, with passion, as though personally involved..." Some light relief, then, perhaps in December. The last book in the pile is Thomas Kuhn's *Structure of Scientific Revolutions* and the professor has pinned a separate note to it: 'You may think this is the best of the lot, old chap.' Roy sighs and doubts he'll even get that far down the pile.

The first thing to do is to get changed into clean clothes and everything is there in the wardrobe and chest, although in a completely different order.

He has been cleared out and then, sympathetically, reinstated. Still, for all that the pieces may be coming back together, there is a dark hole in this room now — given what has happened here — and the puzzle of life can never be complete.

He wanders down to the café for a late lunch, suddenly aware of how ravenous he is, and gets a vegetable pasty with chips liberally covered with vinegar and ketchup. At the counter, Jane smiles a welcome and, despite her youth, knows better than to ask any personal questions. More than most, she knows that people come and go; in fact, in her experience they usually just go so it's nice when one comes back. After a few minutes, she brings him over a coffee and quietly removes the plate.

He checks his watch and hurries back to his room for his greatcoat, taking the stairs two at a time to get to the dry cleaners across the road before it closes. No sooner has he returned than Graham's unmistakable, brilliant finger style can be heard drifting down the corridor, working on a Fleetwood Mac song. The two of them had been close friends last year, sometimes sharing the silence of the Edge, sometimes playing guitar together (Roy struggling to follow) and even for the occasional Saturday afternoon at Maine Road. He knocks the door, waits a moment and enters.

Graham sits on the bed, bent over in concentration, and gives him only a cursory glance. At the table, apparently writing a letter, is his girlfriend Red. She is an English student, real name Christine, but known to everyone for her burgundy hair. It's long and thick and when she tosses her head any man within twenty yards is transfixed by the flood. Her features are thin, classic Geminian like her quick mind and speech, and she has dark gypsy eyes. They look up now and smile quietly at Roy. The two of them have shared some, ah, history together, this being the late-sixties, but she and Graham suit each other beautifully. The rough, exuberant young man who used to attack life headlong with eyes firmly shut had become calmer with this girl whom all other male students watch pass by. He even enjoys their blazing rows over the perennial conflicts of art and science.

"'Need someone's hand to lead me through the night, need someone's arms...' you're back, then? Thought you'd baled on us again."

"Graham!" Red admonishes him. "Sorry, Roy. Are you all right? We know about it..." He raises an eyebrow and she shrugs. "People talk."

"'...when the lights are low, and it's time to go, that's when I need your love so bad.'" For a wonderful musician — and a shoe-in for a First in Engineering — he can still be incredibly insensitive. He completes the riff on top E and lays the guitar to one side, looking up at Roy for the first time. "Christ, mate, you look crap."

"Thanks. Funnily enough, that's exactly how I feel."

Graham gets up and moves the guitar to a corner, gesturing Roy to sit in his place, before standing to look out of the window at the gathering gloom of evening, his back turned. A cool shudder passes through Roy as he recognises the orchestration of the scene, he below, his friend above, preparing some pronouncement. It doesn't take long.

"You just have to let it go. The teacher says that we must not base our lives on what others do. What we truly are, whether we are happy or sad, is our own responsibility. Life doesn't have to be a struggle or a tension. It doesn't have to be suffering, that's not the true nature of life. Life is bliss."

"It's bliss, huh? And this would be Maharishi's idea, I'm guessing."

The guru-of-the-moment had held his first public meeting in the city earlier in the year and Graham had become absorbed in the message, proclaiming it the best thing since the Clifton Suspension Bridge. To hear him now, he was already halfway to cosmic consciousness.

"Yes, but it's an ancient teaching. The Brihadaranyaka Upanishad tells us what our hearts already know, that this life is not the reality and enlightenment leads us out of the darkness."

"Well, it would."

"Self-realisation transcends all sorrow."

"You should put that in a Christmas cracker. Got any more?"

"Your self-realisation is the greatest gift you can give the world, Roy. You may laugh, but on the day of liberation—"

"Have you actually sold your brain to the Maharishi?" The window was open and Roy was beginning to consider a different kind of liberation for his friend.

"No, no, that's Sri Ramana Maharshi."

"Silly me."

Graham turns back to the room now, an untroubled expression on his calm face, almost certainly believing that he is helping his friend. He doesn't notice Red's glare or the icy chill settling around them all.

"See, Roy, we know what happened was... a bit upsetting. But (a) it's gone now, (b) you didn't do it, and (c) in the great scheme of creative consciousness and natural law it means nothing. Nothing."

"Simple as ABC, eh? Maybe B minor?"

"Through meditation we reach pure consciousness, the Atman, where we know ourselves as the infinite field of pure being. Our thoughts and feelings are like waves on the surface of the ocean but our minds dive beneath to the deeper, quiet levels until thought is transcended and there is just silence. And peace. And there's nothing new about this, it goes back millennia. Shankara's Dasa Sloka says it perfectly: when we are self-realised we are neither above nor below, neither inside nor outside, neither middle or across, we are indivisible and all-pervading." He pauses and smiles at last. "I hope that helps."

Roy is already on his feet and heading for the door.

"In the Tao it is written that the Tao is forever and he that possesses it, though his body—"

The door slams.

For the next several minutes, raised voices can be heard along the corridor. Roy tries to shut everything out and sits on his bed with head in hands, wondering how it has all changed so completely. This was stupid, imagining that he could simply pick up the old life, write essays on Gilbert Bloody Ryle and his ghost, drink beer in the Union and write songs. Prof is well-meaning, a good man, but he really has no idea. It would have been better if he'd just left him to walk the street until he'd figured out... something else, somewhere to go, or...

His thoughts don't get any further than this. Perhaps he's sinking below the waves of the ocean after all. But then Graham's wrong because it isn't peaceful and there are just dark, shapeless beings lumbering around him with huge grinning teeth.

Small feet come padding along the corridor and there's a timid knock on his door. Red doesn't wait for an answer and slips inside, closing the door gently behind her. She stands sheepishly in the dark with head bowed.

"Sorry, Roy, am I disturbing you?"

"No, it's all right. I'm not doing anything."

She's wearing a thin green dress, her long, thick hair falling around bare shoulders and when she moves to stand by the window the early evening streetlamp outside ignores the material and picks out her beautiful slim body. She doesn't seem to be wearing anything else.

"I know he can be a real prat sometimes," she observes quietly. "And he's become obsessed with the whole transcendental thing. It's Vedic this and sutra that. Meditates twice a day for half an hour — I mean, where does anyone find the time? — and even then he's weird afterwards until he's had something to eat. I'm sure he was trying to help, though. In his way."

She comes to sit demurely beside him on the bed, hands clasped on her knees, and pauses for his response. There isn't one.

"Look, it's horrible. I can't imagine how you... But we are still your friends, really, and we'll get you through. Back on your feet. 'Whether 'tis nobler in the mind to suffer the sli—'"

"Don't you fucking dare quote Shakespeare at me, Red."

She giggles and moves closer, resting her head on his shoulder and taking one of his hands in hers. He lifts the other one briefly above his head.

"I'm all up to here with advice, thanks."

The turbulent energy of the room begins to settle now, her gentle warmth scaring away most of the dark, shapeless beings, and he begins to feel indescribably tired again, all thoughts shrinking back into their caves and refusing to move. So, for this and other reasons, she chooses the wrong moment now to edge her face close to his and lift his hand to her breast.

"It will be all right," she whispers. But he pulls away sharply, shaking his head awake again, and moving to lean against the window.

"I can't," he says simply. "Sorry, I can't."

She gets up and goes slowly to the door, pausing with her hand touching his green summer jacket hanging there and suddenly remembering those happy times. It had been a few weeks before the Apollo 11 mission and they'd all been completely unaware of its significance, just four young people with wildly colourful clothes and long hair, camping on the lower slopes of Glastonbury Tor. The nearby town was in the vanguard of the hippy wave and they'd bought incense and crystals, walked the Abbey ruins, made the pilgrimage to the Holy Thorn and stood duly reverential at the Chalice Well with its tumbling blood-red water. And she remembers getting a bottle of the holy water and saying to them perhaps it could turn Graham into a human being again... Everyone had laughed.

"Why do you stay with him?" Roy asks quietly across the shadowed room. She shrugs.

"He's very clever," she says. "And when he's all done with his meditation, he has fantastic, er, energy. If you know what I mean."

Φ

I left the cabin and walked around behind it, finding a narrow track that led steeply up the mountain through dense woodland, all the while with the overwhelming sense that I was revisiting somewhere within myself. Even the normal bright light of the island could hardly penetrate the canopy, still yet breathing rhythmically, silent save for the rustling of small memories that came to stare at me, some smiling, others accusingly.

In this darkness, not knowing where I was going, my mind's eyes began to clear. Shadows moved among the trees and

I knew that I was being watched, though no more so than by myself. One creature did accompany me, a black, silky butterfly that glided a little way ahead, sometimes hovering as though to check I was still following. On each wing, a bright golden circle enclosed the letter E.

Brushing aside long, stinging grasses and grazing my forehead on low branches, I kept moving and resisted the growing fear that I may be entirely lost. Or that I may find an awful truth. Indeed, there was now light at the end of this tunnel, growing brighter.

I emerged and had to stop suddenly, finding myself at the very rim of a volcanic crater, and then laughed at myself for imagining that I might fall. The butterfly moved on and I followed it down smooth, black stones to sit beside the silent, unmoving waters of a lake. Strange though it may seem, for the first time I now felt very, very alone.

Beyond the ring of tall trees standing guardian of this place, a single, thin vaporous cloud stretched out lazily overhead like a sleeping body on its deep blue sheet, arching slow limbs to gather in the space around it. Its reflection slipped across the surface of the water, where I strained my eyes in vain for the merest ripple. Nothing else moved here. Everything was waiting for a response from me.

"Perhaps I could have—"

Where did those words come from? They implied a past, a time that had rhythms, even a coming and going of seasons, those mistresses of nature who call the tune, invite the guests and dismiss the uninvited. A past when decisions could be made with unstoppable consequences, since it's all worked out ahead.

We believe that we decide, blinded by the pain of our experience to the simple truth of how things have to be. We believe ourselves free, then see that freedom's loss is one more test of all that remains. And all our words are meaningless, falling from our empty heads like grains in a sand timer that pile up in another space until it's time to reverse them.

Suddenly, like a moment before Creation, I felt entirely empty. I realised that I was nothing. There was nothing to know. Nothing to be. It was beautiful. I no longer needed to understand why I was here, what had been or what came next, because there is no time. Just unimaginable peace.

It couldn't last, of course.

Out of the nowhere, an almighty storm of grievous thunder rolled uncontrollably around the void that was me and exploded with excruciating aggression, firing jets of flame throughout my whole body and threatening to tear it apart. I fell onto my side, curled up like a foetus at the edge of the lake, gasping for breath as the water gently enclosed and held me. And when it all finally subsided, there was a new and terrible pain within, where my heart should have been.

It wasn't a memory, I still didn't know what had happened in that implied past, what pointless decisions had been made. But I felt it. And it was love.

And it came to me that we are all so very foolish, needing and demanding love from others in the vain belief that they can make us feel whole, filling up those empty spaces we are born with so that the sands of time can slip through us. In our total self-interest, love becomes just another habit to be put on each morning, shapeless and colourless and reducing our identity to nothing. Every so often we will change the clothes, burn them to ashes, and look for a new path where another traveller may take pity on us and cover our nakedness. So we go on, each breath bringing new life and destroying it in the same moment.

"'Such sweet dreams are made of this... some of them want to abuse you, some of them want to be abused...'"

Where did that come from?

Beside this silent and unfathomable lake, enfolded by the trees, utterly alone save for a silky black butterfly waiting patiently on a rock a little way off, I felt like a small child again in church, unsure what came next in the order of service, when to close my eyes or put my hands together. Slowly, I saw my thoughts wandering lost through narrow, empty cobbled streets that weaved between blank stone walls until at last they opened out onto vast, unmapped steppes full of life and greenery beyond the boundaries of anything I'd known before.

I was here because of love. Because love is never to be found in any attachment to another, which will always disappoint. Yes, it may reveal itself more and differently with each one, but it transcends our searching. Alone here with just my self, all resistance broken by the power of the storm, I knew it as my own deepest being. I knew it as nothing to do with good times or bad, with joy or despair.

It is.

Awareness of one's self.

And right now, it hurt like hell. Because I didn't know any of this before.

I stood up, limp as a wet rag, and wished the silent lake would open up and take me down. To disappear. I felt tiny, just a drop of water in an unknowable ocean.

"No," said the butterfly, "you are the ocean."

THIRTEEN

It's Saturday morning and Roy is looking forward to a calm weekend, although he should know by now that anything can happen at any time. This is given.

He takes a shower, pulls on jeans and sweater, and wanders downstairs for breakfast, sitting alone at an empty table near Graham and Red. They'd been the closest of friends last year but things have changed and Roy has been keeping his distance since the onslaught of the Upanishads. Indeed, he's been keeping his distance from life in general for several weeks now, at the forefront of his mind that Professor Meeks has gone out of his way to give him a second chance. Actually, it's probably his third or fourth chance.

His last essay came back with a B+, the margins peppered with the professor's habitual purple ink, the occasional smiley face but more frowning ones, alongside pithy comments such as, "Justify!" and "This is disrespectful!"

Feeling the rebuke keenly, today he plans to rewrite ahead of Monday's tutorial. In the afternoon he'll take a bath listening to the soccer on the radio — the Albion are playing Burnley today — then in the evening he'll work on the new song that's beginning to trickle out from unconscious depths. This one is introducing itself from the beginning: notes G – B – E repeated twice, then C – E – G before the chords F – C – Dm7 – G7 lead into the first line.

"When this is over... and the dark night flies..."

But all this depends on whether the headache at his left temple calms down.

"You're not actually going to eat that, are you?"

The girl's soft voice over his shoulder cuts into his thoughts and he freezes, fork in mid-air, before turning to look with genuine shock at his sister standing behind him.

"Helen! What on Earth are you doing here?"

"That's a nice welcome. Can't a girl visit her big brother?"

His surprise is because they've had almost nothing to do with one another for years. Theirs is a family of four separate individuals with entirely different personalities whose lives rarely intersect. Helen is three years younger and a different species, living in a girly world.

"That looks disgusting." She points to the scrambled egg on toast and baked beans.

"It does for me."

"It probably will."

She takes off her dark raincoat and drapes it over a chair, then tosses back her long, curly auburn hair before sitting beside him. His eyes widen as the short, black, leather-look skirt rides further up her thighs. She wears black tights and a thin green blouse with a low, lacy neckline.

"Don't worry, veggie brother, the skirt's fake."

"I wasn't thinking that. I was thinking you've got nothing on in December — and in Lancashire."

"Eat your awful breakfast, Roy. I'll go and get some for myself. You won't have to look at it if you're careful."

Graham and Red have been watching with fascination and now, uninvited, come over to sit at the same table. Red already suspects that this attractive young girl could be a game-changer and makes the first move as Helen returns with a plate piled high with everything on offer.

"I never knew you had a sister, Roy."

"Neither did I. Not this one, anyway." She looks very different to the anonymous girl he's seen fleetingly during the holidays, certainly not a child now. And there's a bright light in her eyes.

He lapses into confused silence and picks at his cooling beans as the others start grilling Helen about her life. She skilfully fends off all the personal questions with a light voice in between large mouthfuls. She is either very hungry or very private or both. Nonetheless, Red plans to take her under a wing.

"So, what are your plans for today?" she fires at Roy.

"I, um, need to go back over Kuhn's work and rewrite—"

"Forget that, what about me? I've come all this way to see you — and anyway it's the weekend."

"Hmm." He looks at her with narrowed eyes. After all, this is the first contact with home since August. "Why today, then? You've got an ulterior motive, haven't you — is it a boyfriend?"

"Don't be silly," she giggles. "Oh, all right, if you must know, my favourite band is playing at the Students' Union tonight so I thought you could take me. That's okay, isn't it?"

"Ha, I knew it wasn't me you came for. Who's the band?"

"Family."

He laughs out loud at the irony.

"They're prog rock, jazz fusion, that sort of thing. They're the best live act out there now but I've never seen them... pleeeease, Roy?"

Nineteen sixty-nine is a good year to be a student. There's been the groundswell of political activism and an explosion of culture that has brought one well-known band after another to the Union. Admittedly, virtually all of this has passed a secluded Roy by, except for when he'd been one of the sparse audience for Third Ear Band who played improvised versions of their *Alchemy* album to a meditative room of students sitting on the floor with heads bowed. It had helped him, the strange rhythms soothing and reorganising his mind.

"If they're that good, there won't be any tickets left," he objects. "You should have—"

"No problem," Graham suddenly interjects, glad to make a contribution. "I know Dave Sykes, the Social Secretary. He'll get us in."

Helen squeals with pleasure and gets up to throw her arms round his neck. Red is not to be outdone.

"And I'll take you into the city, Helen, then Roy can do his cocoon. We could, um, get you some new clothes, yes?"

Roy finally smiles at his little sister in surrender. After breakfast, they go up to his room where he reaches for a sock in the back of a drawer that contains his emergency money. It's a habit he'd developed in childhood after desperately wanting a soccer magazine but finding that his pocket money had run out.

"When it's gone, it's gone," his father had said, refusing to hand over any more. "You have to learn that." Since then, he's learned that the aphorism doesn't only apply to money.

"Call it your early Christmas present," he says with a grin, "for the next three years." He fishes out a ten-pound note and she hugs him and is about to skip away to meet Red when she remembers something.

"Oh, by the way... I noticed your post box was bulging. By the front door. You might like to check it out."

He hasn't given the post a thought for weeks. There's a clutch of multi-coloured flyers advertising long-past events, an official buff envelope — the MOT and road tax on his car are overdue — and a couple of personal letters with months-old postmarks. One is from Nora, expressing in her inimitable style that he's late for the new term and should get off his backside. With a sinking feeling, he turns his attention to his mother's letter, standing stock still among the throng of students heading out to enjoy the weekend, his hand trembling slightly as he tears open the envelope. There's the usual stuff about eating properly and a rather odd suggestion that he should go to the cinema more often.

"We think—" she continues, though it's obvious this is his father's contribution, perhaps toned down, "—perhaps you should count your blessings and not dwell on your problems. A lot of people go through bad times and we all have to get on with..." There's more about difficulties making us stronger and maybe he could take out that nice girl Kate at Christmas.

There's a handy waste bin near the post boxes.

When Helen returns later, eyes sparkling and skin glowing, she is now wearing tight lilac jeans, slightly flared — "I wanted the ones with blue and yellow stripes but couldn't carry that off back home" — and an arresting full-length jacket with interwoven coloured panels.

"And look—" she thrusts her hands out excitedly "—Red has painted my nails." On alternate blue and purple backgrounds, each nail sparkles with a different silvery rune symbol.

"Mmm, you may have a bit of a problem with those at school next week." Graham is as good as his word and in the evening the energy in the hall is electric as Family settle into their set, drawn mostly from their new album. They're good, and Roger Chapman is holding these several hundred students in the palm of a hand with his unique vocal style.

"More like a bleating goat," says Graham, less than impressed.

The music is raw and intense and, despite the crowd and the noise and his headache, Roy's spirits lift to see his little sister having the time of her life. She's pushed her way to the front, dancing with abandon. When he finds her at the end, she's completely exhausted, has somehow managed to drink several glasses of wine and can barely stand. Red helps him get her back to the guest room at Fallow Court.

"Is she all right?"

Red has put her to bed and now sits beside him, the bright half-moon outside bringing a glow to his otherwise darkened room.

"Fast asleep and very happy. She may not be quite so energetic in the morning, though."

"Thanks for everything. You've really helped."

He turns towards her, their faces close, this strange and uplifting day melting softly towards its end. Maybe things are changing. A turning point. She tosses her hair and opens her mouth to… but no. His eyes are cold.

Helen doesn't surface until after midday and she knocks his door, blurry-eyed and sheepish. He's been at his desk for a couple of hours already, rewriting the essay, and she looks over his shoulder.

"Tell me about your famous Kuhn, then."

He gives her the gist of *Structure of Scientific Revolutions* and she seems to take it all in, sitting thoughtfully on his bed while he finishes. As they walk downstairs for lunch, she looks him up and down appreciatively, rediscovering her brother. Roy is tall and slim, strongly built, and he carries himself well. The long hair and beard, of course, mark him out as a student of the late sixties and she can't help smiling — no one would recognise this as the fresh-faced young teenager with a side parting in the photograph on the mantelpiece at home, the boy their parents probably wish he still was.

"You look good, brother," she offers, "and you seem a bit cleverer than I always thought."

"Thanks," he smiles. "We don't know each other, do we? And look at you now, all grown up and doing A levels. What are they, fashion and psychedelic rock?"

It's ill-judged and she lapses into silence, a little hurt, until halfway through their meal he says they'd better find her a train home before it gets dark. Her face changes as a big frown settles over wide eyes.

"I don't want to go back today, it's been soooo good here. Pleeease! And I haven't seen the university yet, not properly. I know, I could come with you to your tutori-thingy tomorrow, couldn't I?"

"I'm not sure that's allow—"

"Pleeease? I have to do my UCCA this year anyway so I can tell everyone it was an Open Day."

He doesn't know how to argue with her and senses that he wouldn't win anyway. So while she phones home to say she'll be back tomorrow — their mother doesn't seem at all concerned or surprised — Roy goes out to check the car's oil and water since he hasn't used it for a few weeks. It's a surprisingly mild day with a wan sunshine doing its best so they're going to the Edge for a couple of hours. He makes a flask of coffee, takes a spare blanket from his room to sit on and begs Amy, along the corridor, to lend Helen her wellies.

Φ

The woodland is as peaceful as ever and they have it to themselves. He helps her over the stile and along the muddy track down to the carved rock, retelling the myth of the wizard like a tour guide. Finally, they settle on the sandy bank beneath the birch, nature silently holding them, breathing with them and giving thoughts the space they need after yesterday's noise.

Roy has always come here to calm his mind but today that's not working so well. And Helen is no longer a little girl.

"You can tell me about it," she says quietly, reaching out a hand to his.

"It's just… when I came here before…"

"It was…"

"And now, everything…"

"Changed. Yes, I know. But the place is still…"

"Nothing's the same. Nothing."

"You are…"

"Nothing. I don't know who…"

Then she says something remarkable.

"You can tell me, you know. After all, we've only just met. I'm a stranger."

He smiles for the first time since they got here.

"Not quite. You know. And you're in…"

"The enemy camp? Is that what you think? Maybe for you nothing's the same, but nothing's changed at home. I'm not…"

"Sent here? You came…"

"Because of Family."

"Yes."

She withdraws her hand and turns her head away and he doesn't know if it's because she hasn't been honest or because she's offended. So he pours coffee and they warm their hands around the mugs until she stands and walks slowly around the clearing, composing herself before returning to settle down and look into his eyes.

"You know… it's not easy for anyone. Being human, I mean. Everything changes eventually — our bodies change, our thoughts, relationships, families…"

"Not ours."

"Eventually. There are always endings… and beginnings. We think we're clever and we make all our plans, then…"

"Life happens."

"Yes. But it's fighting against it that hurts. Life is just what it is. When we don't accept it, think it's unfair, that's when it hurts."

"When did you get to be so wise?"

"I'm a girl."

He takes a bar of dark chocolate from an inside pocket, breaks it in half, and they share it in silence until she owns up.

"All right. Actually, that's Buddhism. I think. I'm doing Comparative Religion. They say these are truths and we have to accept them 'cause it's the only way to be strong and happy. Accept the things we can't change… and, um, have the courage…"

"To change what we can. Yes. That bit was actually a Protestant priest in the forties."

"Oh."

"But you're right about the truths. The thing is, though, you're wrong too."

"What do you mean?"

"Life didn't just happen. It was me — I made a decision. And then…" He spreads his hands as though that's all there is. But she isn't letting go.

"You know, big brother, for someone so logical you're not so clever after all."

"Eh?"

"We're always making decisions, aren't we, and usually it's not really our decision anyway, it's because of circumstances."

"You're going to tell me it's all fate, are you?"

"'Course not. But we can't control everything, we just do our best. And we can't know what's coming next. It's not your fault that everything changed. You didn't have any, um…"

"Obligation? Who have you been talking to?"

"I don't know what you mean. Look, anything can happen to anyone. It's a given. You have to stop…"

"Feeling sorry for myself?"

"I was going to say… being sad."

The light is fading fast now and a cold wind is rustling the piles of wet, fallen leaves. They pack up and head back to the car while they can still see the path, then sit for a few minutes with the heater on. When they set off, she tries again.

"You know, life can be good again. Things can turn round. You'll have new opportunities, meet new people. If you try to stop focusing on…"

"Myself?"

"I was going to say… sadness. I mean, not that long ago you were soooo happy."

"And look what I did with that."

"Just sayin'. Miracles happen."

They spend the evening at a quiet corner table in the Fallow Court bar with Red, Roy again withdrawn into his own world while the girls are deep in conversation about the relative merits of Deep Purple and Led Zeppelin. Finally, he excuses himself to put finishing touches to the essay.

Several eyebrows rise when they enter the tutorial room next morning but Alan Meeks merely nods — whether or not he believes it — when Roy whispers to him that Helen is really interested in Philosophy.

Jack Croft is the first student to be singled out to give an overview of Kuhn's work, probably because he is the quietest member of the group and hardly ever offers an opinion on anything despite his sharp mind. He and Roy respect one another's introspection and have become friends in the Department. He's a local man still living at home and has come through a rough Comprehensive. However retiring, he stands out by his short, curly hair and his clothes — "It's proper," says his father — never in jeans, always in a smart jacket.

"So... he, um, challenges the idea that science progresses in, um, a linear way," he murmurs. Meeks encourages him to continue with a smile. "Well, scientists do their experiments and collect their data... but, um, most of the time they're all just supporting a theory they all think is true anyway. And it's safer to ignore anything that doesn't fit."

"Anomalies," chips in Marcus, never one to be left out of a debate. Yet even he has only achieved his top grades by playing to the rules. His thick, black hair is trimmed neatly at the neck and his personal signature is a multi-coloured cravat that he's never seen without. "Eventually there are too many of 'em and someone has to come up with a new theory that changes the truth. Kuhn calls it a—"

"Paradigm shift," ten voices echo, everyone wanting the professor to know that they've actually read the book.

"Quite so," says Meeks quietly, seeking to tease out whether these eager students in an arc before him have actually got the wider message. "But what do those same scientists then do to save face? After all, to some extent they've all been proved wrong." He waits in the silence, slowly scanning each face in turn before settling on Roy's. Shifting uncomfortably, Roy realises he's been caught in the headlights.

"They, er, rewrite history, sir."

"An example, please."

"Well, in Newton's *Natural Philosophy* he says that Galileo discovered the gravity equation — about the constant force. But Galileo never said anything about forces, he just did experiments. The new theory only came a century later when physicists started asking different sorts of questions."

"The, um, answers you get," weighs in Jack, "depend on the questions you ask."

"And Dalton's chemical atomic theory only came together right at the end of his career when he applied chemistry to different questions. But the way he wrote up his work made it sound like he was onto it from the beginning."

Several sheepish faces shrink into their chairs at this, having glossed over that part of the book. Meeks makes some mental notes.

"And has anyone thought," his calm, authoritative voice putting everyone's nerves on edge, "that perhaps Thomas Kuhn is making a subtle, more general point about human behaviour? That we all believe what we want to believe? We rewrite history, as Roy put it, to suit our own interests?"

"I've been reading about False Memory Syndrome."

The new, soft voice makes everyone sit up straight and turn towards Helen. Eyebrows are getting a lot of exercise this morning as the entire energy of the room changes. Again, Meeks smiles encouragingly.

"Well, it seems a lot of people have strong beliefs in their memories of some traumatic experiences that actually didn't happen at all. It's been proved. It affects their whole lives, how they relate to other people. But our memories are hardly ever true, they're fallible and unreliable because what we remember depends on how attentive we are and on our expectations and emotions at the time. Sorry..." She smiles shyly at the sea of faces trained on her, including her brother's. "I, er, I'm doing Psychology."

"Don't be daft. That's not at all the same thing as scientific revolutions," objects Marcus, annoyed that he's being upstaged.

"You're right, it isn't," concedes Meeks. "But on the other hand, it does go to the heart of the matter. Thank you, Helen. What is truth?"

"Truth is whatever we want to believe," observes Jack, with a touch of bitterness. Helen has touched a raw nerve of some experience he doesn't talk about.

"Or perhaps," Meeks offers, to deflect attention from him, "what those in authority tell us to believe?"

"People like you, you mean?" comes a small voice at the back. Everyone laughs, including the professor. It's easy to see why he is so well loved by his students, holding the reins yet always self-effacing and willing to listen. Perhaps that's why this subject is so dear to him and central to his teaching.

"Indeed," he agrees. "And hasn't that been the cause of most of humanity's conflicts?"

"On the other hand," Roy can't hold back, "sorry, but isn't that also the reason why scientists behave as they do? Why everyone does it? I mean, people go along with the status quo precisely to avoid conflict?" A telling glance passes between him and Helen, sharing personal experience at home.

"That's right," adds Jack. "Scientists depend on funding grants and publication of their papers for their livelihoods. And reputation. They can't rock the boat. And people love to join clubs and societies—" he glances around at the others nervously since they all belong to one or the other "—and churches and political parties because they just want to fit in. If you think for yourself, you get labelled, ostracised."

"Yes, but if you want to come up with a different truth, you have to provide the evidence." This is Siobhan, a short, overweight girl with heavy-rimmed glasses who has also had to overcome prejudice to get here.

"Evidence is easily ignored," Helen counters, emboldened by being given permission to speak. "Has anyone here heard about Rhine's experiments with telepathy at Duke University?"

"Oh, come on! Parapsychology isn't even a proper science," Marcus snorts. But she's unmoved and turns to him coolly.

"And yet telepathy does happen. Some of Rhine's subjects scored impossible results with the Zener cards, odds of, like, billions and billions to one against."

"Exactly, it's impossible."

"Um, aren't you guilty of ignoring the evidence, mate?" Jack has probably spoken more today than in all the term's tutorials put together. "There are all kinds of unexplained things in this world."

"Like Marcus getting three top grades at A level, you mean?" whispers Siobhan.

Meeks brings the discussion back to Kuhn before wrapping up the tutorial and the students filter out with some laughter and argument continuing along the corridor. Roy hangs back.

"Thank you for letting Helen sit in, sir."

"My pleasure, old chap. She certainly livened things up. I hope we'll see her again in due course. Ah, what's this?" Roy has taken the new essay from the document case he always carries, a gift from his father. ("You have to look the part," he'd said.) The professor smiles and nods. "I think I was expecting this. Well done."

Just before the ticket barrier at Piccadilly Station, Helen turns to her brother and hugs him.

"Thanks for letting me stay. I enjoyed getting to know you at last."

"Me too," he grins. "It wasn't quite the weekend I had planned."

"Good." The train is about to leave so the guard hurries her. Over her shoulder, she can't resist a parting shot. "Remember, big brother, the truth is only what you want to believe."

Φ

I have no idea how I got back to the cabin from the lake but I fell onto the bed and slept fitfully for goodness knows how long, a phalanx of dream fragments flashing through my mind in ragged formation and firing off meteorites at the closed shields of my resistance. It was open warfare, with one state of mind insisting on telling me something whilst another state refused to listen.

When I awoke, I stumbled outside to find Iggy pausing beside the stream and looking at me pityingly. I sat cross-legged on the ground nearby and reached out a hand towards him; I needed a friend just now and he was the only one around. Well, he didn't nuzzle me or anything but in my head I clearly heard him before he ambled away.

"You'll soon be one of us."

I can't say that helped much but something had changed between here and the crater, as though a light switch had been flicked, if only a low voltage one in the basement. I was a little more in tune with my strange world. And as my eyes followed Iggy away and back into his forest, I realised that the mist was definitely beginning to thin out.

A small sound from one of the orioles made me look up. She was there again, the old woman just beyond the arch, and I could see her more clearly. She was holding the baby and smiling at me, a light of recognition in her eyes despite the squint. But, of course, as soon as I got up and moved towards her she faded away to nothing like before. So, in the oddest way, I wasn't alone here after all.

I drank from the stream, its waters cool and crystal fresh, and out of habit ate some fruit for breakfast. The tomatoes and bananas were especially delicious. I had hardly eaten anything since I arrived and didn't need to, my body feeling lighter and more energetic with every passing...

Look, I suppose I have to address this point. For long periods, the light was bright and clear although I never saw the sun. Nor were there any clouds, save for the thin haze over the lake, and without rainfall I would wonder how the flora grew so profusely and the streams ran with such energy down the mountainside. And then the light would dim when I began to feel tired despite there being no moon or stars to be seen above. So we may as well call this day and night, for want of any other way to describe the rhythm of life, although I had lost track entirely of that since arriving.

Like food, perhaps time is a habit.

So imagine my pleasure when I discovered some candles and a box of matches at the back of a drawer in the bedside cabinet, which I'm sure had been empty before. Anyway, this enabled me to continue writing my diary in the evenings. And with a flourish of joy, I was now able to light up one of the *Petra* cigarettes too, although it didn't taste as satisfying as I hoped.

All of these things could be added to a long list of incomprehensibilities but they didn't trouble me. When you grow up in a communist regime, it soon becomes ingrained that you don't ask too many questions about the ridiculous, the inhuman and the irrational. You just want to fit in because if you think for yourself you get labelled, ostracised, and that can be dangerous for your livelihood, or your life.

Yes, I had pieced together from the dreams that I had lived in another place too, a place where people could think freely and become individuals. But even so, there were always unanswerable questions. 'When was the beginning of time?' So it didn't bother me that I had lost track of it altogether. I had quickly learned that, in whichever country or world I found myself, the truth is only what you choose to believe.

Yet some new truth was beginning to press itself insistently at the admittedly porous boundaries of everything I thought I knew since returning from the lake. I was here because of love.

Slowly, but with the inexorable force of the tides, I was re-member-ing, piecing together the broken parts of my history. This new awareness had something to do with another person, yet in the same breath it had nothing to do with this person, whilst because of this person love had revealed itself. The still waters of the lake had spoken to me of transcending persons, of having nothing to do with good times or bad times, with desires or opinions, of becoming aware of one's own deepest self.

And just as it had back there, as I wrote this the pain in my head throbbed again as if to split me apart. Better not to think about it too much, then. No doubt this new anomalous truth will find a way to reveal itself in due course, and then I shall have to think differently.

To distract myself as much as anything else, I set about exploring this island. I began close to home, following narrow trails through the dense trees that covered the mountainside, pausing to sit on a fallen branch in a clearing, all the while feeling ever closer to the beings around me. It was easy to walk even up steep paths and there were moments when I would look up far ahead of myself and just somehow find myself there. The familiarity of putting one foot in front of another was comforting, though.

Other creatures accompanied me on some of these journeys, at least that's how it seemed because, whenever I stopped to look around the forest, there would be a thrush eyeing me curiously with head on one side from a high perch or a distinctive large frog hopping along a nearby ditch. Images came to me then of teenage adventures in the holidays, cycling through the Krkonoše National Park in Hradec Králové, along the Devil's Valley and looking up to the snow-covered Sněžka. It had seemed to me the most beautiful place imaginable. Yet one was always a guest in nature like this, not part of it, much like we Czechs felt like visitors to our own lands under Soviet dominance. And, just as we were always wary of strangers, the wildlife had kept its distance from me.

"Are you one of us, then?"

I distinctly heard the soft, low voice, like a breeze rustling the long drooping leaves of an old mango tree on the far side of the clearing. A dark, formless shape flowed around its lower branches before settling within the canopy as if to study me from a safe place.

"I... um, I'm not sure," I found myself saying aloud.

"It is good here," came the response, before the form faded away. As though my eyes had been directed to look lower, I then noticed an extraordinary orchid with its roots buried into the tree itself, masses of bright yellow flowers in their starfish patterns with lips standing proud.

Why had I never noticed that this was my nature too? Why had I only ever craved the conversation, the music, the touch of fellow humans with barely a thought of this deeper communion? Maybe it was a survival instinct, to be part of the group, avoid trouble, feel alive. Now, among these trees, I felt more alive than ever.

Nonetheless, there were of course moments when I again found myself longing for human company. After leaving what I assume had been a hospital — and only briefly there — I had seen no one except an old lady who kept disappearing and the young dark girl with braids. So I set off back the way I'd come to find her. As I almost expected, she wasn't there and nor was there a sign of anyone else. The tumbledown shack was still there though, so I took the opportunity to exchange some of the clothes I'd found in the wardrobe of the cabin for a long, white cotton dress and white canvas shoes. It's amazing, the brief happiness a girl feels wearing new things.

I moved on past the little bay, the pelican now drifting along off to one side, hovering every now and then to let me catch up and watching me with the same curiosity I had come to recognise in other creatures' eyes, and retraced my steps up through the woodland. There was absolutely no evidence of any hospital.

Another unanswerable.

With the coastline to my left, and having seen the rounded tip of the island as I was arriving, I decided to call this area 'north' — whatever that meant here — and to explore clockwise — whatever that meant. Walking was becoming ever more comfortable and I rapidly followed a deep gulley uphill, sparkling water rushing the other way, then down and across a wooded valley to the north-east coast.

I was met with a surprise. So far, everywhere I had been and everything I had seen had been utterly calm but now I stood at the head of almost vertical cliffs looking down on a hostile, rocky shore where waves crashed and splintered with a hellish roar. It was refreshing, and somehow reassuring, to find that the island was somehow more... real. The sea was driving a salty wind up the rock to sting my face and I gulped down its powerful energy, moving right to the edge to bathe in the welcome new experience.

Closing my eyes, just in time a thought from long, long ago arrived with a jolt, that imagination — not even a memory — of the Krkonoše mountain peak, the light-headedness and the arousal of inner being, the forgetting... For those who have lost their way and don't know where they're going, it would be so easy to jump and welcome the loss of thought. I wasn't ready for that.

There was a coastal path running south which I followed, reminding myself that there was much more to know. To the right now, the land was hilly and barren save for clusters of trees reflecting a silvery light as their leaves danced in the sea breeze. I stood for a while to look out over the dark blue ocean, great shadows racing across it into an unseeable distance, and for the first time realised that each part of this island was telling me something about myself.

As yet, I wasn't clever enough to understand its language but this thought was now firmly at home in my mind and intending to stay. What was clear enough, though, was that there were expanses of my self that remained unknown to me. Some of these were featureless, which is to say that I did not have the awareness needed to see their features, much like I have often felt the presence of other people passing nearby as I have travelled this island without being able to see them. I assumed that this was some fault, or immaturity, in myself. On the other hand, there were regions I could apprehend that were much darker and forbidding, even threatening my safety — and, presumably, that of any others who may be close to me. Best avoid them, perhaps, at least for now.

And as if to acknowledge the opening of this small window, the woodlands waved and beckoned me back further inland to safer areas, back among the flowing formless shapes that spoke and the birds and small creatures that had begun to accept me as one of their own.

My eyes were clear and open now and I looked around eager to know them better. What I began to see, though, was altogether different. I sat on a log in a clearing, admiring a spreading shrub much higher than myself whose branches arched in all directions bearing pale yellow and orange tubular flowers that split open into delicate lips. Then something moved within the shrub, something that had a body with limbs of some kind. I shook my head but, no, this was not a mist in my eyes. It was tall, slim and sinuous and, whilst I couldn't make out any features, it was certainly watching me.

"Um, hello..." I ventured nervously. There was no response and the shape curled into a white wisp that slowly faded away to nothing. But I would see it again, often from the corner of an eye or floating among trees a little way off, and knew that I was being assessed. I was not at all afraid. Why should I be, when this land had welcomed me in and was allowing me to know myself a little better?

I returned to the cabin for a while, to rest and consider my discoveries and, well, to enjoy that comforting feeling of simply being at home. All was as it should be, in fact it seemed lighter and the dust had cleared. The pencil beside my diary was sharp. The fruit bowl was replenished. The bedclothes were fresh. Was I being serviced? Not entirely, apparently, because in the bathroom the creamy soap was almost completely nibbled away and my ratty lodger looked back at me guiltily before edging away backwards into his hole.

Iggy would pass by every day and even rest beside me for a while at times, sniffing my ankle with bobbing head and waving dewlap, which I decided to take as a gesture of friendship.

Another encounter, though, was not so welcoming.

It was when I continued my travels over the forested central mountain and, accompanied at a distance by the tall, white wisp, across to the south-east. Throughout, there had still been no sign of human life, which in an odd way was a kind of relief. What people call society, I had learned, is a mere surface tension on the swamp of human emotion and barely natural. Most people are suicidal fish, following where the school leads and willing to grasp any appealing hook that suggests security. Through centuries of invasion from all sides, from Celts to Slavs, Habsburgs to Russians, we Czechs have learned to keep our heads down and go along with it all because we know this or that invader will eventually lose interest or be usurped by another. By and large, I didn't like people much and was enjoying their absence.

Until now.

The landscape here was becoming desolate rather than barren, as though its life was as yet undiscovered. It was distinctly colder too and the air was still, hanging back and making itself difficult to breathe. My wispy friend also left me to carry on alone and presently I reached a kind of natural barrier of thick, tangled brambles. Its thorns pointed at me menacingly and it clearly stretched for a distance. No way through.

Frontiers have never bothered me. The details still escaped me but I was certain I had crossed them many times, by tunnels and through barbed wire, by train and by... aaah, a crack of pain as another fragment returns, of a musty office and — what, a slug in uniform? I composed myself and began to follow this border, searching for its weak point, until I was stopped in my tracks by a huge shadow. It spoke.

"You can't go through. You don't have permission."

The shadow revealed itself to be a very large, very imposing sort-of man. What I mean is, the figure was not really solid, it shimmered and was almost transparent, but it was dark-skinned and clearly very muscular beneath its grey robe. At least, I noticed instinctively, it wasn't armed.

"How do I get, um, permission?" My voice sounded very small.

"You don't. Authorities. Go back, Miss." Well, I suppose he was attempting to be friendly, insofar as a massive otherworldly bouncer can be. I moved one way and another but somehow he blocked my path at each turn until I smiled at him and headed back the way I'd come, already planning a different approach. I don't like authorities in particular.

This island was taunting me.

Wisp was taunting me, too, hanging around more and more often just out of reach and fading to nothing if I approached.

The more I rested — my exploring didn't tire me but my brain kept insisting it had work to do without any interruptions from me — the more the dream pieces began to slot together like a giant jigsaw. But you know the frustration when half the pieces are blue sky with light cloud that all look the same or, when you get to the interesting section that's about to reveal all, you find that some pieces are definitely missing? You search the packaging, you lift up the furniture, you even check the kitchen bin… and resign yourself to having to wait for them to turn up.

There I was, though, clearly moving to Prague, to my parents' frustration, and there was Josef. I think he was a journalist, I know he was my first lover and there was a hint that our relationship, and he himself, ended very badly. The details were missing. There was England, the city of Liverpool and the hospital where Nurse Mallory befriended me, and there was the lovely Welsh countryside of lakes and green hills and… no more. But there was clearly also a university somewhere in the north-west and a young man, slim with long hair and a beard and… the crack of pain in my head woke me up at this point.

I decided I needed a holiday. Or maybe one of those pieces was laughing at me from a dark corner and whispering that I hadn't yet explored the quiet beaches to the south-west.

I followed the dusty path a little way inland as it wound around and over a small hill at the top of which, unbelievably, sat a tiny church. Inside, it appeared to have been deserted with thick dust covering the handful of pews, some of which were overturned. In the chancel, the once beautiful mahogany pulpit was split down the middle and, beyond, the sanctuary was bare. One ray of hope was the bright daylight streaming through the stained window above to fall on my face as I stood halfway along the nave, but the glass was cracked and several panels were gone so that I couldn't identify the scene.

"All right, I get it," I said aloud to no one, "just one more neglected part."

Outside, the path petered out to a narrow, stony and unpromising track downhill but at least I had company here, a small and friendly tabby cat with black and silvery markings that wrapped itself round my legs, looked up hopefully and then trotted along a little way ahead. I decided that she was leading the way, which was just as well because there was no obvious path towards the coast.

We came to a pleasant woodland of white cedar and neem and Tabby went straight in with me following faithfully, winding this way and that towards the distant light that grew ever brighter. At last, we stopped abruptly at the edge of a ridge that swept steeply down over mossy rocks, treacherous stepping stones within another stream of clear water appearing from nowhere. Here, Tabby looked up at me as though to say, "I'm not going anywhere near that. You're on your own now." And she wandered off back through the trees, job done.

I skipped down the ridge and rounded the last of the trees to be rewarded by the loveliest beach of shingle and black sand I had seen so far on the island. It was quite small and utterly private, fringed by sheer grey cliffs topped by woods that surrounded it except for the way I'd come. Patches of colourful wild flowers grew at the base of the cliffs, whilst a group of heavy black boulders near the shoreline offered a comfortable seat from which I looked out over nothing but pale blue water that merged into the sky with no horizon. The water breathed in and out gently in soft waves, slowing down all thought, and all was still except for the pelican drifting past from time to time, this way and that, keeping his check on me.

I hadn't realised how long it had taken me to get to where I should be and the day's light was now beginning to fade. Somehow this only added to the magic, to the peace I felt in a gathering dusk with just the tinkling sound of small pebbles chattering among themselves as they were swept together by the water and left out to dry.

I took off my clothes and walked along the shoreline with cool water up to my knees, something within urging me to drink this as deeply as possible while I could because ... When I returned to my boulder there was someone with me. A presence. Invisible, yet very real. Right next to me, yet equally aware of me only as a feeling.

I began to shiver but not with any chill. The waves were running through me, chapters of a story that hadn't quite begun yet despite everything I had experienced so far, and I stared out over the sea watching young shadows hop and settle on the waves as all thoughts disappeared away on the ebb towards whatever was surely coming over a horizon that I couldn't even see.

Then the music started. It was an acoustic guitar being played far, far away, barely audible but insisting on being heard. At first there were just three notes being picked out and repeated over and over as though each one were questioning the last, before a chord hovered and resonated in the still air like a small animal nosing its path through woodland. As the unseen fingers gathered confidence, the music began to flow slowly and with the rhythmic breath of the waves. And words began to enter through a back door of my mind, each one introducing the next with bowed head as they drew themselves up in lines.

'When this over...
And the dark night flies in the face of our dreams,
When nothing we know is the way that it seems now...'

And with an almighty flash of searing pain in my head, I fell unconscious onto the black sand.

When I came to, goodness only knows how much later, it was uncommonly dark, far more so than anything I'd seen so far, and it took a while for me to realise where I was. Holidays invariably fail to live up to our expectations, don't they?

Ridiculously, I now felt foolish being naked. Having dressed, I searched the shoreline for the gap in the trees through which I'd come but everywhere was now shrouded in dark shadow until... yes, there was Wisp, shimmering dimly beyond the sand. I had no choice but to trust him.

My body now weak and my senses shaken, the ascent up the ridge over the wet and mossy stones was difficult but the pale white shape hovered within the trees just to one side and ahead as though checking my progress, until finally I scrambled clear to be greeted — why was I not surprised? — by Tabby. She led me back to the petering path up towards the desolate church where I stumbled inside, brushed the dust off a pew and lay down.

When I awoke, I was on my bed in the cabin, curled up in a foetal position and shivering.

This would not do, I decided. Until now, whilst having no idea where I was or why, the island had been a relatively pleasant experience. But pain, dark dreams and a ruined seaside holiday had changed all that. Clearly, there were 'things that needed knowing', important things at that, and some instinct told me that an answer of sorts must lie beyond the brambles where I was not allowed to go because I didn't have permission. Well, another instinct told me that this had never stopped me before. Moreover, it looked like I had some help now from other beings nearby, even if I didn't know who they were.

I rested outside in the restored bright light, writing my diary and saying silent thanks to my surroundings. The fresh water from my stream gave me new strength and Iggy's visits lifted my heart.

Finally, the moment came when I sensed the opening of another small window.

Approaching the border from a different direction in the south-west had seemed like a good idea but perhaps I should have known better. Yes, scanning the dense undergrowth from a safe distance on a low, biscuit-coloured hill, I could see a gap where some kind of old road led through. I approached cautiously, looking left and right, and of course almost walked straight into the same huge guard who'd appeared from nowhere.

"You can't go through, Miss. You don't—"

Well, I reasoned, what's the worst that could happen? I simply carried on walking, passing right through him, and found myself on the other side.

Quickening my pace in case reinforcements were being called up, I headed down the rutted, narrowing track, turning here and there as other paths crossed in a naïve attempt to lose myself from those who may want to stop me, eventually pausing to take stock of this new and very strange environment. I was on a hillside that sloped steeply down towards a distant view of the sea, in what might have been open common land and fields save for a few buildings scattered here and there. This may not seem very unusual.

Except that everything was grey. I mean, everything: the grass, the sparse trees and hedges, the buildings and, curiously, me. But it was by no means a dead region because I could sense its people and animals, passing me on the track or apparently working a little way off in the fields. I just saw their vague outlines and felt a sort of electric shiver within when they were close. They paid me no heed. At one house, I knocked the door and my hand went through it so I followed inside. There was furniture, a sideboard with family photographs in wooden frames, a table with an ashtray in the middle, a kitchen with pots and pans, all grey, and there was the owner of the house moving about oblivious to me, an elderly woman.

I began to understand why I might need permission to be here, very much a stranger in an unrecognisable foreign land. Yet I still trusted the instinct that it held some kind of answer for the darkness I'd been swallowed up in, so I moved on across the landscape far away from its shadowy inhabitants and searched.

Inevitably — I can say that now — I came upon an archway of sorts. It had once perhaps been part of a field wall that was long since broken down and now stood incongruously alone, two thick and rotted wooden uprights with a precarious, charred spar across the top. Just beyond it the hillside rose steeply up towards a craggy cliff, but someone had taken the trouble to cut seven steps in the rock. An invitation if ever I saw one. Beyond the steps, a narrow stony path continued on to another set of hewn steps where the climb was harder.

The mist was returning to my eyes now and with my surroundings entirely grey it was almost impossible to see the way ahead. So I just followed where the path would lead me until at last it evened out and I found myself hugging the side of the cliff, feeling my way along and trying to ignore the sheer vertical drop to my right.

My left hand closed on nothing. There was a door-shaped opening in the rock and actually, as I focused through the mist and my surprise, there was a door. It was mahogany, bound by heavy ironwork and with small carvings that I couldn't read, and it was slightly ajar. I entered a dark cave with a high roof and smooth walls, for all the world the entrance hall of some grand house except that trickles of water ran quietly down the rock and traces of copper, cobalt and perhaps silver provided the lighting. I had left the grey behind and the air here had a special freshness that sent a surge of vitality through me. It brought to mind that day hiking with my friend in Liberec across the Ještěd-Kozákov Ridge, and I instantly felt the same warmth of companionship, the same youthful happiness of discovery and the same deep sense of peace.

Nothing about all this seemed at all odd to me, given all the other oddnesses, and I knew I was where I needed to be. So naturally I followed the tunnel that led from the depths of the cave as it twisted and turned ever deeper within the cliff, ignoring other small caves as they appeared to the side of me like anterooms, intent on finding whatever was drawing me in. As I almost floated effortlessly along, the tunnel was becoming ever brighter as a distant light approached. With a burst of exhilaration I reached the end and another partly open doorway that warned me to pause. I crouched down behind it, making myself as small as possible, and peered around the edge.

There was a vast cavern, bathed in that light with mineral colours flashing in the rock and a pool of the clearest white water at the centre. Seven white stone steps led down from just beyond the doorway to an arched bridge over the pool that led in turn to wide ledges cut into the rock like the seats of a Roman amphitheatre.

And there were five people sitting on them.

Φ

He never liked family parties. It's not just that he's shy, more that these are not the sort where people actually enjoy themselves. By some natural law, the sun, if no other god, has shone without fail on these birthday parties for as long as he can remember. Yes, it is July but this is England so that's no explanation. Yet despite the weather, the men are all suited and tied and their women are in long dresses, heels and hats and a considerable weight of jewellery. They stand stock still across the grass, spaced out in carefully chosen groups like a grotesque Art Deco installation created by his father, frozen in time with crustless sandwiches held halfway towards fixed smiles.

The flowerbeds are organised by size and colour, the curves of the lawn are semicircles and Mr Carter is himself circulating — the only apparent movement — with a tray of punch that he's invented, enjoying himself on the fringes of the gathering while actually controlling it and not having to participate. He didn't get to be company director without talent.

Roy stands at the far end of the garden by the small pond, looking out over the field to the middle distance where lost thoughts live, vodka in hand and willow leaves trailing over a shoulder, as goldfish nose about happily until a frog plops noisily from its lily pad and scatters them.

"Who's a clever boy, then?" The arms enclose him from behind in a fleshy belt and the overpowering scent of Yves Saint Laurent Rive Gauche Eau de Toilette announces Lucille, his mother's friend. She is a widow and therefore uninhibited, despite being almost forty years older than him. "You got a First, I'm told. That's pretty unusual, isn't it? But then so are—"

Roy politely untangles himself and turns to face her undisguised scrutiny. He's thinner than he used to be and the blue suit is hanging loosely, but if anything the hair is longer and flows over his shoulders. She looks at his drawn features, stubble beard and shadowed eyes.

"You're still not…?" she murmurs. No one really knows what to say to him these days.

"Thanks, Lucy. Yes, it was hard work but it's all over and I did what I could."

"And now you're going out into the wicked wide wor—" She bites her lip but it's too late. Fortunately, Mr Carter's tour has brought him close by and she reaches out deftly for a glass. "Good party, Ray," she chirrups. "You always put on a nice show."

"Thank you, Lucille. Yes, everyone's enjoying themselves. Although—" he doesn't hide the disdain as he looks at his son "—you can't always tell the boys from the girls sometimes." Appearances are more important than the family's first university degree.

As Lucille trots away in search of a more willing victim, Roy is joined by Helen and Jack. No one would have any trouble telling that Helen is turning into a beautiful young woman. Her long auburn hair frames a face full of vitality with clear green eyes and no need of make-up whilst, asserting her independence, she wears a short, low-cut cotton dress and is barefoot. None of this seems to trouble her father.

It certainly doesn't trouble Jack Croft, whose arm she is clinging onto and who is very obviously smitten. He fits in rather better today, in sober grey suit and pale gold tie that almost matches his curly hair, trimmed short. When they'd met in that Manchester tutorial room there had been an immediate spark between them, fanned by a mutual dislike of the high-flying Marcus, and Helen had somehow found frequent excuses to visit her brother ever since. It had taken Roy the best part of a year to work out what was going on, their meetings covered up by a conspiratorial Red.

"Hi, Jack, glad you made it. You two lovebirds still going strong? And brought together by Thomas Kuhn, eh?"

"Our very own paradigm shift," laughs Helen, if possible clinging even more tightly to her man. Jack grins sheepishly. Working class and introvert, he feels awkward at this foreign event; yet he is a clever man and soon learned that this girl was a more valuable prize than any degree (although he did get that too) and his best strategy was to go along with whatever she says. (He's still working on appreciation of progressive rock.)

They chat about university for a while, staying well away from difficult subjects, yet Roy has become highly attuned to clouds on horizons. Helen is waiting for A level results and has an offer from Manchester, but doesn't seem as excited as her brother expected.

"Thing is," Jack begins awkwardly, "I've been offered a job. Here. By, um... your dad, Roy." Having given up on his own son, Mr Carter has clearly seen a gap in the market. "It's good, too, well paid. But your sister and I would be... I mean, wouldn't be... I don't know what to do." The grip is becoming painful. "I'm supposed to talk to Mr Morris this afternoon."

All three glance across at the slug. Arthur Morris is the company's Training Director. He is short and very fat, with strands of hair greased down across a bald dome and cynical eyes betraying his natural disinterest in young people. How he got the job is a mystery to everyone. Just now, one large, hairy hand is stroking the bottom of the woman standing next to him. She's not his wife.

As though alerted by the telepathy that cannot be proved, he suddenly removes his hand and turns towards the group of young people, bulbous lips forced into what he hopes will be taken as a smile. True, he's been put on the back foot by Roy's determination to leave the company but here is a ready-made replacement. Moreover, it's one that offers social possibilities with the lovely Helen.

"There's a decent motorway between here and Manchester," Roy observes. "If the job's really that good, I mean. And if you stayed up there, my little sis would only get, er, distracted from her studies." Helen scowls at him, clearly looking forward to distraction. "And don't worry about Morris. He's a very stupid little man and basically does what my dad tells him. Just be cool and ask for fifty per cent more than he offers. Settle on twenty-five and he'll think he's won."

Roy looks around this perfect garden and his parents' perfect lifestyle and a sharp flash of pain hits him above the left temple as he remembers this self-same party two years ago that had indeed almost felt perfect. He hadn't been alone then. The wickedness of the wide world had been tamed and the future... the future would crash and burn within a month.

He excuses himself, saying that he's going to help his mother in the kitchen, and walks slowly across the neat lines of grass unaware of the sidelong glances from each group — some of pity, some of judgement — yet completely aware of another presence walking beside him.

Wyn Carter has just taken a large tray of scones from the oven and is hovering over the kitchen table with arms outstretched like a priestess unsure of the blessing.

"Cream first with jam on top?" she asks as he enters. "Or the other way round? I never remember which is right."

"I can't see that it matters," mutters Roy, reaching for the aspirin in the First Aid cupboard. "They all go in the same hole together. And they all come ou—"

"That's enough of your vulgarity," she snaps. "Where do you get it from? America, I suppose."

Her son gets a glass of water to wash down the tablets and bites his lip. He recalls the supposed cosy family evenings of long-gone years, watching British comedy programmes on their new, proudly owned Baird colour television set. The only moments that had made his mother laugh out loud were the toilet humour. Of course, this was in private, not when there were twenty or so guests waiting to be fed. She slashes the scones in half with her new electric knife — a birthday present — and sets about spooning the cream onto them.

"Isn't Paul coming?" she asks without looking up.

"Yes, he'll be here soon. He never misses a free feed."

With the pressure of Finals, the two school friends haven't seen one another since Christmas when they'd had a few frames of snooker at the otherwise deserted local club. Yet the understanding that comes with real friendship meant that they had barely talked except to bemoan the Albion's poor form. Only six wins in twenty-three matches and they'd even lost 1-2 at arch-rivals Wolves. Roy had taken Double Maths at A Level and knew all the angles but his poor concentration let Paul win comfortably.

Still standing by the open window at the sink, overlooking the garden, he is the first to realise that the atmosphere has totally changed. The low hum of voices has been completely silenced by the arrival of two new guests.

Nikhil is tall and slim with short dark hair and sharp brown eyes. Only about a year older than Roy, he is devastatingly handsome. And Asian. He wears a white suit and shirt with a royal blue tie that matches the sari of the woman at his side. She is a foot shorter and four years younger than him, with elfin features and beautiful, long jet-black hair. She looks about her nervously, in contrast to Nick's natural confidence.

They reach the middle of the lawn and stop.

Time stops.

All conversation has stopped.

The deepest silence comes from Arthur Morris.

In a split second, Roy recalls their early friendship as apprentices when Nikhil's family had recently arrived as refugees from Kenya. One day, Morris had wandered into the Training Centre and come across them discussing their technical drawings.

"What'yer jawing 'bout, darkie?" he'd scowled, standing full square in front of him with hands in jacket pockets and belly thrust forward. Nikhil had been completely unfazed, knowing his own intelligence and having had plenty of experience in his short life of judging character.

"Metaphysics, Mr Morris," he'd answered evenly.

"Metterwhat?"

"Yes, what do you think Archimedes would have made of this Hellenic screw?"

For people like Arthur Morris, skin colour was more important than intellect and his prejudice had only deepened over the next couple of years with Nikhil's meteoric rise to Assistant Director in the new Systems Analysis department. The company had invested in a room-sized IBM mainframe and discovered that this young man had the unique ability of not only being able to talk to computers, they also talked back to him.

There had been a notice on the wall of the Training Department: 'Communication only happens when you understand what the other intended you to.' The grammar might have been ropey but Nikhil was the embodiment of its sentiment.

And when Bell Laboratories then produced the UNIX operating system, enabling networking, he was first to understand it and begin revolutionising the company's manufacturing and marketing. Morris had no idea what was going on, except that he was being made redundant.

Snapping out of his shock, Roy quickly pours two glasses of orange juice and hurries outside, relieved to see that Helen and Jack have already moved in to welcome the arrivals.

"Good to see you again, Roy," Nikhil enthuses, shaking hands and standing back to study his friend. "Where did you buy this?" He fingers Roy's hair lightly and laughs.

"Hello, Nick. The world seems to be treating you well."

"Oh, as well as I deserve. You haven't met my wife Asha, have you?"

She lowers her head and smiles demurely. More heavy memories crowd into Roy's mind as he takes in her beauty and youth. He and Nick had had long conversations about this arranged marriage. Newly in love, Roy could not understand his friend's equanimity.

"We Indians live in families, so before we marry we look at another family to see if we have the same standards — socially, financially, culturally and so on. That makes us compatible."

"But what if you meet someone else... nicer, prettier?"

"I won't."

"But don't you want to be free? What if you don't love her?"

"You have a strange way of thinking, my friend." Nikhil had seemed genuinely surprised. "I am free. Love is simply accepting one another and being at peace. Asha has been chosen for me. In any case, your way of doing things is so complicated, full of worries and doubts."

Roy couldn't argue with that, even if the idea of his family choosing his future was incomprehensible.

They talk about Nick's work and his new, small house in a quiet suburb while Helen takes Asha aside to talk girl things. Mrs Carter arrives with scones, hovering at a distance as though afraid of catching colour.

Clouds and horizons. Roy leads his friend to the end of the garden and asks him what's wrong. There's a full minute of silence before Nikhil accepts his trust.

"Do you remember our conversation about passion," he begins, "and me saying it was no reason to get married? You'd had a beautiful experience with... and I said that feeling couldn't last and sex wasn't so..." His voice drops to a whisper and his face becomes ashen. "I meant what I said then, that Asha and I would come to know one another because of our hundreds of years of tradition..." Roy waits patiently, holding this safe space. "Well, the truth is... Asha is very different to me, after all. Yes, we are both Vaishyas and believe in the dharma — living honestly, doing no harm, you know? But she is very... independent-minded. And—" he takes a deep breath and looks around to make sure no one can overhear "—she refuses to... you know, consummate our marriage. She says she's too young. Says she had to accept our marriage but that I... I wasn't her choice."

Roy reaches out a hand to his friend's arm but Nikhil moves away, in too much pain even to accept comfort, so he tries words instead.

"Believe it or not, Nick, I do remember our conversations very well. In fact, I've replayed them in my mind many times these last couple of years. And something else you told me back then was that I shouldn't get so hooked up on love. Love is everybody's destiny, you said, it's where we're all going in the end. The most important thing is to suffer as little as possible — and cause as little suffering to others as possible."

"You don't get it, Roy. The same hundreds of years of tradition that brought us together are now hanging round my neck like... what is it, a millstone? Now that I'm married I'm expected to produce children, preferably a son. But I can't. So I'm not a man. And I am ostracised by our families, just like—" he waves an arm towards the rest of the gathering "—I am by all these people." He takes a fresh, new handkerchief from a pocket, turns towards the field and quietly dabs an eye.

"And you know what, Roy? I used to tell you that I was free because I had accepted my life. I knew that I would never be able to do what I wanted because nobody can, because we have our destiny and freedom is acceptance of that. Well... I know that you've been suffering, my friend, and I'm sorry. But how I envy your freedom now."

"And I suppose you're going to say next that all this is your karma?"

Neither of them have noticed that Jack has come to join them and has overheard the last few minutes' exchange. Nikhil becomes rigid in defence and glares angrily at him until Roy reassures him that Jack is a good man.

"You probably think that you deserve this," he goes on, yet his challenge is softly spoken and friendly, "because of your... mistakes — or your family's or your past life mistakes or something, yes?"

Roy is shocked, his mind immediately computing the reasons for his own misfortunes. There have been a few mistakes, of course, as Jack puts it. But what could he possibly do about his family's?

"It's that way of thinking that imprisons you, Nick," Jack continues, without waiting for a reaction. "You can never be... I don't know, karma neutral, when you don't even know who to blame. This tradition — your family's beliefs — keeps you stuck in samsara and guilt. You can never escape. Never achieve moksha. Don't beat yourself up, Nick."

The other two young men stare at him in sheer surprise, one because no one has ever spoken to him like this before and the other because he had no idea his friend was so well versed in Hinduism. Jack winks at Roy.

"I may be a pleb, as Marcus put it, but I've done some reading." He turns back to Nikhil and offers a hand to the shoulder, which is accepted this time. "I suppose you know your Mahabharata, Nick?" He nods. As a child he had to read all two million or so words. "So, Karna asks Lord Krishna about the injustices and suffering in life, yes? And what does he reply?"

"He talks about his own poverty, his privation, being blamed by everyone for their troubles. Yet now he is universally loved."

"Go on."

"No matter how unfair and tough life is... our disgrace... how often we fall... what matters is how we react. There's no excuse for not walking the right path. Happiness is not created by the shoes we wear but by the steps we take."

"'S right. So hold your head up, Nick. You're a good man, you've done nothing wrong. And by the way, don't worry about Asha — Helen's working on her."

Φ

I settled down low behind the door and watched through a narrow gap the extraordinary scene unfolding in the cavern. The figures were talking softly amongst themselves although somehow I heard them clearly within my head, without being able to tell at first which one was speaking.

Three of them wore simple, long, white robes and looked androgynous, although I guessed that one might have been female to judge by the lighter voice. Maybe it wasn't wise to form opinions like that in a place like this. A little way off sat a kindly-looking monk in light brown habit — Franciscan? — and a more austere bearded figure in black robes who reminded me of pictures I'd seen as a child of Lutheran ministers who breathed fire and brimstone over their congregations. These two remained silent as the three in white robes shared their lament.

"The eagle soars and the hunter with his dogs pursues in a perpetual revolution of fixed seasons and habits…"

"An endless cycle of ideas and actions that bring them knowledge of motion…"

"But not of stillness…"

"Of speech but not of silence…"

"And all their knowledge merely brings them closer to ignorance."

"Indeed, in living they have lost life…"

"And in knowledge they have lost wisdom…"

"Ever further from the source…"

"Nearer to dust."

"Wastelands."

"Garlands of fat words strung from mouth to mouth…"

"Voices blaring…"

"Droning…"

"Yet in the end, silence endures…"

"A knife drawn at the moment when their backs are to the wall…"

"And they're alone."

"Only in silence will they learn the meaning of a lifetime."

They seemed to be quoting poetry, some of which I thought I recognised as Holub, but now they became quiet, staring deeply into the glistening pool. At length, it was the monk who spoke next.

"Yet are we not all afraid of silence — that silence of the space after our prayers… that silence of an empty room filled with grief… the silence of those who fear and of those who turn their faces away? Are we not afraid of the silence of the dark night when our souls cry out — and of the silence of the answer that returns to us?"

"Aah, you are too kind, father," replied one of the white robes. "There is little kindness in their house of being."

"And yet, as ever, you put your finger on the matter..."

"It is fear that drives the human heart."

"Suppose they knew the truth..."

"Some of the truth..."

"Some of whatever truth there is..."

"The truth that doesn't undermine free will..."

"Then, evidence of the truth..."

"Some of the truth..."

"Fear remains endemic..."

"It undermines the power of those who have authority..."

"And people always bow to authority..."

"Ignore what doesn't fit..."

"Rewrite history..."

"Join clubs and churches to fit in..."

"Avoid conflict..."

"And in the end..."

"Their truth is what they want to believe anyway."

"Because of fear."

"Ahem..." There was a sudden change of atmosphere, the conversation hitting a wall, as the minister-in-black spoke for the first time. "Unless," he continued in an authoritative voice, clearly unafraid of being side-lined, "they know love."

The white robes sat up straighter, their eyes turned to him, whilst the monk was clearly fighting to suppress a smile.

"Can we get to the point?" the minister asked.

"Aah, yes..."

"Your, er, girl..."

"Young woman."

"Indeed. What is the state...?"

"How is she...?"

"Do we need to decide...?"

"She is outside the doorway. Perhaps we could invite her in, since she has taken the trouble — and had the courage — to get here?"

With that, the door opened by itself and I found myself with trembling limbs walking down the white stone steps and across the arched bridge. One of the white robes waved a hand inviting me to sit on a ledge just below them. The minister came over to sit beside me, somehow not austere at all now. He smiled and patted my hand reassuringly, no doubt aware that all my senses were rigid with... no, not fear... with awe at being in this presence. The energy of these people (were they people?) swirled around and enclosed me like a cloak of light and my usual confidence — my acceptance of whatever should befall — shrivelled away to nothing.

"Don't worry, Evička," the minister said. "We're here to help."

Were I not held tight by awe I might have fallen over in surprise. Hardly anyone knew my pet name, and only those very close who knew me very well.

"Yes, here to help..."

"Always here..."

"After all, there are decisions..."

"To be considered..."

"And time passes there..."

"So it is thought..."

"So does she know...?"

"How much is she aware...?"

"After all, she is here..."

"Despite the borders and..."

"Everything."

"Yes, that takes some courage..."

"A strong mind."

"Or recklessness."

"So how much...?"

"Not everything," the minister replied, patiently waiting his turn. "There have been many dreams. Experiences. She is putting it together."

"What was broken..."

"Everyone must be broken," offered the monk quietly, "for the light to enter..."

"Yes, we know that."

"Yet there is responsibility..."

"Consequences."

"There is... obligation."

"There are... others involved."

"But she is not to be blamed." This was the monk again, seemingly in the role of balance.

"There is no blame..."

"No blame."

"Yet... there is responsibility..."

"And there are decisions..."

"To be considered."

"She needs to be aware..."

"To know..."

My head was spinning back and forth from one to the other, trying to make sense of all this. Of course I was not fully aware of what might or might not have been... my responsibility. I didn't even know where I was. Or why. It crossed my mind that the least they could do was tell me that, whoever they were, since they seemed to know so much about me. What was I not to blame for? What were these decisions?

"I think it's time we got to know one another better, Evička," the minister said. "Would you like some tea?"

TWENTY-ONE

Having shown their faces, Nikhil and Asha walk slowly across the manicured lawn arm in arm, smiling to all the half-turned glances as they leave. There is an almost audible relaxation of shoulders. With the afternoon dragging its feet, the next test is for Jack to introduce himself to Arthur Morris. Nervous as a schoolboy, still conflicted and having to be given a gentle push by Helen, he walks with small steps towards the dark aura, which detaches itself from the group and takes him aside. No need to worry. Morris is in a very good mood. He hasn't had to speak to Nikhil and his wandering hand hasn't been rejected. Within only a couple of minutes, Jack's own hand curls behind his back and gives them a thumbs-up.

"You've got a good one, little sis," Roy smiles. "And don't worry, Goodyear will lay plenty of rubber down on the M6 in the next three years. You'll get plenty of distraction."

"I certainly hope so." She takes his arm and turns them away from the garden to look out over the fields. "And you know, don't you, that what he said to Nick was meant for you, too. Please hold your head up."

"Mmm. It's not easy when it hurts so much."

"You're still getting them? You need to see a doctor, big bro."

"I did, at uni. Two of 'em. They said it was stress. Gave me Valium." She has a strong grip on arms today. "Don't worry, they went down the toilet."

Just as the last of the tipsy and perspiring guests are falling into their cars and heading home to get into something more comfortable, Paul arrives.

"Sorry, sorry, my uncle was visiting and I had to play families. Have I missed all the food?"

Roy slaps him on the shoulder and heads to the kitchen where he's hidden away a plate of sandwiches and scones and a bottle of vodka. Glasses are draining by the sink and his mother has her hands in a bowl stacked high with plates. You wouldn't know it was her birthday today.

"Have a word with your father about dishwashers, will you?" she says. One pink-gloved hand emerges from the water and points to the table. "There's a clean tea towel there."

Ten minutes later, he is sitting beside Paul on the stone steps of the terrace watching Helen and Jack, who have been put to work picking the lawn clean of cocktail sticks and cigarette ends. He waits in silence, knowing better than to interrupt his friend when he's hungry. When he's satisfied at last they talk about Finals and leavings and Paul's on-off girlfriend Sally; it looks like she's another leaving but Paul doesn't seem too upset.

"No, in the end my heart wasn't in it, as they say. We'd been drifting for a while. She was all fun and adventures — which is great, don't get me wrong — but over the last couple of years I've been changing. A lot, actually. Stuff I haven't told you, not because... I dunno, maybe I wasn't sure myself. And it never seemed the right time."

Always thoughtful and a little introvert, Paul rarely says much and Roy realises there is more to come, probably with a question at the end. He stays quiet and nods encouragement.

"Well, you know what I used to be like. Rabid Socialist, workers' rights, Tory Eton wankers, that sort of stuff. Joined the Soc Soc as soon as I got to uni. They did do a good party on Friday nights, then we'd drag ourselves out of bed at lunchtime and go selling *The Worker* in the main square. It was all 'Read the truth they don't want you to know' at the tops of our voices. Our own Trotsky permanent revolution.

"NP was the loudest — never found out what his real name was — and he was just so... convinced, angry. Then one day towards the end of the year he says he's organising a coach for us to go to Leicester next week because the National Front bastards are having a rally and we're going to kick some heads.

'Put yer boots on, it'll be great craic,' he said. Well, he laughed. He was really looking forward to it."

He pauses to finish the sandwich he's been saving and munches slowly to make it last, looking around at the garden, now perfect and clean again, taking in the regular curves, the trimmed hedges, the summer colours. However lovely, life is not this neat.

"That's not you," Roy murmurs.

"No. No, it's not. Back then I didn't even know what craic meant — splitting heads open, maybe? And NP was an Indian too, an immigrant. I always thought they were peaceful people. No, I wasn't born for violence. Actually, I'm a devout coward if it comes to that. And for all the shouting and the dialectic, I'd much rather just get on with people really."

"So you left?"

"It wasn't easy. They don't let you go easy. I just kept making excuses — you know, essays due, parents ill, Sally thinks she's pregnant… Eventually they gave up on me. I did feel a bit lost, tell the truth, for a while. But then…"

"Then?"

"It was that September. I guy I used to know at school died suddenly. He was only young, just a horrible accident. I came back for the funeral and… well, the whole thing blew my mind. There was his younger sister singing a solo hymn, standing up proud and strong, and some guy from his uni course gave the most incredible eulogy. It was brave, said how they actually didn't get on but he really admired the guy and we must all look past our differences and care for one another. And everyone was singing away like it was a real celebration while I was hiding away at the back, all choked up, thinking what was it that all these people had … this faith, this strength. I wanted some of that."

Roy puts a hand on his friend's shoulder, knowing that this isn't easy. It's more than Paul has said at one go in living memory and it must have been building up for a couple of years. The afternoon sun has faded now and there's a chill in the air with a strong breeze making the willow branches dance above the pond. Helen and Jack have done their duty and left, hand in hand, giving them a happy wave on their way out to enjoy the rest of the evening. The garden breathes a sigh of relief at being allowed to get on with being itself. Roy pours them both another vodka.

"Why didn't you tell me any of this before, Paul? I'm your oldest friend. Gosh, the stuff we've shared in the past, eh?"

"I know, sorry. But there was everything that you were deali— it never felt... appropriate. And anyway, epiphanies might happen in a moment but it can take a bloody long time to work out what they mean. In practice. I mean, in that first term the God Squad had been everywhere touting their business, knocking on doors in halls, stopping you in the street outside the Union. 'Do you know that Jesus loves you?' Oh, fuck off and let me get on with changing the world. Mind you, Julie was very pretty with her golden curls matching the ostentatious cross on her... tight sweater..." His eyes go dreamy just for a moment but then he shakes his head and turns to look Roy in the face. "How could I admit that I'd flipped the coin?"

"'S not such a biggie. If it's what keeps you going. Yeah, there were those Bible readings every day at school with a half-hearted hymn and a droning prayer before the Beak gave us a sermon about running in the corridors and graffiti in the bogs. We all knew that was crap. But what you're say—"

"No, there's more. There was a phrase that got stuck in my head that day. 'Come unto me all that are heavy laden and I will give you rest.' That's Matthew, by the way—"

"'Course it is."

"—and I just needed someone to talk to about it. So a few months later I went back to the church to see the vicar with all my questions about faith and strength and cynicism. He just pointed to the stained glass window above the altar with Christ looking down and said, "See, his arms are open and he says 'Come to me.' It doesn't matter what you've done or if you're struggling, know that you're loved and accepted with all your faults. You're not lost, you are found." And I just blubbed. I felt at home."

"Hmm, I see." He doesn't really. It's not just that Paul's attitudes, his beliefs, have changed so dramatically. It's more... why did he never notice any of this himself? Has he been so wrapped up in his own pain that Paul couldn't talk to him or write to him, just say something? This stuff is really important. His oldest friend has been going through his own grief and huge life changes and he hasn't noticed a thing. He's really let him down. "My turn to say sorry. I've been way too self-interested. So now... where do we go from here?"

"I know where I'm going." Paul stands up and takes the three stone steps down to the grass before turning to smile at Roy with a clear and determined look. "I'm doing a Masters in Theology and Religion at Birmingham. Starts September." There's a total silence in the garden as though all the flowers, shrubs and trees are struggling to take this in too.

"You're... what?"

In the next three weeks, it seems to Mr and Mrs Carter that nothing is happening and their son is going nowhere. Heavy hints are dropped about getting a job, contributing to the housekeeping, inviting that nice girl Kate out. This is in the rare moments when they actually see him, since he's shut himself away in his bedroom for days at a time and only appears to get some food from the fridge that his mother — always a mother — has left for him.

But under the surface and behind the closed door of his life, a great deal of work is being done and a future planned, albeit a sketchy one for now. First, he rearranges the furniture so that the small desk is under the window that looks out over the garden to the fields and the bedside lamp is rerouted to sit at one corner. He carefully rearranges the books and files on the shelves in the corner, throwing out everything from a past that has no relevance anymore along with most of his childhood toys except for the model aeroplane, a Lancaster bomber, he'd proudly made and painted himself from a kit when he was about ten.

Everything unwanted goes into large plastic bags that he takes down to the Oxfam shop in the village. The assistant there raises an appreciative eyebrow at the quality of the offerings. One of the qualities ingrained by Roy's parents has been respect for property. Then he goes to the newsagents nearby where more eyebrows are raised at his request for six large writing pads, six biros and a carton of Consulate menthol cigarettes. Nobody buys those around here and they've been sitting on the shelf at least a year.

Then Roy disappears behind his shields and begins writing an account of everything that's happened. Everything. From the moment he wakes until late at night, he writes in daylight and darkness, smokes one cigarette after another and drinks one coffee after another from flasks his mother makes up. He feels compelled to do this despite the idea nagging at the back of his mind that it isn't necessary since surely everything is recorded... somewhere.

Φ

Rookery Road in Selly Park is just off the A38 and close to the university. It has several small shops and long rows of terraced houses, nearly all let to students. Paul has moved in early and taken the better bedroom that overlooks the small back garden and his books, papers and used coffee mugs are already strewn across the sitting room.

His Uncle Ron was why he was late to the party. Ron is the black sheep of the family since he makes very good money by not actually doing any work himself. This is not a proper post-War British attitude. He buys up old housing cheaply, gets a builder to do some minimal repairs, then sits back and collects rents. But something Ron did very well was turn up for an unexpected visit just as Paul was trying to persuade his parents to rent a flat near the university. Instead, he got a house at family rates. And by the time he left the party, he had a housemate too.

Sometimes, the right thing happens at the right time.

When Roy arrives, heaving a large suitcase through the door and dropping it at the foot of the stairs, Paul is sitting in the more comfortable armchair, bent over his guitar.

"You made it, then. Welcome to the castle. Listen, I've been working on a new song…

'This is a time for the closing of books,
the smoothing of pages and searching for room on the shelves.
And now, holding you from me,
I don't understand how I could hold you to me
in other tim —' Oh shit, sorry."

It's plaintive, melodic and insensitive. Roy throws his jacket over the other chair, stands his own guitar case in a corner and sits with a tired sigh.

"It's all right. Can't keep walking on eggshells. Actually, it sounds pretty good."

"Oh, thanks, shall I—"

"Another time. Just need to clear my head. Bloody traffic. Listen, do you think my car will be safe outside? This road's a bit rough."

"Who'd want to steal that? And I might remind you that this road may be a bit rough but we've got a cheap house to ourselves. Not quite Heaven on Earth, granted, but let's clothe ourselves with compassion for Selly Oak, forgive Birmingham and be at peace. St Paul said that, almost."

"Indeed. Well, at least it won't sway in the wind like that caravan we shared in Wales. And I won't be able to hear you snoring."

A week later, they've established a routine of sharing chores and bathroom. They've made friends with the smiling Pakistani man, Imran, who runs the local convenience shop. And Paul is making friends with the two lovely young women who have just moved in next door and spends days encouraging Roy to show an interest.

"Linda's even doing Maths. Just your type." It isn't working. He comes downstairs on Monday morning determined to help his friend move on. Roy is already in the kitchen.

"Bugger."

"What's up?"

"Having a bit of egg trouble."

"I thought it was cheese on toast today, with beans for you and sardines for me. It is Monday, isn't it?"

"We haven't got any cheese. Or sardines."

"Well, good job you weren't in charge when the five thousand needed breakfast. 'Sorry, Lord, fishes are off. Will a couple of eggs do?'" He peers over Roy's shoulder at the thick yellow sauce. "Too much milk."

"Yes, I'd worked that out," mutters Roy, breaking another egg into the pan and stirring furiously. "And by the way, the Bible jokes are wearing a bit thin."

"Sorry. Bit of an occupational hazard, so to speak, trying not to take things too seriously."

"Some things are serious."

"Point taken. Anyway, why are you all dressed up, shirt and tie?"

"Got an interview at the Council, Education Department."

"Oh, great. Good luck. God, my uni interview was excruciating. There were three of us students and one girl misunderstood the question about what she was most looking forward to. They meant on the course. But she said she couldn't wait to meet Moses and St Paul."

"I doubt they'd signed up."

"Quite. But instead of putting her right the tutor said, 'Well, let's just hope we are all remembered by God.' Wondered what I was letting myself in for."

"Don't worry. I'm sure you'll be remembered by God."

After the first month in the job, Roy understands why the Council finds it hard to recruit Welfare Officers. It's a daily grind of missed opportunity and thoughtlessness that's hard to shake off when he finally gets back to the house in the evening and collapses into a chair, barely able to take in Paul's happy prattle about his day. They'd taken him on because he's intelligent and well-spoken; no other qualifications seem necessary.

In the early weeks he has toured all the schools in his patch, getting to know teachers and reading files on absent children, then launched into home visits where his gentle persuasions have been met with singular disinterest by parents. Typically, he has parked his old green Ford in the road, walked past a smart BMW on the drive and been shown into a sitting room with thick carpet and black leather suite on which lounge an obese father and his smirking teenage son watching a Telefunken twenty-six inch colour television.

"I never 'ad no education an' it ain't done me no 'arm."

It's hard to argue with that.

He's even braved the Bull Ring to look for the children hanging around in groups, laughing and smoking, in the Bus Station and Manzoni Gardens, or even working on market stalls, only to be met with abuse and fingers.

"Keep trying," says Paul one evening, seeing his friend's face across the table, the Indian takeaway untouched. "Even if you just get through to one or two... you know, prodigal sons and daughters, they all deserve love—"

"Not a lot of that around these streets."

"—and Jesus says to forgive them, for they know not what they do. Luke twenty-three thirty-four."

"Well, Jesus should get himself down to the Bull Ring, then, and try it."

Paul puts down his fork, opens his mouth to respond then closes it again. Academic theory, however well meant, is crashing into reality here. True, these are his felt beliefs, but words have little power where there is no feeling. He tries again.

"Suffering is the human condition — you know that yourself, better than most. One Corinthians thirteen four, 'Love is patient. Love is kind.' And that means to yourself, too. You can only do so much."

There comes a day when Roy thinks he can really do something.

He eases himself from the car, stretches, sighs at the Out of Order sign on the lift and begins to climb the stairs. Three floors, five floors, becoming dustier, darker and smellier, sweet wrappings and wet leaves in every corner. Breathlessly, he presses the bell on the eighth floor. There's a hollow ring of mock church chimes and a slow shuffling of feet.

Meeting Mrs Graidy is to come face to face with inevitability.

Like drawing breath, her pain is second nature, burrowing throughout her body, flooding her eyes with emptiness and draining down through parchment cheeks. She wears tension like a suit that's too tight to undo, like the khaki uniform her husband had once worn at Waterloo Station and had never taken off again. Some things have always gone too far and cannot be cured, cut out or untied.

He follows her slow steps to the sitting room, expecting poverty and filth, a door warped by damp, blackening Sellotape on window cracks, the bare light bulb and cigarette ends mounting in saucers — and finds none of these. The oak sideboard is polished and has a collection of silver-framed photographs and there are pressed linen coverlets on the armchairs. Yes, there's a path worn across the carpet, a water-stained wall and cracked plaster — he's alert to all such signs of decay by now. But what he is not prepared for is the shroud of death that hangs about the air and is seeping into his pores.

"You're from the Social." Her voice seems to require great effort and reaches him hesitantly across the gloom, though her eyes watch him steadily. "You can recognise them, like plain-clothes policemen." Thin lips twist into a smile. "I wrote to you," she prompts.

"Yes, Mrs Graidy, you did." He recovers himself and fumbles in his briefcase for the paper, scanning the spidery blue words spilled across the white page.

"It's not for myself, you understand. I wouldn't ask for myself. I can manage, always had to, times have always been hard... since Tom went... There's always others worse off. You have to manage the life you've chosen, don't you, young man?"

"Um, I suppose so. But maybe there are things I can—"

"No, it's my granddaughter, you see." A spasm of pain crosses her face and she waits for it to pass. "She lives with me, well, you know that. Her mother—" she pauses again, shaking her head as though still in disbelief "—she only lives near The Green, not two miles away. But Tyrone left and the other one moved in and... well, the drugs just took hold of her. Heroin. She's eight now, poor child. Or is it nine?"

Roy is gripped by her clarity, her defiance of the mustiness in the air, and sits on the edge of his chair unable to shake off the sense that this visit, which ought to have been straightforward, is some kind of turning point. There will be decisions to make, but they won't matter because life unfolds to its own rhythm.

"What will she do, Mr...?"

"Oh, call me Roy. What do you mean?"

"I mean, what will she do, Roy? I'm over eighty, not long left. They won't let her stay here, the Housing. Or your lot."

The normal thing to do here is make some banal protest such as 'Come now, you've got plenty of years left' but that's pointless. Her every breath confirms that she's right.

"And I can't pretend things are easy for us now," she continues. "We do struggle... with the rent and food and the electric, not that we have it on much. The nice man from the Housing said they'd fix the damp... but he hasn't been back. And the girl needs clothes and shoes. School things are so expens— oh dear, do forgive me, I haven't even offered you a cup of tea."

He hovers above the chair, about to offer, but she waves him back down and shuffles along the worn track towards the kitchen. He stands anyway, grateful for the chance to move his limbs, and studies the room carefully whilst making notes of what he thinks she needs. Perhaps he hasn't heard her after all. He moves over to the window and looks down to see two young boys crouched beside his car, tucking pieces of broken bottle beneath a rear tyre. Across the road is an identical building, its twelve floors defined by block upon identical block of precast concrete. On a rusting balcony, a woman is stringing washing between large nails driven into the mortar, her hair rolled up tight in plastic curlers.

There's an unsteady rattle of china and Mrs Graidy is back, bending stiffly over the table with a silver tray.

"I'm not complaining, Roy. I chose my life and I can manage. No, the girl's my responsibility, you see, her mother's my daughter. Milk? She deserves better than this... a lovely girl, despite everything. And she's very bright." With great effort, she settles back in her chair with the tea and then smiles wistfully. "Takes after me, you know. I was at Bletchley Park in the War. But I've done all I can now. That's all we can do, isn't it?"

Roy drains his cup, puts the notebook away in his briefcase and leans forward, shaking himself free of the shadows.

"Well, Mrs Graidy, there are several things I can do."

He stumbles back into the late afternoon sun, stiffness of mind and body evaporating as he takes deep draughts of fresh air, then carefully removes the broken glass and throws the disappointed boys cowering in a doorway a contemptuous look before driving away with foot hard down. Finally, he knows, he can make a difference.

"Don't waste your energy, mate. At the end of the day, you can't change anything," says Mike, his Team Leader. He has grown up in the Liverpool docks area and is experienced in life's limitations, content to keep lids on pots and have a job.

But Roy's on a mission. The couple of qualifications that got him the job have enabled him to make some good contacts at the Council and now they fall into line almost without realising that they're each part of a plan. It's not a matter of bending any rules, rather of simply persuading those with the power to do things that it would be a good idea to do them. Guttering is fixed and walls dried out, cracks repaired, window seals renewed and floors carpeted and the lift is repaired. It is suddenly discovered that Mrs Graidy has not been claiming all the benefits she's entitled to and her granddaughter also qualifies for a maintenance grant. A home help calls three times a week.

Just as he pulls up outside the block a month or so later and glares at the two small boys hovering in a nearby doorway, a young girl is approaching with a shopping bag in each hand and a satchel on her back. She is of mixed race with long black hair in braids, wears a smart dark green school uniform, white socks and shiny shoes, and somehow looks vaguely familiar although he can't put his finger on why. They reach the lift together and she looks at him with hostility as they wait for it to open.

"You're from the Social," she says. "I can recognise 'em, like plain-clothes policemen." Inside the lift she puts down the heavy bags and presses number eight.

He can see now that there's a dirty brown mark down one sleeve of her jacket, a tear in her skirt and a bruise beneath her left eye. He thinks he should say something but the atmosphere between them is strange and cold and he's still wrestling with it when the doors open. She refuses his offer to carry the bags and strides ahead of him, leaving the door of the flat open and disappearing towards the kitchen, so he wanders into the empty sitting room, puts down the briefcase and takes in the detail of all the remarkable changes with an already practised eye. The furniture hasn't changed — it's old but has always been well cared for — yet there's a new lilac carpet, walls have been replastered and papered and window frames repaired and the heating is on. The room is still and quiet and, on the face of it, comfortable. So why does he again feel death crawling over his skin? Why is it so... empty?

In the kitchen, cupboard doors are being opened and closed and crockery is being rattled. Then, in a slight pause, he hears a faint cry and long exhale of breath from a nearby room. Moving silently to the partly open door, he can just make out Mrs Graidy lying on her bed, sleeping fitfully, her grey face tense with waves of pain.

After a few minutes the girl returns with tea on the silver tray, which she almost drops onto the table beside his chair, making the cup spin on its saucer.

"Nanny always says as 'ow we got to offer guests tea," she says abruptly. "'Elp yersen." She goes across to the sofa, climbing on with her legs tucked beneath her and settling back as though wanting to be swallowed up. Roy dutifully pours himself some tea — it's thick and dark — and inwardly takes a deep breath. He's responsible for the conversation now, although it doesn't quite work out like that.

"So, this all looks so much bett—"

"Are you daft, mister? You've gone an' made everythin' worser."

"What... what do you mean?" He waves a hand around the room. "You're warm and dry now, you've got more money, everything's changed."

She actually laughs derisively.

"Nuthin's changed, not really. Not for Nanny any'ow. Everythin' were already set for her. No one could of changed anythin' for her, tek her out of it all, and in her way she were 'appy the way things was. There's nuthin' you can do for her. Nobody can. She were copin' — it were me she were worried 'bout. Things might look different on the outside, I'll give you that, but you ent changed anythin' what matters. On the inside. An' now she feels worser than ever."

His confusion is beginning to give way to anger and he struggles to control it.

"You mean she's dying now because I changed everything here? She did ask me to help, after all."

"Mister, she's always bin dying. No one can 'elp that, not you, not me. Yes, she asked you to 'elp but not like this." It's her turn to wave an arm around. "See, my teacher always tells us that..." she frowns, trying to remember the right words, "as 'ow nuthin's 'appened if one person don't hear what the other actually says. You may of listened, mister, but you didn't hear."

"So... what did your nan want from me?"

"'S obvious. She wanted you to tell her she's done a good job, what she calls her duty, an' make sure as I'm all right. After she's gone." She looks across the gulf between them with the same directness her grandmother had a few weeks ago, her eyes boring into his. "But that ain't gonna 'appen now, is it?"

"What do you mean?"

"They'll send me back to my mother, now that Wayne's gone an' all."

"Surely not? I mean, Social Services know all about her... her issues... and why you came here in the first pl—"

"Nah, she can put on a good show, my mother. As long as it ent early morning. So I'll just be back where I started, with a mother 'o's off her face, in the same shitty city an' at the same shitty school. An' my face'll still be black."

Defeated, there being no answer to that, he eases himself up and wanders over to the window, looking out at the identical building of block upon concrete block opposite. On a rusting balcony, a woman is stringing out washing, her hair rolled up tight in plastic curlers. Down below, a sullen boy picks up a sharp stone and walks slowly alongside Roy's car, carefully scoring a deep line in the paintwork from end to end.

"I'm sorry. I'll see what I can do." He turns back, picks up his briefcase and makes for the front door with heavy steps. But she hasn't finished yet and slips in front of him before he can leave.

"People like you can't do nuthin', mister. It's like you ain't even really 'ere. Never 'ave bin. You didn't do nuthin' for us, you did it all for yersen. To make yersen feel better. What're you feelin' guilty 'bout, Roy?"

The lift isn't working and her eyes dig deep wounds into his brain as he walks along to the stairway. Was this all a penance, giving himself to meaningful good works in the hope that the pain might relent? It never does. Maybe lives and deaths are precast, block upon block that can only be masked by carpets and wallpaper but never changed. Everything's already worked out ahead of us.

Where has he heard that before?

"You're human, mate, there's only so much any of us can do," says Mike, trying to make him feel better back at the office.

But the fire that was meant to cleanse away the old overgrowth has burned itself out and any seeds that lie patiently beneath the surface will have to wait. Meanwhile, Roy reverts to the departmental fallback position of form-filling, letter-writing and script-parroting. Yes, there is one notable success when sheer latent frustration gets the better of him and he serves the O'Rourke family with legal papers for the Juvenile Court and, miraculously, young Sean is back in school the next day and is still there, making progress, a fortnight later. They even hold a small celebration in the office and the Director herself comes down from above to congratulate him for sorting out the Council's most intransigent problem family. But it fails to lift his mood.

"You're human, mate, there's only so much you can do," says Paul in the evening. "But blessed are the poor in spirit, for theirs is the kingdom of Heaven. And blessed are the meek, for they shall inherit the Earth. Matthew five one—"

"Well, they're bloody welcome to it. You're not helping, Paul."

"Sorry. Oh, by the way, I forgot. There's a letter for you, came this morning."

It's been redirected by his mother and takes him by surprise. He hasn't heard anything of Marian for a few years now, not since she steamrollered Eva that evening at the pub with a spirit message about her grandmother and a stillborn child. He'd tried to get in touch but she was always… unavailable. Had she always known what was going to happen? Anyway, she says she wants to meet and see how he is. He calls the number and leaves a message on her new answer machine.

On Friday evening he's back in Sandwell at The Mermaid, picking his way past the upturned barrels and between the draped fake fishing nets and cardboard cannons to the bar where the landlord never forgets a face.

"Hello, young Roy, good to see you. How's things? You look bloody awful, by the way."

"Thanks, Adam. Things are fine. It's people that's the trouble."

Despite the chill in the air, he takes his beer outside to one of the wooden tables near the carpark. She's late, having been giving an evening demonstration at the small, white-painted church in Union Street, Stourbridge, where her recycled talk about Swedenborg hasn't gone down any better than last time she tried. Eventually, the red MG sweeps into the carpark much too fast and pulls up with a screech of brakes nearby. In her mid-forties, the flaming hair, short skirt and fur jacket are still turning heads.

As she approaches Roy, her smile freezes and an undeniable shadow crosses her eyes. She sits down slowly opposite, still studying him closely as though not really sure he's there. After an uncomfortable minute or so, Roy gets up to buy her a drink.

"Martini soda, please, Adam, two cherries. And a Bourbon chaser for me."

"Ah, the witch is back, is she?"

She's not her usual voluble self tonight and seems troubled by something she can't quite put a finger on, so contents herself with asking what he's been up to.

"I've got a job. Education."

"Oh, that's... good."

"Not really. I get daily abuse and don't achieve anything much."

"I told you before, Roy, don't you remember? You have to stop caring what people think. When you start out on the path, like you did, you leave a lot of people behind. A lot of people. Friends, family, lov– You can never go back, not in this world or..." Her voice trails off as though she's already said too much and she chases a cherry round her glass with the cocktail stick.

Half an hour passes excruciatingly slowly in trivial conversation about this and that, Marian skilfully deflecting any mention of what happened two years ago. And all the while she is watching him closely, eyes shifting between the outline of his body and the top of his head. It's unnerving and he begins to feel annoyed that their past good friendship seems to be evaporating. After all, she said she wanted to see him. And inevitably, whatever one's good intentions and pleasant expectations, when the atmosphere of a meeting collapses into something else entirely one becomes defensive and is apt to choose the wrong words and the wrong subject.

"What about you, then? How's life? Last I heard you were getting married — your doctor, wasn't it? So I guess you've been keeping fit."

"He died, a year ago. Pancreatic cancer. It's the worst kind, you know, extraordinarily painful."

"Well," he just can't help making it worse, "you didn't see that coming, did y— oh, I'm sorry." He's never seen her face so dark. She drums her fingers on the table, spears the last cherry violently and crunches it between bared teeth.

"And I also told you before, Roy, it's not my job to tell the future, not yours, not mine. Just pick up the pieces afterwards. In this case, mine."

She stands and pulls the jacket tightly around herself, reaching into a pocket for her keys, then turns away towards her car with Roy following lamely behind like a chastised child. She fires the engine into life but then winds down the window, despite herself, for a last attempt.

"I will just say one thing, though, Roy. There is someone coming for you... to help you."

Wheels spin and the car spurts away much too fast, leaving him in the gathering cold and darkness. He buys a couple more double Bourbons and sits at the wooden table, feeling very alone, until Adam comes out.

"Time, gentleman and wi— oh, she's gone. You all right, mate? You know you can't drive tonight, don't you?"

His parents' house is only a little way down the lane so he decides to risk it, slowly and carefully, until he pulls onto the drive behind his father's large Morris with a sigh of relief. It's short-lived. The lights are on and a curtain in his mother's room upstairs twitches as he gets out of the car and sorts through his keys. But the locks have been changed.

"What do you want?" Mr Carter opens the door and stands there blocking the way, the expression he uses for union negotiations frozen on his face.

"Hello, Dad. Um, I thought I'd—"

"No, you don't live here anymore. We're sick of your childish dramas. Your mother's not well and I won't have you upsetting her again. Find someone else to mess up."

The door closes, the lock turns and a bolt slides into place as Roy stands dumbfounded, wondering what just happened. He'd thought this awful evening couldn't get any worse and was just hoping to sleep it off. There's nothing else for it now, since the whisky is about to take complete control, but to crawl onto the back seat of his car and lie down as best he can.

Cold wakes him early in the morning as a thin late November daylight begins to creep hesitantly, wondering if it should bother, across Birmingham. His knees are locked bent and his neck isn't working properly but a rising anger forces him wide awake and he crawls out, stretching each muscle in turn very carefully. A curtain in his mother's room upstairs twitches. He ignores it and gets back into the car, forcing it hard into reverse and spitting gravel out across the manicured front lawn.

Paul is making breakfast when he arrives.

"You dirty stop out, was it a good eve... Grief, you look blood—"

"Yes, I know. Any coffee going?"

Paul is a good friend and knows when to keep quiet. For a while, anyway. He makes egg on toast for Roy and refills his coffee mug twice.

"It appears that I've left home," Roy offers eventually, "according to my dad. He was pretty nasty, wouldn't let me in. Slept in the car."

"That's crap, mate, sorry. Still, 'spose it had to come some day, one way or another. And you're not actually homeless, not until next August anyway."

"Comforting, thanks. Right now, the bed is calling."

"I'm planning on going to the Hawthorns this afternoon for the old enemy. Alice is coming, you know, short dark hair and shorter skirt next door. Finally succumbed to my charm. We could make it a foursome with Linda, yeah? Just your type."

"I don't have one." Roy eases himself up from the table, still aching, and carries the breakfast things to the kitchen. "I need a bath. And sleep."

"So how was Marian? You haven't said."

Roy pauses on his way back and leans face down on the table.

"She was weird. Kept looking at me strangely. Like I wasn't really there. She did say something odd, though, when she was leaving, about someone coming to help me soon."

"Ah, well, that'll be me then. I made you breakfast. No, she's bad news, mate, stay away. Do not believe in the prophets' false visions and divinations and the delusions of their own minds. That's Jeremiah fourteen fourteen."

Roy stops halfway up the stairs and calls back over his shoulder.

"And I raise you he that prophesies speaks to edify and comfort men. One Corinthians fourteen three."

"Good God, how do you—"

"I can read, you know."

His decision to write off the day turns out to be a good one and he's much brighter by the time Paul returns, slamming the front door.

"You would not bloody believe it. Two down at half-time, then Browny gets a pen and Bobby Gould equalises and it's all set up for a barnstorming comeback until Wagstaffe flies in with their winner. That sort of speed should be illegal. Don Howe was spitting feathers. And Alice was bored, just didn't get it at all. Said I was overreacting. I mean, it was Wolves."

Φ

He touched my forehead lightly, took my hand, and I found myself sitting outside the cabin at a table on a wooden veranda that hadn't been there before. The minister sat across from me and on the table were two cups, a teapot, a sugar bowl and an ashtray.

"Do you take milk?" he asked. "I don't remember."

I shook my head, dumbstruck by the incongruity of the scene and the fact that he was now wearing a colourful, short-sleeved shirt, knee-length grey shorts, white socks and sandals. He couldn't possibly look less like a Lutheran minister. To confound me further, he then produced a packet of Woodbines from the top pocket of his shirt and took out the small picture card inside.

"Ah good, I haven't got this one. Look, it's Kate Tyrrell. Irish girl. Captained the Denbighshire Lass. Quite the pioneer, a bit like you, Evička. Would you like one?" He offered the pack to me. "Of course—" he waved a hand over the table "—we can't, eh, actually taste them or any of this. But old habits die hard, eh?" He rummaged in a pocket of his shorts for an old petrol lighter and lit up our cigarettes. He was right about the taste, which was just as well.

There were words in my mind, lots of them, but so far they were having trouble making their way to my mouth. It didn't matter.

"You're no doubt wondering who I am, how I know you, what we're doing here, who those chaps in the, eh, robes were and what on Earth, so to speak, they were talking about."

I managed to nod, at the same time trying to get my head round his broad accent. At this moment, Iggy turned the corner of the cabin and, I'm sure, did a double take when he saw us. He then hurried on without taking his usual drink from the stream and disappeared into the trees, pausing just before he left to throw me a distinct look of disappointment.

"Well, let's start at the end," the minister said. "The chaps in white robes are what we call elders. They're supposed to know, eh, everything that's anything, 'though to be honest I don't understand what they're going on about half the time. Still, they keep an eye on us, as it were, and get us to, eh, move things along when they think it's necessary. What you had there, lass, was what I believe nowadays they call a case conference."

So I was a case? It occurred to me that I may not know much about elders and the like but it would have been a courtesy, at least, to let me know that earlier.

"You have a point, lass. But on the other hand, as you say, you don't know much about us. I mean, you've not given us any, eh, thought, have you? To be honest, it's a bit, eh, dispiriting, seeing as I've known you for so long."

This was altogether too one-sided for me and I was beginning to get annoyed by the implied rebuke for something I didn't have a clue about. I mean, who the hell did this man think he was?

"Ah, yes, sorry, lass. I should've introduced myself. They call me Jamie."

"Is that your name?"

"One of them."

"And if you know me so well, perhaps you could tell me where I am?"

"Of course, Evička—"

"I'd prefer Eva, if you don't mind. We don't know each other that well yet. Or I don't know you."

"All right, lass, sorry. Well, you already know this is an island and I must say you've been most, eh, resourceful finding your way arou—"

"That doesn't answer my question."

"You're not making this easy, Eva. Perhaps I should have, eh, expected... What I was going to say is that everywhere you go and everything you think here is, eh, important in finding out who you really are and what's going on."

"I've been working on that. I've kept a diary."

"Yes, that's good. 'Though you don't need to, of course. Everything is recorded anyway... not in books, naturally. I mean, there aren't any great marble libraries full of... well, they'd have to, eh, keep rebuilding them bigger, wouldn't they? And think of all that paper. No. But it's all recorded anyway. Somewhere. Still, Eva, you've done well so far."

"And what about all the others here? I mean, wherever I go I can feel other people somewhere nearby, especially in that grey area that I wasn't supposed to enter. Where are they?"

"I should've thought that was obvious, lass. They're, eh, somewhere else. This is your island, to all intents. A place for remembering."

"Well, there are still lots of gaps in my mind. Things I don't remember. Bad things, I think."

"Ah yes, human memory, so fallible, so unreliable. Even believing all manner of things that, eh, never happened. People only remember what they want to, what they expect, depending on how they feel at the time." He sat back and clasped his hands together, looking wistfully into that middle distance people go to when they've switched off or lost track of the conversation. "It's all images, eh, passing through a mind pointlessly trying to fix them in time. Yesterday is an eagle that dives down and, eh, tears at the neat fabric of today. Tomorrow is a ghost that's almost alive but always far away. Feelings here and then gone... words dissolving in the air like, eh, the sugar in our tea... phases of a moon that's full, then gone... all images passing through glassy eyes and disapp—"

"I have no idea what you're talking about, Jamie. You seem to be saying that I'm refusing to remember what's really happened. Or accept the truth."

He drained his cup and leaned forward with elbows on the table, looking straight at me with piercing grey, rather intimidating eyes.

"Eh, some of the truth, whatever that is. You see, lass, most people spend all their time deliberately hiding away from life. They get up in the morning and, eh, put on a mask so no one knows how they feel. They get through the day, they survive, by putting on second-hand clothes to, eh, keep out the cold. You get by. Everyone else can look out for themselves. You keep your head down. It's comfortable like that, a habit you learn—"

"Speaking of habits," one of which seemed to be Jamie's sermonising, "who was that monk?"

"Ah, he comes later, lass. No, what it is, you're finding it hard to recall the, eh, reason for you being here."

"No kidding. Why don't you just tell me, since you know me so well?"

"It, eh, doesn't work like that, Eva. All right, so let me ask you to try now. Close your eyes, cast your mind back through all the images... the hospital... the journey here... falling through the soft mattress... the young woman in a dirty, ragged smock... the filaments of light streaming from your body... the cave and the silen—"

"Aaaaah..." The pain throbbed like a heavy rock bass and lightning flashed across my eyes. "...so much pain."

"Good, lass. Well, it's not too surprising, is it? After all, you did, eh, shoot yourself in the head."

There was a very long silence between us as I waited for it all to subside and for his words to take root. Jumbled pictures like frames of a film flickered through my mind, gradually settling down on a wide screen. I watched from the front row as a young woman in a fawn, soft leather jacket walked casually across the cobbles of Václavské Náměstí and stood beneath the statue. It looked like a warm summer morning. A large group of students were sitting quietly to one side and there were perhaps thirty others in the Square, a couple of them wearing long, light raincoats and grey hats despite the weather, apparently scanning the area. A single shot rang out.

"Oh. Was that me?"

"Yes, Evička." His voice was softer and more fatherly now and he reached a hand across the table to rest lightly on mine. "I'm afraid it was."

"So you're saying... so I'm dead, then?"

"Do you feel dead, lass?"

I considered the matter carefully for a while. After all, this was a lot to take in. As if there hadn't already been a lot to take in since I found myself here. I slowly looked around at the beauty of the forest, the pair of orioles observing us keenly from beside the wooden arch as though hanging on every word, the wooden cabin behind us that somehow definitely looked bigger and in better condition than when I'd left to go exploring...

"To tell the truth, Jamie, I don't think I've ever felt more alive."

"That's my girl. Now we're getting somewhere."

The images of memory were coming thick and fast now, still fragments but falling into place with one another, and not so much tearing eagles as squawking sparrows grouped around a bowl of seed that someone had placed in the centre of my brain. They gather together into a red MG that pulls into the carpark of a pub where I'm sitting outside with someone. A middle-aged women with flaming hair and deep green eyes climbs out, turning heads, and comes over to sit at our table.

"Who is Tomáš?" she asks me. Then, "Your grandmother is with you, your father's mother, dark hair and a squint in her left eye. Her name's Marie. Says she had another son, stillborn..."

"Oh, the woman standing beyond my gate?" I asked Jamie. He nodded. "She kept disappearing. Where is she now?"

"Not here," he said, unhelpfully.

Some sort of logic was beginning to take over, though, as other people's thoughts — not mine — edged their way forward from the wings of the stage.

"So... this is the spirit world?"

"It's an... other world, lass." He shrugged, as though not really taking responsibility for his answer. "There are many worlds, if we have to, eh, call them that."

"Then it's..." I searched through those others' thoughts, "it's the afterlife?"

"I thought we'd already, eh, agreed that you're still alive, lass." Jamie sighed, like a teacher despairing of ever getting the concept of a subjunctive into the head of a dull teenager. He poured another cup of tea, drained it, then got up and moved his chair to sit beside me. "Would you like me to show you?"

As before, he touched my forehead lightly and took my hand. The heavy mist had returned when I opened my eyes, looking down from far away at a busy city scene in shades of grey. With a jolt, I recognised Fakultní Nemocnice Bulovka, the Bulovka Hospital near the White Rock outside Prague, and felt myself being drawn towards the old, baroque Vychovatelna building. There was a presence nearby — Jamie? — and we drifted as though clinging to ceilings through a maze of corridors, turning this way and that, through locked doors and up winding stairways, until finally reaching a small private room. It was white, sterile and shadowed, one curtained window looking down over neat gardens, and in the middle was a bed with three people sitting around it and electronic equipment quietly beeping nearby. A young woman lay on the bed, attached to a web of tubes and wires. None of this meant anything to me.

A white-coated doctor entered the room and all three people looked up at him expectantly.

"Pan a Paní Novák... a Aleš," he began, nodding to each of them and doing a poor job of disguising the concern on his face, "Musím říct..." But I couldn't make out what he had to say because now I was drifting back all the way I'd come to find myself, with some relief it must be said, feeling so much lighter, back on my veranda. Jamie was watching me quizzically.

"You didn't recognise them, lass?" he asked quietly. His voice was distinctly more steely now, challenging.

"I couldn't see clearly. And I was beginning to feel nauseous before you brought me back. What was I supposed to — just a minute, where on Earth did I get a gun from? I should have thought you'd know that I hate them."

"You stole it."

"You have to be joking."

"From a Russian officer. He ended up in a labour camp."

"All's well that ends well, then. But exactly how did—"

"We'd better not go into that now, lass. The thing is, you really have, eh, no idea what led up to all this?"

"None."

He got to his feet slowly and stretched his legs, looking out pensively over the trees towards the pale sea as the light began to dim again. I had that naughty girl feeling again. At last, he turned to tower over me, as austere as when I first saw him.

"It seems there is still some way to go on this journey, lass. You need to, eh, work a bit harder. Work it out for yourself. As the elders said, there are decisions... to be considered... I shall come back when you're, eh, ready. I'll leave the teapot for you and there's tea in the kitchen."

With that he strode towards the gate, changing back into the black robes as he went, and faded away beyond the arch. I sat for a long time, completely stunned by all that had been said and seen. More and more of the pieces were falling into place now. But on the one hand, Jamie's intervention had significantly expanded the puzzle — in fact, it was no longer even two-dimensional — and I had many extra pieces to find. The more you know, the more you realise how little you know, that sort of thing. Apart from the known unknowns, there was a whole new collection of unknown unknowns. Which, I can say, is very uncomfortable when the final picture is yourself.

And on the other hand, I was hardly any closer to solving the first version. I mean... me, stealing a gun? And turning it on myself? And when Jamie took me on that disturbing excursion that filled my body with heaviness, sickness and pain, was he suggesting that I should recognise those people? Was it me in the bed? Yes, thinking about it now at a safe distance, there was something familiar about them but they weren't close to me, the me that I was here.

After a while, I went back inside the cabin, lit some candles and made myself another cup of tea. Like he said, old habits can be comforting however pointless. I looked around and was no longer too surprised that each time I'd returned from exploring the island my return found the cabin a little bigger, a little more comfortable, brighter and cleaner with some comfortable furnishings and nice new clothes in the wardrobe. There wasn't much soap left in the bathroom, though.

On the kitchen table sat my diary with page upon page of scribbled notes. Something else pointless, apparently. Everything is recorded. Somewhere. I shrugged and snapped the pencil in half before taking the tea and a candle out onto the veranda. Jamie (if that was really his name) had taken his picture card with him but left the pack of cigarettes on my new picnic table. Oh well. They were even rougher than my Petras but they couldn't do me any harm, could they, since I was in a... other world.

Where was this world? How many worlds were there, for heaven's sake? The questions merely begged another one — what is a world? And another — was I stuck here in this one until some decision had been... considered?

In the gathering dusk, as I liked to call it, I settled back in my new garden chair and eventually realised that I was smiling. I may not have known the details, especially the important ones, but I did know deep within myself that my life until now had never been easy. There had been oppression and denial, constantly watching one's back because others were always watching one from behind, judging and planning. There had been the journey of study as others continuously closed off the more interesting roads and turned side paths into earthworks. But then somehow, at a carelessly unguarded crossroads, there had been a breakthrough, a vision of change and new possibilities... aaah... there was the pain again but as it flashed through it illuminated images of an English city, a university, laughing people...

So it hadn't been altogether terrible, whatever had gone before. And the gun — yes, I saw it now, a Tokarev TT-33 semi-automatic — had landed me in this rather beautiful, peaceful place full of interesting surprises. I might even have been quite content if I hadn't gone exploring where I wasn't allowed to go and met people. I wasn't at all lonely, the company of others can be very overrated. A lot of time and good experience and opportunity can be wasted in idle chatter and going out to do things for the sake of having a laugh and watching screens in the hope of being entertained and distracted from what you could more usefully be doing. In any case — and I knew this for certain — many others simply can't be trusted. Some use their false smiles and weasel words to get in close but only for what they can get, their self-satisfaction or survival. Some mean well, yes, and may even try to keep faith with the right things, but sooner or later life's troubles will chill them through to the bone. And in the end you're always left alone again, with all that you lack.

In the final release, you pick up your own pieces.

Yet here I wasn't alone. There were tiny pinpricks of light in the shadowed undergrowth and tree canopy around my yard, many of them, and I sensed a gathering of small creatures taking up position to watch me and wait for the next chapter. I tried to stare some of them out but they didn't move, just blinked.

So I drank my tea and closed my eyes to run through all these recent unsettling events in my mind. It was a new habit that I'd developed here, whenever I came back from exploring and was preparing to rest. I would visualise stepping out through my arch and retrace my steps along the winding paths of memory, pausing at each encounter and expressing gratitude — not to any deity, since this place seemed distinctly lacking in those — for everything new I had learned. Almost everything. There were always sights that lifted my spirits and other things I could feel but couldn't understand. Yet I knew that all of them were important and would make sense sooner or later. This would calm me and prepare me for sleep's light show, scene after disconnected scene of a poorly scripted play that the frustrated director sitting in my brain was tasked with reorganising into a meaningful story.

It turned out that the next performance had to be unavoidably delayed.

"Gone has then he?"

The deep fruity voice startled me out of my meditation and I turned to see Wisp floating gently around the corner of the cabin and approaching me. He (for want of a better word) was, as before, misty and almost translucent as he glided slowly right up to the other chair where he settled himself down and coalesced into a more or less solid form that was more or less human in shape.

Yet this was the most beautiful being I had ever seen. Very tall and slim, his pale skin was tightly drawn around a perfectly proportioned aquiline face with piercing silvery eyes. Long, straw-coloured hair hung around the shoulders of a finely stitched full-length white smock tied at the waist with green rope, a long hood hanging down behind. He leaned forward slightly to rest tapered fingers with light green, pointed nails on the table, then frowned as he noticed the cigarettes and flicked the pack away onto the ground.

"Habit bad," he observed without moving his lips.

"Um... I suppose so," I managed to squeak. "They were Jamie's."

"Fuckin' insufferable. I fillin' you bet he's guilt been with remember because you everythin' don't, yes? Holier fuckin' thou than."

One of the things I really enjoyed in my English studies was clause analysis, separating subject and predicate, verb and adverb and the like in compound sentences. It was pure logic and made this richest and most complex of languages so much more welcoming. (Oh, by the way, you may have wondered, as I did, why everyone from humans to elders to wisps on this island spoke English, or a form of it. I just reasoned that this was for my personal benefit, since hardly anyone speaks Czech.) Our teacher Mr Gwyn Parker was, ironically, Welsh and had the sort of habitual facial expression that you just want to slap, but he also had a zealous passion for linguistics that he was determined to embed in us. He would say things like, "What you hear someone speak is not necessarily what they have actually said" followed up by, "Communication has only taken place when you have received and understood what the other has intended to transmit to you." In the Prague University of the communist era, this was a critical message that we all took to heart.

However, clause analysis was not helping me much just now as I tried to unravel Wisp's words. Nor did I remember many obscenities in Dickens. But Mr Parker's teaching came back to me and I realised that the issue was mine, not Wisp's. It was my responsibility to unpick this lock.

"Don't words fuckin' we use I'm best doin' my," he confirmed.

Indeed, not only was I not hearing, he wasn't speaking. The face was impassive, with a slight trace of smile, and the words were arriving silently in my head. My brain went into overdrive, synapses on fire as they rearranged electrochemicals and sent neurons this way and that in search of order. Very gradually, our conversation began to settle down and with a flush of pleasure I found that I didn't need to speak aloud either.

"I'm sure Jamie's doing his best," I said. "He clearly cares about me."

"Enough not to tell you you're here why, though."

"He says I have to work it out for myself, which seems fair."

"Fillin' you with I suppose free will shit all that?"

"Well, yes. It's essential to living as a hum—"

"Crap it's. Simply every livin' thing in its nature does what and must the result accept. You people are what ifs full of. Always tryin' to nature change. It's all fuckin' blame and shame with you."

That last bit came through clear enough. I was still struggling a bit but I definitely got that this was much the same as the braids girl had said. And even though I hadn't given my conversation with her that much thought since, it was dawning on me that this idea was going to be my biggest challenge here — or wherever I ended up. Anyway, who was this foul-mouthed being to tell me what to think?

"Oh, sorry," he said, "that's what you call polite bein', isn't it? They call me Ashly." His voice was resonating around my brain more softly now with a definite attempt to be friendly.

"Is that your name?"

"One of them. We don't names have generally."

"And who are we? I mean, who are you — the spirit of the trees?"

"Don't be daft, girl. You really got it haven't, have you? Every fuckin' human thinks so important they're. Separate from the rest. Your own name. Your personal own life. This mine is, that yours is... No, Eva, I am the trees."

This was the first time he'd used my name, someone else who seemed to know all about me, then. How many more were there? It could make one paranoid.

"Would you like some tea?" I tried, thinking I could go into the cabin for a while and buy myself some time while I tried to absorb what Ashly had just said. He stood up for a moment to have a stretch, his limbs virtually disappearing into the air before settling back down.

"I'll give it a try," he really smiled this time. "By the way, you've realised that probably look like this we don't normally. We can shift into anythin' have to we. I didn't want frighten to you. I am tryin', you know."

He didn't actually drink the tea and merely raised one eyebrow when I picked up the pack of cigarettes and lit one. I inhaled deeply, or attempted to, and glanced a little nervously around the clearing, noting that the pairs of tiny pinpricks of light in the border shadows had definitely moved closer. They weren't intimidating. I mean, they weren't the seven hundred and fifty thousand troops, six and a half thousand tanks and eight hundred aeroplanes of the Warsaw Pact that decided to disturb the peace one August — but there were a lot of them and I didn't fancy my chances if it came to a fight.

"Don't worry, Eva," Ashly said. He made an almost imperceptible gesture with one hand and the lights retreated. "No one wishes fuckin' harm you any here." There it was again, my name.

"How do you kno—"

"It important is to know about ourselves everythin', isn't it? You come here have so, yes, we you know. We always have you known."

"I don't get it. I mean, I've only arrived here recen—"

"No, you don't get it really, do you? Let me this way put it... You think arrived you have from that other place, yes?" I nodded, still disconcerted by his ability to know my thoughts before I'd finished expressing them. "But that place doesn't have a — what do call it you, a monopoly? — on nature. And we everywhere are. I am trying you to tell that only one world there is." He paused and seemed to take a deep breath, making a real effort for me. "Until you get it, Evička, there will always be so much you just see can't... so much you do can't... so many places, if you like, you go can't. Beautiful places."

Like a baby being weaned with its first spoonful of puréed parsnip and broccoli, I wasn't sure whether to take this in with the excitement of a new discovery or spit it out as a foreign taste.

"But Jamie said this was an... other world."

"Jamie's a man, isn't he, sort of? Got a fuckin' job and told what crap to say."

"And I'm a—"

"Woman, yes, of course. But you always don't do what you're told you do?"

That was a fair point. Even as a small child I'd been rebellious. I'd be constantly sucking a finger, for example — I don't know why, perhaps some inner lack of fulfilment — and my parents would always be trying to get me to stop. "It's not natural" and "It's for babies", that sort of thing. But I would simply argue my case in the stubborn way of all Czechs, who cannot accept criticism, and by the age of five I'd learned resistance. Come to think of it, that wasn't a bad thing, given what was coming later.

"I'll stop if you don't tell me to," I'd say, which had seemed perfectly logical back then. But naturally people just can't help themselves telling you what to do and what not to do. The finger got replaced with cigarettes. And all their health warnings and expressions of disgust only made the habit more entrenched, because I'll always do what I'm not allowed to do. That's why I cross borders.

"It gets you into trouble," conceded Ashly, "but that's not a bad thing always."

These memories, and his warmth as he leaned — well, flowed — across the table towards me, were softening my thoughts. Perhaps the broccoli wasn't too bad, even if the parsnip was just a step too far for now.

"We want to help you," he went on, "since you've found yourself you don't fuckin' know where but you've the trouble taken to get us to know. You notice us."

"Yes, there are many lovely, er, natures on this island. Many things I had never really seen before. I do feel kind of at home here. With all of, er, you." There was an audible whisper of appreciation from the shadows.

"Mmm, odd that, is not it, given your attitude towards vegetarians?"

"Where I grew up, if you didn't eat meat you didn't ea—" The pain crashed through my head again and I slumped forward, banging a fist on the table while Ashly looked on impassively.

"A clue, that," he observed simply though not unkindly. "Shitty I know. But you others have had, no?"

The pain had been with me from the beginning although mostly it had lurked in dark corners of my head like an untrained Rottweiler, manageable as long as it was ignored and fed on scraps of memory. But there had been moments when I seemed to have provoked it with unwise thoughts... someone offering me an ice cream on a beach... a red MG sports car... walking naked on the black sand hearing snatches of a song... There had been the lake, too, although then it had snarled with bared teeth in my chest rather than my head. And now it was a simple reference to meat. So these were the clues.

"Are now you putting the fuckin' story together?" he continued gently. "What the thing is all together linking them?"

It wasn't a thing.

It was Roy.

Φ

"Wassup?"

They've established a routine for Sunday mornings with a special breakfast of egg on toast with beans and garlic mushrooms, a sausage for Paul and an extra egg for Roy, and a side plate of extra toast with thick-cut orange marmalade. It's a quiet and comfortable time when they can put the last week behind them and throw around unlikely future ideas before Paul heads off to church and Roy retreats to his diary. But today is silent.

"Dreams," says Roy, almost inaudibly.

"Ah. You shall not listen to the words of that dreamer of dreams, for the Lord is testing you. Deuteronomy thirteen three."

"Book of Daniel."

"Okay, call it a draw. Do you want to talk about them?"

"They've been going on for ages, more than a year anyway, same sort of thing almost every night. But I could never remember them in the morning — just a vague feeling. Disturbing. Then since that evening with Marian it's been getting clearer, like... someone's trying to tell me something."

"What happens, then?" He finishes off the last piece of toast, washes it down with coffee and reaches for the day's first cigarette.

"I'm on some sort of island. It's surrounded by this pale blue sea that goes on forever and it's covered by forest. So last night I found myself walking through the trees up the side of a volcano or something, and there was this beautiful lake in the crater."

"Wow, a lucid one, then? I mean, you knew you were dreaming."

"No, don't think so. Weird. It was just like I was actually there."

"Anyone else about?"

"And that's another thing. Yes, I think so, at least I could kind of feel one or two people nearby but I couldn't see them. There was this sort of mist everywhere."

He borrows Paul's pass and spends much of the rest of the day in the university library where the assistant is only too pleased to help a polite, good-looking young man with an interesting subject. It turns out that neurologists have little or no idea why we dream or what they mean, if anything. Probably nothing. But dream laboratories were born with the discovery of REM sleep in the fifties and Calvin Hall's theories produced a flood of alternative research, mostly ignored by the mainstream.

Common wisdom seems to be that there are distinct kinds of dream and, late in the afternoon, the assistant triumphantly produces a small batch of niche magazines that nobody else has ever asked for. The night's first dream, someone suggests, is a jumble of recent events being scanned to see what's worth remembering. Roy writes 'Filing' in his notes. Then older memories are revisited to see if anything links up or can safely be sent to a dusty storage bin in the far depths of the mind. 'Spring Cleaning'.

Ah, now here we go... With all the routine work out of the way, the inner mind tries to tell us things it has discovered that we ought to know, like a kidney going wrong or the boss at work about to stick the knife in. These are dramas that make us wake up shit-scared with thumping heart. 'Therapy dreams?' But late in the depth of night with metabolism slowed right down — Ingmar Bergman called this the hour of the wolf and, in his film, Johan is visited by demons in his sleep — it's as though we travel beyond ourselves to strange places and futures where other beings, for good or ill, have things to say. What shall we call this? Roy taps his pencil repeatedly on the desk, to the annoyance of the last two engineering students left in the library, then writes 'Consciousness'.

So is his dream number three or number four? He shakes his head to clear it, stares out of a window to the middle distance, then sets about writing everything he can remember from his night travels until the assistant reluctantly tells him that they have to close.

There was something else, though. One article suggests that we can create the dreams we want by focusing on our problems just before going to sleep. Apparently, Mendeleev discovered the Periodic Table like that, although Mary Shelley also met Frankenstein at night. Hmm, hit and miss, then. But maybe worth a try.

December can be an unforgivingly dull month with even the brightly coloured leaves of autumn now reduced to a wet sludge on pavements as people wake up in the dark, go to work, and come home in the dark. In the Council office, nothing stirs except pieces of paper in a silence broken only by the occasional sigh of frustration. Everyone knows there's no point in going to school when the holidays begin soon anyway.

End of term does, however, bring one more opportunity for an increasingly exasperated Paul to save his best friend. The girls are having a party next door before everyone disappears home for Christmas and Alice has invited Paul on condition that he doesn't talk about football or God.

"It does limit me a bit," he confides to Roy, "but I'm going to try. Oh, she also said that Linda would like you to come."

"You're lying."

"Well, yes. But do just give it a go. For me."

To be fair, the music is pretty good — Led Zeppelin, Doors, Moody Blues — if too loud for Roy's wounded senses, and the pervasive scent of hash is making him feel nauseous. He parks himself in a corner of the kitchen, pressed back as far as he can without actually getting into a cupboard, with a plastic cup of warm Red Barrel, and wonders why he's so different to all the others enjoying themselves.

"Earth to Roy," says Linda. She's a pretty girl, tall and slim with long blonde hair in tresses, and she wears an Indian print cotton dress that's so thin it's almost irrelevant. And she is now standing very close to him.

"Um, what? Oh, hello... Linda, isn't it? You're doing Maths."

"Yes, but I've heard better chat up lines."

"I'm sure... no, it's just... I'm not good with that sort of..."

"Paul told me you're a bit weird. A recluse."

"Ah, thanks, Paul. 'Spose I am. Reclusive, I mean. Um... I do like Maths, though. What's the course like?"

"You've really been working on your lines, haven't you? Well, this term has mostly been group theory and algebraic topology."

"Oh. I have no idea what those are."

"Come and dance with me, then."

"Ah, I'm not really—"

With one hand she skilfully takes his cup and puts it on the table as the other hand takes his arm and drags him into the next room. She's a strong girl. The room is dark and packed with swaying bodies although out of the corner of his eye he sees Paul giving him a cheerful thumbs-up as Linda takes his hands and puts them on her hips before her own arms lock around his neck. She is very, very close now. She smells nice. Her skin is soft against his cheek. Her body is pressed against his. They're playing *Stairway to Heaven*.

And none of it has any effect on him.

"You're weird," says Paul next morning.

"So I've been told."

"Linda was quite upset, you know. Did her best on you."

"She's a nice girl, I think."

"Nice? She's stunning, mate. And for some unearthly reason she seems to like you, despite you. I mean, sometimes it's like you're in another world."

"That seems to be what Marian thinks, too."

Yuletide is the pagan festival of the god Jól, celebrating midwinter with the sacrifice of cattle and much drinking of blood once blessed by the chieftain. This tends not to happen in Birmingham these days but any pagans around would be honouring the defeat of darkness and the new rising of the solstice sun. Samhain. The time of rebirth.

It doesn't seem to be working for Roy although, to be fair, perhaps new life begins deep inside and takes a while to show its face.

Paul has gone back home to his family for a few days at Christmas. He's invited Roy, who has no home to go back to, but no, he's not good company, thanks. Instead, he rereads *Siddhartha* by Hermann Hesse, to lose himself in lyricism, and passes the evening with a Chinese takeaway, a bottle of Bourbon and the Morecambe and Wise Show on TV, to lose himself. He does actually laugh, though, for the first time in weeks.

"Extra bamboo shoots and water chestnuts?" asks Paul when he gets back. Roy nods. "You're so predictable."

Three days after Christmas he receives a card in the post. It's written by his mother, who hopes he's well. It's not signed by his father.

If December is unforgiving, then January is predictably frustrating, still cold and dark as that promised new life busies itself invisibly underground. Roy is only going through the motions at work now, whilst writing in the evenings and drinking to dull the persistent headache. This doesn't help him to create dreams and although he is visiting the island regularly the mist is not clearing. There is one night when something changes and he can just make out, through a kind of arch made by bowing trees, a figure who seems to be watching him. It's his mother and she has tears running down her face. But then that's just psychological, isn't it?

We need to be patient. We must let the seasons run their course. And then, perhaps, the right thing happens at just the right time.

Another thing Uncle Ron did very well was turn up for an unexpected midweek visit in the early evening of the first day of February, to see how his odd but favourite nephew was getting on (and check that he hasn't trashed the property). Today is Imbolc, the fire festival sabbat dedicated to Brigid, the goddess of healing, and a time for personal growth, renewed energy and spring cleaning. These facts entirely pass by the occupants of the house in Rookery Road yet will turn out to be absolutely appropriate, except for the bit about spring cleaning. Very strangely, and just as appropriate, as it will also turn out later, this is the day that the HP-35 is introduced, the world's first scientific hand-held calculator.

When Roy comes home, drained and frustrated as usual, Uncle Ron is perched uncomfortably on the edge of the best armchair sipping distastefully at the tea that Paul has made for him. He's wearing a hunter green Burberry suit with shawl collars, an open neck cream cotton shirt and two-tone Lanx shoes. And long, thick sideburns. In his mid-fifties, he might have misjudged the mood of the generation a little but he wears his success well.

For all the show, he is actually a rather kind man who cares about the welfare of his tenants, especially the young female ones next door. Now, putting down the cup, he springs to his feet and offers a hand to Roy.

"Good to meet you, son. I'm Ron. How are you? Jeez, you look—"

"Yes, I know. Hello, sir. How's everything going for you?"

"Never mind me, son. Paul here tells me you're Assistant Director of Education now. Well done."

"Ah, well, your nephew is sometimes given to exaggeration. Quite often, actually. No, just a humble social worker."

"So labouring ye support the weak. Acts twent—"

"Give over, Paul. Can't you see your friend's knackered? Go and make him a cup of tea — no, make it coffee, and one for me."

Ron gestures Roy to sit and plies him with insightful questions about his work, all the while subtly looking him up and down with an eye practised in judging character. Paul returns with the drinks and perches himself on the arm of Roy's chair, observing the exchange with interest. His uncle's up to something.

"Look, son," he gets straight to it, "here's an idea for you. A proposition, if you like. I'm diversifying my portfolio, see. Student rents are all very well and I don't mind saying I've done all right." He runs a finger down his suit collar to make the point. "But now I'm going into new-build, for housing associations, like, giving something back to the community." And considerably enhancing his professional status.

There's a small estate being built not too far away and Ron's short of labour. Just down the Pershore Road, through Druid's and round Solihull to the Heath. Half an hour, tops. Yes, it's hard work but it's worthwhile — think of all those young families and their kiddies getting a fresh start — and the pay is better than the Council's. Healthy, too. Roy looks like he needs some fresh air. And Ron's builder is a first-rate decent chap, Carlos Duartes.

Not for the first time lately, Roy is dumbfounded. Such an idea would never have entered his head but, once it has, it burrows down, makes itself comfortable and smiles contentedly. It's now his turn to spring up and offer a hand.

By the time he has worked his notice, the outline of the site is in place with roads, paths and plots marked, and as he pulls onto a gravel patch serving as a carpark he can see men and diggers at work cutting out the utility trenches. From here, with no structures up yet, he can see the plan: two short rows of terraces either side of an open communal area with pairs of semis on a third side and a scattering of bigger detached houses nearer the tree line of the heath. In the nearby field, a gaggle of small caravans sit like grazing metal beasts and on the door of one of them is a handwritten sign, OFFIS.

Carlos has watched him approach and emerges with a look of disbelief. Once again, Roy finds himself being looked up and down until the man reaches out a hand to feel his arm as though searching for a muscle.

"Meu Deus! I seen more meat on a potato. You's Ron's boy, then?" He shakes his head mournfully and kits Roy out with boots, gloves and a shiny new spade. "You break it, you pay," he growls, then his face breaks into a broad, gold-toothed smile. There's clearly more chance of Roy being broken.

Uncle Ron had not been wrong about hard work and it only takes two or three days for Roy to begin wondering whether he will actually survive here. Firstly, for all the human body's quite wonderful organs and systems, the spine is not well designed for hours of continuous heavy digging and lifting. And it's perfectly obvious that Roy is a good six to eight inches taller than any of the other men and far less well-built.

Secondly, it's not just physical. Intellectually and culturally, he may as well be an alien and soon realises that there is a definite caste system on site. There may be no Brahmins, as such, and the skilled Vaishyas have not been needed yet, but Carlos is Kshatriya, the king, and the rest of the men are the Shudras. Yet the subdivisions don't stop there. There's a small group of Brazilians who follow Carlos from job to job and only talk among themselves, and there's a pair of Scotsmen who don't talk to the one Welshman. None of them talk to Roy.

On the plus side, he's beginning to pick up some language skills.

"Filho da puta!"

"Puta de merda!"

"Vá pro caralho!"

These phrases may not be terribly useful in other settings, though.

The days are long and wearing yet it's satisfying to see the progress being made. The drains and electricity cables are now within their covered trenches, popping up at intervals like spindly mushrooms as standpipes and switch boards. Roads and plots are level with footings marked out by tape. Roy's skin is clearer, muscles have given up their stubborn resistance and have agreed to start growing, his headaches are a little less frequent and he is happier than he has been for a couple of years. In his small way, he is achieving something.

But at what cost? Fighting through the traffic with blurry eyes, he arrives back at the house exhausted every day and heads straight for the bath. He hardly sees Paul at all, not for a decent conversation, but his old friend admires his determination and quietly does what he can to help, making sure that an evening meal is ready along with an appropriate quip.

"Be strong and do not give up, for your work will be rewarded, two Chronicles fifteen" and "A hard worker shall have plenty of food, Proverbs twenty-eight nineteen. Don't say I don't look after you, mate."

"Thanks, Paul. It's more blessed to give than to receive, Acts twenty."

There comes a point, however, when the sheer effort is getting too much and Roy suggests to Carlos that perhaps he could stay on site in one of the caravans. The gold flashes again as the man realises he can get another hour's work a day out of him, and calls over the Welshman, Ashley, to tell him he'll be sharing from now on. It doesn't go down well. Ashley is quiet, proudly independent and set in his ways and he's damn well not about... until Carlos takes him calmly to one side and delivers a few truths.

"Welcome to the guest house," he growls as Roy heaves his backpack through the door. "Leave me be, right, boyo? An' I'll leave you be."

And so it is. Although Carlos, as if by some secret plan, finds more and more reason for them to work together by day, the evenings are quiet and distant. They each make their own food. Ashley reads his book. Roy writes his diary.

But then, sometimes, the right thing happens at just the right time.

Φ

The first of May is Beltane, a celebration of fertility, the beginning of summer and the flourishing of nature. It's also the day that the Clerk of Works turns up, thin and silent as a rake, in red Wellingtons and plastic raincoat, to inspect the footings for the houses. Roy leans on his spade in fascination as the man prowls the boundaries, tape measure in hand, pausing every few paces to scribble on his clipboard.

"What's he doing?" Roy asks Ashley, putting on his best bemused face.

It's a peculiarity of human nature that people with a bit of knowledge love nothing better than stupid people asking them questions. Roy learned this fast when he worked at his father's company and it's the reason he generally gets on well with others, if they allow it.

"He's checking the foundation trenches, boyo. See, in this soil they 'ave to be forty-two inch, like, no less."

"Then what?"

"Then, 'aving dug 'em all out just right, you an' me are gonna fill 'em all up again with that lot." He jerks a hand over his shoulder to the carpark where two trucks have arrived piled high with something grey and clearly heavy. "That's clinker an' crushed brick, that is. Then it gets compacted down ready for the corbels."

"Cor-whats?"

Ashley glances around and finds six old bricks which he places on each other in three rows like a pyramid.

"Your corbels spread the load of the house walls, see? No clinker, your walls subside. No corbels, your walls fall over. Got it?"

"Ah, like ziggurats, then." He immediately regrets saying it, but it turns out that Ashley is one of those rare people who has a bit of knowledge and doesn't mind a bit more.

"Iggy-whats?"

"Oh, the Sumerians built their pyramids like that. We're talking, what, four thousand years ago. They were huge, more'n two hundred foot long, some. The most famous is at Ur in Iraq, part of a temple dedicated to Nanna."

"You're 'aving a laugh, now, boyo." His eyes narrow.

"The moon god."

And that's all it takes for chalk and cheese to accept one another. They smile and get back to work, then in the evening Roy makes coffee for them both and Ashley offers his Silk Cut.

"What're you writing, then?"

"What're you reading, then?"

Ashley is in his early thirties, losing himself in physical work and books to escape a past he's never talked to anyone about. Having run away from home in the valleys at fourteen, he is trying to discover what makes an alcoholic minister of the Church beat his wife and son — and how to shake off the irrational cloak of guilt he wears. Bit by bit, the two men realise they have a safe space to open up.

"What I learned, boy, is that every ruddy soul's life is full of the unexpected. Maybe some happiness, more'n likely sorrows.

They all sweeps in an' clear us out. But we 'ave to be grateful, see, 'cause they's all helping us know ourselves, like."

"That's Rumi, you old sod," Roy smiles.

"Ah, so you ain't as stupid as you look, then, boy."

Ashley's eyes narrow again, this time with respect, as he seems to be weighing up the risk of his next move. He gets up slowly and reaches into a narrow top cupboard for a bottle of whiskey and pours two generous glasses. Then, after another moment's hesitation, he removes a few books from his shelf and brings out a thin volume wrapped in gold cloth that's been hidden at the back.

"This is special, boy, only came out last year. von Durckheim. Most important book I ever read." He unwraps it reverentially, checks that Roy's hands are clean, and passes it across. He refills their glasses as Roy opens the book gently at the pages marked with strips of newspaper, but doesn't wait for him to read.

"'The first necessity', he says, 'is having the courage to face life.' There's no point running away from hard times, looking for an easy life, like, 'cause it's only when we open ourselves to annihilation, that's his word, that we find our true indestructible nature, see."

"So that's like Rumi."

"Yes, boyo, but this goes further. When we confront the world's threats... give it here—" Roy passes the book back for Ashley to find the page he wants "—we reveal the true depths of who we are. Transformation, see? We become something greater."

Beneath the bone-dry tinder overgrowth of guilt and regret, a tiny ember flickers and Roy senses that, yes, perhaps there is after all a way to start again. Become new. The seed stirs, yawns and stretches. He drains his glass and smiles at the philosopher-Shudra across the table.

"Thanks, boyo. Time for you to break out, too, yeah? It's only a great man who's hard on himself."

"That's Confucius, you young sod."

It's a little before Litha — since the seasons are variable if you're not sure which world you're in — when Roy looks up from the controls of the digger to see a strangely familiar figure get out of a Wolseley at the far end of the site. Carlos has finally given in to his begging and allowed him to clear up some of the areas that will eventually become gardens.

The man pauses to look around at the clean brick walls, hardwood window frames and tiled roofs before setting off to stride purposefully straight for Roy. Carlos sees him coming from the office window and steps out to remonstrate but stops in his tracks. He can recognise a Brahmin when he sees one. The man is short and tubby, with silvering hair and bright round eyes. He wears a light grey French linen suit and is cursing the splatters of mud on his black brogues.

"You're a hard chap to find," says Professor Meeks. "Do you have any idea how many builders called Carlos there are in Birmingham?"

Φ

Ashly left me to my thoughts, saying that I needed rest and he would meet me again at the lake when I was ready. He eased himself up, smiled at me with those eyes that bore into my head and soothed the pain, then gathered himself back into a misty cloud that floated around the corner of the cabin. The points of light retreated back into the shadows again until everything was still and silent and I was alone with my epiphany.

A flurry of pieces had fitted themselves into the puzzle but there were still big empty spaces, not to mention the extra surrounding areas that I hadn't known were part of it until recently. I sat for a long time, smoking one cigarette after another and hoping they would do something to me, even make me cough. But no, this was not a proper body.

Sleep came easily and astonishingly, given recent experience, was the most peaceful rest I had known since arriving on the island. Perhaps that was because I knew that I now had a real friend here, albeit one who didn't have a proper body either. If I could just get my head around that, there might be some more answers — even a way out. When the light came, I took a long, refreshing shower, watched dispassionately by the rat, and breakfasted outside on passion fruit and the honey-flavoured Greek yoghurt that had appeared in a kitchen cupboard. Well, it said honey-flavoured on the side of the pack.

The orioles were chattering more loudly than usual, for all the world directed at me, encouraging me to get a move on. Then Iggy arrived, took a good look round to check the coast was clear, and curled up by my feet. When I'd commented earlier to Ashly on how lovely nature was here, he'd nodded in appreciation.

"That's good to hear, Eva. You know, animals and birds and trees—" he'd swept an arm around as though to include the whole island "—and even the rocks and waters gentle souls are such. We don't criticise or judge or complain or control. We simply to be want."

I'd had plenty of experience of the other sort of behaviour, and even Jamie and the elders seemed impatient for me to sort myself out so that some sort of decision could be... considered. The rest of nature was just happy to go along with me.

And go along with me they did, literally. When at last I couldn't put off the next step any longer and set off along the winding path up the mountain towards the lake, Iggy shuffled happily a couple of metres behind me and the orioles flitted from branch to branch, showing off their skills as the light flashed off their bright orange plumage, whilst rustling in the undergrowth suggested I was being accompanied by a whole troop of wildlife.

The black, silky butterfly again led the way through the woodland tunnel until we emerged to overlook the silent, unmoving waters of the lake where, a lifetime ago, I had felt at once so aware and so small. I settled down on the black stones at the water's edge and waited, knowing that this time some sort of truth was expecting me. The others melted away to a respectful distance, all save the butterfly that lowered itself gently on top of a large rock nearby.

Silence.

More silence, deeper.

I looked around at the rim of the crater, noticing how much more colourful it was this time, my eyes having lost their mist and become attuned to the island itself. Vibrant scarlets, shimmering crimsons and the purest white framed by a hundred shades of green. The clear sky an even pale blue. The still water silvery and translucent.

Silence.

More silence.

Then it began.

A single B harmonic note opened up the water and drew me in, leaving my self behind and becoming a drop of water that became the unknowable ocean.

I was on a sandy beach where cool waves rippled over shingle and a couple of small laughing children flew kites, watched by parents huddled on a picnic blanket. My body felt heavy yet it was young and feminine and full of a different kind of life. A foreign country, though a safe one. Still, I had a decision to make and it had to be soon... go back to everything and everyone familiar, where there would undoubtedly be suffering, or...

Then the young man approached. I knew he was nervous because he was trying not to look nervous, but he had a nice smile, offered me an ice cream, and someone was racing around in my stomach giving orders to my bloodstream.

"Um, do you have a cigarette, please?" he then asked softly. His own pack was peeping out of his shirt pocket and I pretended not to notice.

It was one of those days when the Earth stands still and the air is full of expectancy. It was one of those moments when you can't do a thing because there isn't a doubt that your life has changed. You've stumbled on something. And everything's new.

It was one of those days when the world has decided to begin and to end. And everyone stares at you, wondering how people can be so close. And I wanted him so much to touch...

This was Roy.

This was where it had started.

Another single harmonic opened the water and I drew back, finding my self sitting on the black stones, my body light again.

"You now see, yes?" Ashly's quiet voice brought me back to the moment and I turned to find him hovering to one side. This time, he hadn't bothered with the human form yet I could feel his eyes searching mine. I smiled and nodded.

"I think so." I was still feeling warm, securely held in that moment of never having to be alone again, of having sensed the inner being shared by everyone and everything, of transcending those unanswerable questions. He wasn't going to let me enjoy it, though.

"Humans do of very stupid things all kinds," he mused. "The fuckin' lies and the secrets. The fights and the monies. Nature tearing apart..." He paused, his voice trailing into sadness, and the butterfly took flight, startled by his thoughts. Then he turned back to me. "But probably the most fuckin' stupid thing is that to away throw — what you remembered just."

"I did?"

A grey cloud began to drift high over the rim of the crater and I felt it settling around and chilling me.

"You people let things small become to you so important. So crap it is. If someone different looks, different speaks, different believes or isn't sure what believe they… you away throw them. You lose all the fuckin' good of alive being is there."

It was the closest I'd seen him to anger, or perhaps deep despair, and the emotion was messing with my brain and jumbling his words up again. I struggled to get to grips with it, feeling sorry that my friend was hurt, and finally realised the point.

"I threw Roy away?"

I hung my head as a picture unfolded. I was back in my room at Trutnov and he was there. But now he looked very different, long hair and beard, and there was a quiet argument about, I don't know, about being different. Then he was gone. And when I realised—

"You tried yourself to away throw."

A gunshot.

"Turns out, yer aim ain't very good, though, Miss."

The deep, guttural voice took me by surprise and I jerked upright, seeing that another figure had settled himself cross-legged beside Ashly and was observing me with kind, dark eyes. As if in sympathy, Ashly now coalesced into his more-or-less human form too.

The man was small and wiry, with nut-brown skin and a bearded but ageless face. He was barefoot and wore baggy green trousers just below the knee, a loose shirt of every colour imaginable and strings of shells around his neck. On his head perched a black bowler-type hat, hardly matching the rest of his clothing except that a beautiful, long sapphire blue feather was tied to the rim with dried grass. The outline of his figure shimmered slightly as though he wasn't fully here, but that might have been my eyes. I could feel tears in them.

"'Allo, Ashish, meu amigo," he said. "You called us?"

My friend, who apparently had several names, bowed and offered a vaporous hand that our new visitor took lightly.

"Thank for you comin'. The child here, Eva her name is, may your help needing be." He turned back to me. "This my friend is, José Duartes. He what you call is a…"

"Um xamã," breathed the man. "What you say… shaman."

"He from where you call is Brazil, I think."

"'S right. In the north, near the Tapajós, well, tributary. Atodi people. Healer. Spirit friend, see?"

"Pleased to meet you," I whispered politely, "if you are a friend of Ashly… er, Ashish… So have you come to give me, um, healing?"

He spat out the stub of tobacco he'd been chewing and gave me a huge, toothy smile.

"Not much anyone can do 'bout that, Miss Eva. The bullet took off a bit of yer frontal lobe — on the left, see — an' skimmed the temporal. Big pressure wave. Haematoma too. Got it?"

"Mmm, sounds bad," I agreed with a kind of objective curiosity, since I still seemed to have all my head.

"'S bad all right, Miss Eva. Done fer yer thinkings, talkings, control of yer body… You'se a cabbage."

"But I'm not dead?"

José Duartes looked at Ashly and raised an eyebrow.

"No, she fuckin' got it hasn't yet, my friend."

"Miss Eva, 'asn't Ashi 'ere explain? You can't die. Not fer the life of you. We's talking 'bout the other you."

"Oh, I think I do get it now. So that was me, in the hospital? And that's the decision those elders were talking about… considering. Those people want to turn off… the other me."

"She got it. 'Course, it has effect on this you, too. You probably got pain, yes?"

I nodded, although I couldn't say I understood it all. Maybe that was because I'd damaged my thinkings… and why I still found it hard to understand Ashly's conversation.

"Naaah," José smiled again — clearly, actual talking was superfluous with him too — "that's jus' ol' Ashi tryin' to sound mysterious. He does that to new peoples." He turned and slapped Ashly on the back, his hand passing right through the vapour. "You'se perfectly able to speak proper, meu amigo, ain't you?"

Ashly looked sheepish and turned away from me. I bristled slightly but let it go, with some relief, because now I had two friends who could perhaps sort things out. We shared some silence, gazing out over the still, clear water of the lake, and I became aware that the other small creatures and birds had returned nearby. In fact, Iggy was nuzzling up to José's feet. All the pain and disturbance and chill I had felt some moments before had passed now and I relaxed into contentment. Until...

"Hang on a minute," I turned to the other two accusingly, "just how do you know so much about me, anyway?" That paranoia again.

"Naaah, she ain't really got it after all, Ash," José sighed. "Look, Miss Eva, folks like Ashi 'ere is everywhere. This you, other you, whatever you — make no diff'rence. 'Fact, there's only one you anyways and you'se everywhere too, see?" I didn't. Not yet. "An' us, folks like us, we go anywhere too, 'ere 'n there. Well, 'ere us is, see? It's how us do healing."

Every time I thought I was getting a handle on things they seemed to change and the jigsaw of things I didn't know I didn't know expanded.

"Soooo..." I began hesitantly, "what I still don't get — one of the things I don't get — is what is this place? This island? Who was that pilot? Sister Nora, the border guard? Why has the hospital disappeared? And where—"

"All shit," Ashly cut in. "It's just what you expected to see, Evička. As I think you might've heard... people believe whatever they want. Like, I don't know, like karma crap, you have to pay for everythin' shitty you do whatever that means even if you didn't fuckin' know you did it so you can never pay for it and you have to get born again and again but no one tells you how to get out of it all and if somehow you manage to get out of it you'll go some fuckin' place else and sit on some god's hands forever. It's comfort, that's all."

I was shocked by this uncharacteristic outburst but José patted my hand and smiled.

"Don't worry 'bout Ashi, Miss," he murmured. "Nosso amigo like to go off on one sometime. He's pretty much right, though. No wonder people is so screwed up. We'll talk 'bout it later, you an' us. An' by the way, Miss Eva—" he fixed me with those penetrating dark eyes "—you asked 'bout the island, yes? Well, who says you 'ave to stay here? That's where us comes in."

With that mind-blowing, throwaway comment, he sprang nimbly to his feet and said he needed to be somewhere else but would come back when Ashly let him know I was ready, whatever that meant. Ready for...? José Duartes shimmered, raised a farewell hand to each of us, and faded away. Ashly, too, wrapped himself up into his mist and disappeared towards the tree line that surrounded the crater, having assured me he would always be nearby and all I had to do was ask for him. Of course, I had always been quite used to people just disappearing.

I decided to stay where I was. After all, I was not alone, many of the small creatures had decided to stay too although, with dusk beginning to fall, the birds had made their way home to rest among their leaves. And now I could pick out the tiny points of light and flashes of colour beneath the water's surface as fish darted this way and that. The air became cooler but was still pleasant and I had no need of sleep yet.

For one thing, I was loathe to leave this beautiful place. I might have had a few harsh realities pointed out to me here and the charge list of my crimes had grown longer — including illegal border crossings, theft of firearms and, worst of all, throwing away — but I had also experienced the beauty, the peace, the magic and the utter freedom of touching the inner self, of being at one with another.

One of those days.

I wanted it again, so badly.

Many memories started coming back to me now. Released from their cages of fear, they queued up patiently to tell me their stories and settle back into their rightful places in my mind. I welcomed them all, even the difficult ones that glared at me as they arrived and fidgeted uncomfortably — causing only a little pain — until they were calmed by their surrounding companions. The tapestry they all created was quite beautiful, if a little rough and scorched at the edges.

Many of those days.

When the light returned, I decided, I was going to dive into those waters again and leave my self behind for a while, become a drop in the unknowable ocean, relive that touch. Because that was the greatest experience I had ever known and it must never be lost, I thought, even if that were impossible. I wanted it with every part of me. And it was perhaps in that moment that the tiny germ of my idea was born...

For another thing, I wanted to rerun all these recent conversations and the pronouncements of my new friends in my mind. What they had said, of course, was their own view of life and they were both, even José in his way, different forms of life. Not human. And even if they had been, I'd had plenty of experience of not believing what others told me, usually for very good reason.

I'm not suggesting they were not truthful. But truth dresses itself in many different costumes, according to the seasons. And when someone is so scornfully dismissive of others' beliefs, as Ashly had been unable to disguise, it often suggests their own insecurity, their own believing what they want to believe. Another memory arrived, puffing out of breath having been left behind by the others, of an arrogant man who called himself

Inspector Jones and kept suggesting that I must be some sort of agent for people with different beliefs. And he was followed by... oh dear, my own family, and Roy's too, living on opposite sides of the cold and never accepting that we could be...

Fuckin' beliefs, as Ashly would say. Yet what else did I have to go on?

There was no doubt that the spirit of trees, as I chose to think of him, and um xamã did care about me, had my interests at heart and wanted to help me in some way. Not for the first time, I wondered why. Perhaps it was simply because I had touched the unknowable, which so few are fortunate enough to do, and a greater awareness of nature was growing in me. That included them, and all the others dozing contentedly nearby.

What could their help mean? José had hinted that I could leave this island, go somewhere different, perhaps even be something different? I gazed at the mirror-smooth surface of the water and as the brightness faded around me found that I could see my own reflection. It was the first time I had seen myself since being in that hospital room, wiping away the blood, and I was surprised. Come to think of it, in the light of shape-shifting intelligent wisps and goodness knows who else I was yet to meet, human beings do look a bit odd, with their sticky-out ears and noses and slit mouths and eyes at the front when what you really need to look out for is usually behind you. Perhaps I really could be something else, redesigned, efficient and streamlined and beautiful like Ashly... the thought excited me.

"Naaah," Iggy opened one eye and still managed to make it pitying, "you'se jus' 'ooman, Miss."

I accepted my lot, for now at least, and rested on the black stones, at peace. Indeed, part of me would have stayed there indefinitely, so gentle was my life, so warm the embrace of this forested mountain and its hidden, magical lake. Other parts, though, were waking up and demanding to be fed and exercised and taken to unfamiliar places with new scents and sights. Before that, I knew there was still more work to be done. I would close the door on those excitable thoughts, sit comfortably and turn within, blur my eyes and stretch out my arms, then wait for the harmonic and dive again into the waters that opened up to draw me in and down to its depths.

I had to know those other days. Including the bad ones.

They came willingly enough, now that I was ready, although not necessarily in an orderly queue. There was the beach again, in a cool evening, and there was Roy beside me playing his guitar. Well, he was showing me his new song but he hadn't got much further than the opening notes and a few words...

> *'...a broken sea calls out,*
> *waves whipped by wind caress the beach.*
> *And I begin to see the end...'*

And then we were side by side at a table strewn with books and papers, trying to look studious while trying not to touch.

Instantly I was in Václavské Náměstí, walking hand in hand with Aleš... Other people always thought that we would... and wasn't there some kind of understanding...? Aleš, the engineer, steady and constant and offering some kind of security as the group of students surrounding us by the statue were closely watched at a distance by pairs of silent men in long grey raincoats. Safety perhaps, yet incalcitrant thoughts kept tugging at a sleeve of my fawn leather jacket and insisting on leaving for another country altogether, another big city and another big university — not so very different, then, except that Roy would be there.

But he wasn't, we were standing in a garden — someone's birthday — near a small pond where a frog plopped noisily into the water and I've never seen anyone look so happy even though half his face was covered by thick long hair and a beard.

It was one of those looks.

And then there was that gunshot again and with a rush I was back on the black stones with the waters closing over.

I knew it was time to go now for there were loose ends to tie and a decision to be... considered. I stood, thinking this might be the last time I would come here, slipped off my clothes and walked into the cool, silent lake to bathe away any last fears.

It wasn't there. I mean, there was no water. I was just standing on black, shiny sheets of lava, feeling silly. A mirage.

"People sees what they wants to see, Miss," came a small, familiar voice. "There's no fish in there, neither. I thought everyone knew that. Even the ducks know, 'n walk round the edge. I had one once, you know."

"What, you had a pet duck?"

"You're daft, a fish."

"Doesn't every kid?"

"Maybe. Blackie were special."

"Why did you call your fish Blackie?" This was the longest conversation I'd had for some time and I wasn't quite prepared for surrealism.

"You can call a fish what you like. It can't hear you. Anyway, Blackie were my friend, that's all. 'Course, she died."

"I'm sorry."

"'S not your fault."

The young, dark-skinned girl with long black hair in braids falling around her shoulders was watching me with an amused smile in her wide, brown eyes. She still wore the streaked floral dress, white socks and trainers with a flapping toe cap.

"Still, I said you'd work things out, didn't I? 'S no sweat."

"Mmm, yes, you did," I mumbled, reaching for my dress. "I'm getting there, more or less. I just have one or two decisions to make."

She jumped up from the rock she was perched on and walked slowly around me with arms folded, perhaps wondering again whether I was worthy of her continuing.

"Whatever you decide don't matter," she said inevitably. "I told you that before."

"You did, yes."

"Like, whatever you decide is whatever you have to decide at the time. Not good or bad, just is."

"But decisions have conseq... I mean, things happen as a result."

"That's not down to you, though, is it? It's all made up in advance." She turned to face me with the mock pose of a teacher trying to get a simple point across. "It's what my Nana told me."

"But I made one decision that's hurt a lot of other people."

"You could of decided something else," she shrugged, "but it wouldn't've mattered in the end."

"So everything's planned out already?"

"Dur, don't be daft, Miss. You still make your own mind up, don't you? You just don't know what's going to happen next. You just decide what seems right at the time."

"Your Nana sounds like a wise woman. Does she look after you?"

"She died too."

"I'm sorry."

"'S not your fault." She spread her arms as though that's all she could offer for now. "Got any biscuits, Miss?"

"Sorry, no."

"Roy gave me his Bourbons."

I was shaken to the core by this casual remark and a surge of something like electricity shot through me at the mention of his name. How in all the worlds did this girl—

"He's all right, by the way, in case you was wondering. Well, he wasn't, bit of a mess tell the truth. But he's moved on. Anyway, I'm off, got friends to meet. 'Spect I'll see you again, Eva."

"Oh, 'bye then... Hey, just a minute, how do you know—"

But she had already disappeared, leaving me in pieces, all my new-found composure drifting away on the still waters of a lake that wasn't there.

When I got back to the cabin Jamie was already there, sitting on the veranda and drumming his fingers on the table next to a cup of cold tea and a half-empty packet of Woodbines. He'd clearly been waiting for a while.

"You can be a hard lass to find," he murmured, looking up with troubled eyes. "Have your new friends been, eh, helpful, then?"

Was there nothing that anybody didn't know about me and all my activities?

"It's kind of my, eh, job." He grimaced, as though he really wished it wasn't, but there was a definite change in his demeanour since we'd last met. He was quieter and despite the gruff exterior I felt his warmth reach out to me. He cared. And something was up. I decided to try and delay whatever it was.

"Yes, I've learned a lot lately. I mean, the pieces are falling into place. How about you — have you been, um, keeping well? Did you get a good one this time?" I indicated the picture card from the cigarette packet that lay on the table. He reached out a finger and flicked it away.

"It's no good to me. John Gray, a fine, eh, Scotsman of course. Master mariner, captain of the SS *Great Britain*. But everyone's got him, I'll never be able to swap him."

The fleeting thought occurred to me that, given all the paranormal things that seemed to go on in this place, surely it would be possible simply to manifest the cards you wanted? Still, where would be the fun in that?

"Eva, my dear, I have to confess to you that I've been under a bit of pressure. The elders, you know. They're a bit, eh, agitated. More than usual, that is. Now… eh, José will have told you—"

"You know José?"

Jamie gave me a withering look. Of course he did. Jamie knew more about me than I did.

"—that your brain is pretty, eh, messed up, lass."

"Yes. Sorry about that. I didn't do a very good job, did I?"

"It's hardly a matter for flippancy, lass. You've done a lot of damage, and I don't mean to yourself. Other people are, eh, suffering. The universe is suffering." He waved an arm to indicate everything the eye could see and much, much further. "And here you are, marooned on this little island with no, eh, family or friends or—"

"I have friends," I objected, my eye caught by Iggy crouching at the corner of the cabin. He nodded vigorously. "And I rather like it here. Although..." I stopped myself suddenly, trying desperately not to think about the idea that José had put into my mind. But you know how it is — if I told you that you must not on any account think of yellow elephants... "And anyway," trying to change the subject with little success, "at the end of the day, as it were, it makes no difference what people decide, does it?"

"Ah, you haven't really got it, have you, lass?" I thought that was Ashly's line. Jamie leaned forward and fixed me with a ministerial look. "I'm sure you must have wondered how it is that, eh, you know there are other souls all around, even here, but you can't see them. You can sense them. But that's all. There are worlds and there are worlds and there are, eh, other worlds, Eva. And what you do in one of them changes things in all of them."

He paused and we both sat back, I suitably chastised and he considering the next move.

"What matters at this moment, Evička—" I let this go without objection because an enormous wave of love flowed from him and washed all around me "—is what happens in the other world. What is about to, eh, happen. See, Václav Černý — your doctor — has called your parents in again. So... shall we go?"

I nodded mutely.

This was one of those other days.

We drifted over the grey city towards the Vychovatelna building of the Fakultní Nemocnice Bulovka, then in and along the maze of corridors and stairways, past cheap watercolours of Prague landmarks to the shadowy private room. I felt a gulp in my throat as I recognised Petr and Amálie, my parents, both in tears as they sat silently at the bedside. Aleš stood by the window, looking out over the gardens. This time, Marie was there too, my grandmother, and we could see one another clearly. She looked straight at me, expressionless, neither comforting nor accusing.

Doctor Černý entered, paused and looked right in my direction, then shook his head and pulled up a chair next to my mother, speaking in soft tones.

I looked down at the machine. Not the electronic one, beeping quietly, its arms and legs snaking out to attach themselves to... the other me... but the extraordinary biological one, once so strong and lithe, self-regulating and self-healing, that had known such fear and joy, sadness and ambition. For all the pain, I had enjoyed being this me.

But there was nothing to be done and it was time to move on. I turned to Jamie and nodded, and with infinite compassion he touched each of the others in the room with a gentle hand. The switch was turned.

I was free.

THIRTY-FOUR

"So I phoned your parents' house first, of course, but your father wasn't any help — quite rude actually — but then your mother called back the next day and told me you were living with your friend Paul and working for some chap called Carlos so I went to the house in Selly Oak but there was nobody there — the place looked empty — and I just had to ask around at any building site I could find." He pauses for breath and looks Roy up and down as he climbs out of the digger. "Is this what a first-class degree gets nowadays?"

Roy grins, takes his gloves off and offers a hand.

"It's just for a while. I'm getting fitter. I'm happy. It's good money."

"That's all very well. Still, I had hoped..."

"Prof, it's good to see you, sir. But you haven't said why you're here. And you've obviously gone to a lot of trouble to find me."

"Ah, that, yes. Well, he seemed to think it was really important. Urgent, he said. And then the other thing came up. More than a coincidence, I thought."

"Professor Meeks, not for the first time I have no idea what you're getting at."

Carlos has been watching the exchange from a distance and now comes over to introduce himself, bowing slightly, and find out what's going on. Meeks says he has vital personal information for Roy and asks if he might take him away for a couple of hours. Carlos Duartes does that thing of frowning darkly then breaking out into his broad, gold smile.

"'Course, professor. Is no trouble. We manage." He turns to Roy and slaps him on the back. "Você é um imprestável um merda!"

"Oh, I wouldn't say that, Mr Carlos," Meeks objects. "Todos têm talento, eh?"

As Carlos stands open-mouthed and rooted to the spot, Roy runs to the guest house to get changed. The professor drives them to The Regency Hotel, just off the A34 south of Solihull, where he's booked a room for the night and insists that Roy has a bath before he's allowed to meet him in the bar. He's waiting there, impatiently drumming fingers on a table next to two glasses, a bottle of Bordeaux Supérieur, Château Saint-Ignan, and a foolscap manilla envelope. He has the look of someone who has no idea, any more than Roy does, why he's here and what he's doing. But then he looks at his favourite student's smiling face and remembers in a flash all the troubles they've been through and all they finally achieved despite them. It's true, this is the first time the boy has looked well and happy since...

"What's up, then, Prof? Don't tell me Kuhn's done a Galileo. Recanted."

"I had a call from your man Cotton on the Wirral. Said he had to get this to you urgently." He pushes the envelope across the table. "Precious, he said. Though what's so important about a drawing I can't imagine. Odd chap, isn't he? Gave me a cup of tea and offered to paint my guide."

"You went all the way over there?"

"He refused to post it."

"That was kind, Prof, thank you."

The envelope contains a charcoal portrait, wrapped in layers of tissue paper, of a Church minister, and a short handwritten note. John Cotton says that he woke up in the middle of the night and was "instructed" to do the drawing and get it to Roy at once. He was also given the minister's name: Jamie McIntyre. It means nothing to Roy, except that he has to trust Cotton.

"What was the other thing? You said there was a coincidence."

When he gets back to the site in the evening, Ashley has disappeared along with all his belongings except that he's left the von Durckheim as a gift for Roy. Carlos has no idea why he left or where he's gone and he's not best pleased.

Two precious gifts in one day, or perhaps three. He pours a stiff drink to deaden the headache that's begun to rage again and rereads the letter Meeks gave him at the hotel. An old friend of the professor's is headmaster of a prep school in Surrey that's short-staffed — there's been some sort of scandal — and he wants to know if Meeks can recommend a recent graduate to teach Maths. It's good money and there's a flat thrown in. Coming on the same day as John Cotton's call it had made the professor think of Roy for the job.

"But it's years since I did any Maths. And I'm not trained."

"No need, it's a private school. And it's only Common Entrance, you'll soon pick it up. Come on, it's a fresh start."

Tonight's dream is definitely one of the fourth type. Someone, somewhere, is telling him something. He's on the island again and walking, more like floating, up a steep, rough path to a kind of archway with a gate. It doesn't open. Beyond, through the mist, is a wooden veranda with table and chairs in front of a cabin. Sitting at the table... are they people? He can't tell, they're more like shimmering pale lights, with some kind of prehistoric-looking animal lying at their feet. Some words, barely audible, drift across to him.

"You really have, eh, no idea what led up to all this?"

In the morning he writes it all down and, over coffee, an idea comes knocking and demands to be let in.

"The show house is nearly ready, isn't it?" he asks Carlos, who looks at him with narrow, suspicious eyes. He's not keen on ideas but nods. "So you don't want buyers to be looking out at a patch of mud at the back, do you? Why don't I work on a garden? You said yourself, I'm not much good at anything else."

Carlos strokes his chin. The point is unarguable but it's going to cost money.

"Twenty pound."

"Fifty."

"Thirty, no more."

"Good, thanks. I'd have taken twenty-five." He just manages to skip out of the way as Carlos aims a punch.

For the rest of the week he throws himself into it, with no experience whatsoever, the design already in his head. There's a paved patio just outside the back door, sine waves of flower borders edging the lawn, a small pond backed by a rockery and a willow tree — no, an ash — and a path with a trellis arch just beyond which has to be a wooden veranda and a small cabin.

The digger makes short work of levelling the ground, cutting out the pond and piling up soil behind it, and there's no shortage of free rocks on site. A couple of the Brazilian labourers stop to stare at him, jeering and tapping their heads in pity.

"Vá pra puta que pariu!" he calls back cheerfully.

There's a decent garden centre on the edge of Solihull, where he gets a good deal with everything delivered. He pays the balance out of his own pocket. It's exhausting work but he's on a mission, leaving a personal legacy on this site. Just as well, because he's not coming back.

The house in Rookery Road is boarded up, the locks changed and the girls' house next door empty. He only has the few clothes, books and papers from the caravan and, thankfully, his guitar — Ashley had suggested that. None of this is making any sense but it seems he has to get used to people disappearing.

Perhaps the charcoal drawing is a clue. Roy heads off to the library again where, although he has no pass, the kind and hopeful young assistant lets him in.

"He's a Scottish Presbyterian," she says when he shows her the portrait. "They kept good records. Um, let me see…" This girl's good and she's back in ten minutes. A minister of this name lived in the 1860s at Walkerburn, a small village in the Scottish Borders south of Edinburgh, about eight miles from Peebles. "Why is he important?"

"I have no idea."

"Well, look, I'm finishing here soon. Why don't you come back with me for some dinner and tell me about it?"

Her Edgbaston flat is small, very clean and tidy and empty of anything with character except a family photograph in a silver frame and a collection of American soul records beside an old turntable. But this evening, Anne is surprising herself. She's shy and introvert, like many booklovers, yet something about this young man is drawing her in. Perhaps he needs her. Or she needs him. There's something in the air, anyway, although not what she's hoping for.

She lets him have a bath and then brings him a glass of wine while she cooks a vegetable curry, but when she brings it out on a tray he's fast asleep on her sofa. And by the time she has to leave for work on Saturday morning he's still there, so there's nothing for it but to put some breakfast things out with a kind note. After all, she'd known there was something about him that wasn't... normal.

'I hope your feeling better today. You must of been very tired. Im going to work so come over if you like x'

You'd expect a librarian to be able to write good English, wouldn't you? Maybe she's not what she seems, either.

Roy could not have woken up if he'd tried, exhausted by the garden work and the strangeness of events. And tonight's dream was a long third type. It's the island again and the gentle ascent to the archway, but this time the cabin and veranda are nowhere to be seen. The gently swirling white mist is now thick, dark clouds from which emerges that odd, horny animal, except that it's no longer small and rather cute. It must be ten feet tall and three times as long, a great thick-skinned beast that lumbers towards him with a roar. It has a long neck and an open mouth of sharp teeth and he can feel its hot foul breath as spiky hands reach out to him. It doesn't seem able to get past the gate, though, so he makes a run for it up the dirt path towards the lake, the ground shaking as heavy, armoured feet follow him, crashing through the trees. If only he can reach the water he'll be safe. He knows that it will draw him in and help him understand everything, in a place where monsters cannot go.

But halfway up the mountain there are the even more terrifying sounds of the Earth herself exploding as the night is set on fire by yellow flames shooting high into the sky and the crash and crackle ahead of burning rocks and red-hot lava rushing towards him. Inexplicably, he watches frozen in fascination as it all passes him by and swallows up his pursuer with a gulp before racing on to destroy every shrub, tree, gate and archway in its path. Finally he is standing alone, mesmerised, on the scorched and empty mountainside with no sign of life anywhere except for a silky, black butterfly hovering nearby. It seems to have a bright golden circle enclosing the letter E on each wing.

He has a bowl of cereal, two slices of toast with cheese and two cups of coffee before he's calm enough to shake it out of his head and onto paper. Then he notices that Anne has a telephone. The first call is to Paul's parents' house of course, but the number has been discontinued. This needs to sink in so he makes more coffee and takes his guitar from its case, hoping that the gentle rhythm and cadence will dislodge the shadows and clarify the decisions that have to be... considered.

'When this is over...
and the dark night flies in the face of our dreams,
when nothing we know is the way
that it seems now...

Will that be the end,
will we still know our lovers and friends?
Will we be the same?'

The song succeeds in taking him to a different place, so he carefully puts the guitar back and rereads the letter Professor Meeks had given him for perhaps the fifth time. Maybe the letter is really from Jamie… It could be a fresh start, a new life in a place where nobody knows him with new things to focus on. A career, even.

The second call is to Helen's university halls and he's lucky to get her when she's just woken up.

"Urrrgh, what time is it? This had better be good, Roy. My head's splitting."

"I need a really big favour, little sis. Too much to explain right no—"

"Good, I can't do big stories this morning."

He needs her to go back home for the weekend and get their parents to take her out for Sunday dinner. You know, the Mount Hotel. Keep them away a couple of hours, make up something about it being a big celebration.

"Well, I did just pass my end of year exams. Thanks for asking. There was a party last night, so… All right. But you owe me big time. I'll leave the keys under that dreadful grinning gnome."

The final call is to Lakeside College and it's answered by a gruff voice that also seems displeased at being disturbed on a Saturday morning. Taking a deep breath, Roy adopts his best friendly-but-firm voice. He knows perfectly well that a caretaker is the most important individual at any school, the one who actually gets things done, and a fledgling career is doomed from the start if one is not in his good books.

"All right, laddie. The flat'll be ready Sunday evening. But ah ken you'll nay last longer'n the last gadgie."

So that's it, then. He's on his way. One more coffee as a spark of hope vies with a cloud of sadness at leaving the Midlands, his sometimes annoying but always loyal oldest friend Paul, his new and mysterious friend Ashley and even his scornful friend Carlos Duartes. Then just as he gets round to feeling bad about having used Anne, albeit unwittingly, the phone rings and he knows it's her, checking that he's all right. No, he can't, she belongs in the old story.

He leaves coins on her table for the food and telephone — but no note — and takes his things out to the car, which he parks round the corner out of sight. Then he catches a bus up to the Bull Ring where the same gaggles of young boys are smoking in doorways. They don't notice him. Uncle Ron had been right about the money and he's able to buy himself a decent suit, a few cotton shirts with matching ties and new shoes. Then he has a good meal and drives back to Sandwell where he first visits Paul's parents' house and is somehow not surprised to find it empty and up for sale then parks the car just round the corner from The Mermaid.

Adam is one of those rare landlords who calmly accepts the owners' every marketing whim, however awful, and welcomes the new faces with their funny clothes and accents whilst remaining loyal to the old ones. He knows when to be gregarious and when to be silent. He has also known Roy since he was twenty-one — well, twenty, but he was tall — and come to realise that this lad's journey has not been an easy one. This evening, he doesn't bother with the cheery insult about how he looks and quietly offers the guest room for the night. In the morning he brings coffee and toast with marmalade and the Sunday paper, followed by more coffee. A good man.

Around midday, Roy takes the sports pages to hide behind as he sits in the car watching the road. The news isn't good anyway. Greg Chappell has made a big ton and Bob Massie has been single-handedly decimating the English batting, so the Second Test is heading for an Australia win that will level the Ashes.

Right on time at twelve-thirty, Mr Carter being a man of routine, the large Morris passes and Roy's eyes briefly meet his sister's as she looks out from the back seat. Within ten minutes he's in his room packing a suitcase with his favourite clothes — not all of them, so as not to arouse suspicion and cause Helen trouble — along with certificates, his radio and some books. He congratulates himself for having kept, for old times' sake, his school Maths textbooks. The Franciscan monk definitely seems to be smiling today and Roy finds old newspapers stored under the stairs to wrap the painting carefully, tied with string from the kitchen. How strange it feels that he knows exactly where everything is in this house and now he's leaving it all behind, perhaps forever.

With one eye on his watch, he visits each room and slowly takes in every detail as though to lock it all in the memory vault marked Past Life. He senses the atmospheres, mostly cold and distant, of all those years and feels no regrets, before a final look out over the garden from the stone patio. Yes, there had once been a happy party afternoon here, when they... but that had soon been lost too.

With the keys back beneath the hideous gnome, he's on his way in an hour and heading south on the A435. He's not using the motorway because it seems important to take in the countryside and count off each passing county boundary as a step along an entirely new path. He's about to be a Maths teacher, so he also notes each road sign and mentally breaks the numbers down into prime factors, the foundation blocks of arithmetic. A46. A44. Past Oxford. A34. A339. A31 towards Guildford.

He turns through the arched wrought iron gates of Lakeside College at six o'clock.

Φ

Wyn Carter sits in her padded garden chair on the veranda and gazes blankly out over the grounds. The lawns have been newly mown in stripes and are fringed by mature beech and ash trees in full leaf, wild betanies and speedwells and poppies at their feet. Poppies are her favourite flower, their brilliant red paper-fine petals and spindly stems reminding her how precious and delicate life is and how easily blown away. But she doesn't see them.

Her senses are virtually all locked within. Whether this is because the breakdown damaged neural pathways, or due to the electric shock treatment, no one can tell. Nor can they say if she will ever recover. The carers are genuinely kind — this is an expensive clinic — and talk to her constantly, taking her into the lounge where others play board games or watch television, helping her to eat meals. But she shows no interest.

She barely even recognises her family when they visit although, strangely, she will talk with her young granddaughter if they are left alone. The doctors are mystified. She has been here a long time now and simply seems to be living in another world.

When they arrive back home in the silent car, Dr Helen Danbury-Jones goes straight upstairs to the back bedroom. Nothing has been moved for years and she makes a mental note to at least do some dusting. There's a thick layer on the table by the window but nobody has touched it for fear of disturbing the two writing pads and four biros sitting there. After all, there is still a presence here. Everyone can feel it.

With tears in her eyes, she looks out across the overgrown, unkempt garden to the swaying willow and the field beyond where a small herd of Herefords are oblivious to human pain. It's not her mother's condition that upsets her, though — as a clinical psychologist she is used to some human mysteries having no solution. But she has never been able to get used to losing her brother before she had a chance to know him properly. She had been too young, absorbed in a girl's world of school friends and music. Anyway, he had been away from home, lost in his own drama.

Now, he is just lost. Tell the truth, the most she knows about him is what she heard at the funeral when Marcus had delivered his eulogy and that friend Graham had played one of Roy's songs on his guitar.

'When this is over
and I finally see why it had to be,
will my spirit accept its necessity?
In the final release,
who will pick up the pieces for me?'

Their father had sat stony-faced next to her and even Roy's best friend Paul from school had been useless, hiding away and blubbing at the back. Well, the one good thing that came out of the whole horrible experience was meeting Marcus. There was a spark between them immediately despite her being so young and unknowing. All too readily — perhaps indecently — he was welcomed to the family and is now secure in the Training Department and fast-tracked to take over when Morris retires.

No, their daughter is another good thing, of course, even if she is a strange girl defying her mother's diagnosis. In one moment, she plays happily with friends and throws herself into netball and athletics, then she can suddenly become silent and unresponsive with wide eyes and cheeky smile. She has gone somewhere else.

An early warning flash of migraine makes Helen stumble and put out a hand for support, leaning against the row of books on one of the deep corner shelves. Oddly, they don't move, as though something is blocking them at the back. So she has a decision to make. It's easy, driven by the need to know her brother she removes the books carefully, keeping their correct order, and reaches into the shelf to find the hidden box. It's full of letters, mostly in blue airmail envelopes with foreign postmarks, and some papers with handwritten songs. Another decision to make.

Her husband enters the room quietly and comes up behind, putting his arms around her gently.

"No, darling," Marcus whispers, "leave them. Let him rest in peace."

"But he's not." She buries her head in his shoulder, smearing his white shirt with tears and mascara. In a few moments she is composed and pulls away, taking the handkerchief he offers to wipe her face. "Is Dad all right?"

"What do you think? He's shut himself away in the dining room with his reports and calculator. As normal. But look, I wanted to show you this..." He hands her the morning newspaper that's he's only now had a chance to glance through. It's open at the report of a young Kenyan man who's been murdered by a National Front mob in Leicester. His name was Nikhil Patel. "Isn't that Roy's friend? The apprentice — he was at the funeral."

"Could be, yes. The photo does look like him, though I didn't know he was an activist. The last I heard, he left the company because of people's racism and went to university down south somewhere."

Helen replaces the box and its protective books and they go downstairs to the lounge where their daughter is sitting beneath the mahogany standard lamp watching Adventures of Morph on television with a plate of chips on her knee. Her floral dress has a streak of ketchup down the front, and she wears short white socks and black trainers with red flashes on the side. The toe cap of the left one is flapping loose.

"Mummy," she says without looking away from the screen, "what did Nanny mean? She worried me."

"Sorry, dear?"

"Don't be daft, 's not your fault."

"I mean, I don't know what Nanny said to you."

"Oh, she said that whatever I decide is just what I have to decide at the time. Can't be good or bad."

Φ

"There's something I don't understand," I began.

"Only one thin'?" José Duartes grinned.

I had returned from the hospital with Jamie a bit of a mess, to be honest. When Doctor Černý switched off... me... my first feeling had been exhilaration. The pain and troubles, the distrust and suspicions, were over and I was free to explore my new life. But they weren't over. I only had to see my parents and feel what they were feeling to realise what I'd done and how much healing there still was to be done.

Jamie left me to my thoughts, saying he had to "report", and I sat there on the veranda for goodness knows how long with actual tears running down my face. The faithful Iggy sat with me, dozing by my feet and occasionally lifting mournful eyes to see how I was.

Finally, after a few cigarettes and cups of tea that did nothing for me, I gathered myself together and gave myself a talking-to. 'Look, Eva, you've seen plenty of death before. All right, not your own, but people you knew and cared about. You've seen all the horrible stuff that human beings can do to each other and you came through it all... well, until you didn't. But along the way you also touched the very best, the deepest, the most joyful awareness of being alive. Until you threw it away.' This wasn't helping so I told myself to shut up and simply resolved, as I had so often before, to do something about it. Put things right.

The tiny seed of my idea began to swell, sensing the coming of spring above ground.

Accompanied by creature friends as usual, I took myself back to the lake-that-wasn't-there, hoping that José would come back soon and give me some answers to the new questions that were lining up impatiently outside the door of my mind and demanding attention. He was already there waiting for me. I don't think I shall ever get used to the fact of others, however well-meaning, knowing everything that's going on in my head.

He still wore the baggy green trousers, colourful shirt, string of shells and black hat with its sapphire blue feather. I wondered whether he actually had any other clothes or if perhaps this was his xamã uniform. He still shimmered slightly but his figure seemed a bit more solid to me now.

"All right," I said, "the first thing I don't understand is... how long have I been here? I mean, yes, quite a lot has happened but it only feels like a short while, whereas I — the other me — must have been in that hospital for, I don't know, maybe years." I saw his eyebrows begin to rise and it crossed my mind that one peculiarity of human nature is that people with knowledge love nothing better than stupid people asking them questions. Now, I just needed to play stupid, which wasn't hard. "Yes, I know there's a lot I don't got yet. But help me out, please."

"Is okay, Evička. Most peoples don't got it, neither.' 'Ow long this, 'ow long that, see, it don't mean much. Not when you sees the big picture. Now, back there, our place, us got sun an' moon so folks like you count the days an' nights."

"Well, even here there's bright times and then dusk."

"Only 'cause that's what you'se expectin', see? There no sun, no moon, no? An' where us comes from, the Tapajós place, we no think like that anyways. You asks us how long upriver to next village an' us says four, maybe five stories. Depend how good stories are."

"I'd like to hear some of your stories."

"Mebbe one day. Right now, you got yer own to work out. This place, that place, other place, 'ow long no mean anythin'."

"Hmmm, I see." I didn't of course. It was still too, well, soon. But I needed to know more if my seedling plan was ever to grow into anything, so I put on my best frown and tried again. "So while I'm here, in my story as you put it, what people call years and years could have passed back on... the other place. All kinds of things could've happened." He wasn't falling for it.

"You don't wanna know, Eva."

A sadness in his eyes that I hadn't seen before told me that all kinds of things were happening in other places and none of them were good. We sat in silence for a while. I gazed out over the non-lake to the beautiful, vibrant colours of the flowers and shrubs that framed it, backed by their sheer grey cliffs, to distract myself from the urgent knocking of those questions.

At length, José came up with a lesson plan. He looked around the black stony beach nearby and found a small rock that seemed to satisfy him. It had rounded edges and smooth, concave sides that made it look rather like a fossilised finger. He put it in my palm, closed my fingers over it and then his fingers over mine, told me to close my eyes and be very still.

For a while there was nothing and I was beginning to wonder what the point of it all was but then the pictures began to emerge within my mind, hazy at first then increasingly real. I seemed to be moving up the gentle ascent to my archway, observing from above, although the cabin and veranda were nowhere to be seen. In fact it was hard to see anything much because thick, dark clouds were swirling around. Then a huge shape began to emerge, maybe ten feet tall and three times as long, a great, thick-skinned beast that lumbered towards me with a roar. It had a long neck and an open mouth of sharp teeth and I could feel its hot, foul breath as spiky hands reached out to me. I knew this wasn't real but all the same I made a run for it up the dirt path towards the lake, the very ground shaking as heavy, armoured feet followed me, crashing through the trees. Then halfway up the mountain there were the even more terrifying sounds of the Earth herself exploding as the sky was set on fire by yellow flames shooting up high and the crashing of burning rocks and red-hot lava rushing down the mountainside, passing me by and swallowing up the beast with a gulp. And all around me the land was scorched and stripped bare.

José released his grip and I opened my eyes with relief, still shaken, staring down at the innocuous little rock.

"See, Miss Eva? Nuthin' dies and 'ow long means nuthin', neither. Even the stones is livin'. 'Undred million year, don't make no difference to souls."

"But those scary creatures," I objected, still clinging on to what I thought I knew, "they were all wiped out, weren't they?"

"Charming, I'm sure," Iggy sniffed disdainfully. "And by the way, we don't eat people. He would only have licked you."

"Us is jus' tryin' to show you as 'ow long means nuthin'. Even back in my place. Look, us show you."

He did that thing Jamie does of holding my hand and touching my forehead, but this time I just saw through his eyes and could still hear his voice. We were in an arid, windy desert with the sun scorching down, a place where nothing can survive. He focused in on a crispy, brown bundle of dead vegetation that trundled over the ground like tumbleweed, blown this way and that.

"We's in Chihuahua," he said. "Is México. See the plant? Is called Selaginella lepidophylla."

"Well, it's dead."

"Watch."

Somehow he nudged the spindly ball into a crevice between rocks and poured a little water — heaven knows from where — over it. The dry twigs began to twitch and unfurl into a green, fern-like plant with white tips.

"Is jus' sleepin'," said José, "an' is millions year old." He let go of my hand and we were back within the crater. "Us mustn't judge by 'ow things look. Us mustn't judge 'ow long by human thinkings. In the Mojave, arbusto de creosoto don't look much but he's more'n ten thousand years old. In the Inyo, is real cold, high wind, an' Pinus longaeva is more'n five thousand year-old."

"But even those trees all die eventually." I was still struggling. Still human.

"Do I look dead?"

I hadn't noticed Ashly float up silently to sit beside us.

"Life goes on and on, Eva," he murmured. "This place, that place... other places. Hello, José, I see that you've given our friend your usual fuckin' lecture about time. And, as usual, it hasn't worked."

"Na sua bunda, meu amigo. It no easy."

Ashly actually bristled. But, possessing timeless wisdom, let it go. He turned back to me.

"Jus' take it from me, Eva. I'm not dead, you're not dead, nothin's dead. Maybe when you leave this place you'll begin to get the bigger picture. Livin' on an island doesn't do much for the soul — same views, same paths, same trees and animals—" Iggy shot him a challenging stare "—however beautiful."

I knew that I was going to have to leave, even though I had no idea yet where to go or how to get there. Yes, I may be 'free', but it wasn't as if I were in an airport with a wad of money and a passport in my pocket, standing in front of the departure boards with a choice to make. I was just going to have to trust my personal travel agent, José. He seemed to know pretty much everything in my head so, as a shaman, he must have seen my little seedling of an idea taking shape. He hadn't raised any objections yet. And since he apparently had the ability to produce water from nowhere in a Mexican desert, I was probably in good hands.

On the one hand, I was excited. After all, I was quite used to crossing borders and finding something better on the other side, however challenging. Being human, whatever our circumstances, means a lot of struggle and uncertainty, a good deal of pain for body and mind, and never-ending unanswerables. Yet it also means joy and creativity and discovery and... love. I knew all these, even if I had thrown some away. That's why I had to do something about it, to make good. It wasn't a question of karma, weighing up the balance of my thoughts and deeds so that I could achieve moksha — I knew Ashly's views on that, but in any case I didn't want to escape. Sorry, Brahman. I enjoyed living too much.

But on the other hand I would be sad to leave this island. It may be small yet it had taught me so much. I had rediscovered my mind and found a kind of peace. And I would be sad to leave behind my sometimes annoying but always loyal friend Ashly, my new and mysterious friend José Duartes, my moody yet compassionate friend Jamie and my cute friend Iggy. Still, wherever I went, if there were trees there would be an Ashly. And I had a suspicion that the others may not be so far away either.

When I got back to the cabin, I wasn't surprised to find Jamie already sitting there, drumming his fingers on the table. Heavens, what does a girl have to do to get some time alone? What did surprise me was that an extra chair had appeared and it was occupied by the Franciscan I had first seen with the elders. Indeed, it felt as though he occupied the whole veranda, so great was the aura of compassion surrounding him. Dressed in a sandy habit tied at the waist with a simple white rope and open, brown sandals, he had piercing brown eyes and the gentlest of smiles. Everything about him told of quietness and lifetimes of experience.

"This is, eh... John," said Jamie. "He has, eh, things to tell you."

"Hello," I breathed, hardly daring to speak, "is that really your name?"

"One of them," he said. Well, no, he didn't. Nothing in his expression moved, I simply felt the words. And now that he was right there in front of me, in the flesh, so to speak, I also clearly felt that I had seen him somewhere before — not in the cave, before that, in another place, perhaps in a painting.

"You have learned a great deal here, Evička," said Jamie, lighting a cigarette and getting straight down to business. "About, eh, yourself. About the worlds. How, eh, things are. And we know you want to move on now. You have, eh, plans." I must have grimaced because he continued, "Everything is known, lass. Somewhere. Anyway, we have to be sure that you're ready. That you've taken full responsibility for what you've done. That you're, eh, penitent. For only whosoever confesseth and forsaketh his sins shall have mercy. Proverbs twenty-eight thir—"

"Yet God hath not given us the spirit of fear but of power and of love. Two Timothy one. Oh! Where did that come from?" I put my hand to my mouth in shock as Jamie first glared at the impassive John and then, for the first time since I'd met him, laughed out loud.

"All right, then, call it a draw," he said.

John now leaned forward and rested his forearms, wrapped within the long sleeves, on the table. His demeanour changed too, no less calm but somehow rather more... human, more face to face, and this time his lips did move as he fixed me with a kind stare.

"You should know about Roy," he said. The voice was melodic and I could almost swear I heard music behind the words. He paused for a while, allowing my mind to settle happily around the memories I had recovered in the lake-that-isn't-there. Even so, I sensed a storm cloud coming over the horizon. "Good," he said, "he's there within you. Now, let me take you forward a little, to your parents' house in Trutnov, Hradec Králové. Do you remember this?"

"Couldn't you make an effort? For them? For me? Is it really so important?"

"It's just... how I am."

My whole being froze in terror as I heard those accusing words come from my mouth and his simple explanation that somehow I couldn't tolerate. I saw myself again standing by the open window and looking out over the rooftops of my home town with my back to him.

"I'm not going to come back with you," I'd said, without turning round. When at last I'd looked at him, he was slumped on my bed with his head in his hands, crying quietly and unable to speak.

"And what happened next?" asked John. This was cruel and I wished he would just stop because all that pain was flooding back with the clouds that grew black and angry and ever closer.

"We went back to Prague the next day. To Ruzyně Airport. He took the Aeroflot flight to London. That's it."

"Well, I'm afraid it isn't, Eva."

The Ilyushin Il-62 lumbers into the quiet night sky like a tired goose and heads west into a gathering weather system near the East German border. Roy sits alone next to a window, looking out at vague shapes below picked out by moonlight, watching his life pass him by through tears streaming down his face. There is a deep, agonising pain in his gut, the pain that reminds you of when a terrible decision was made that changed everything, of when you might have said or done something to put your being back on track but didn't.

The plane rocks in the continuous light turbulence and there are some low, anxious murmurs from others behind him. An overhead locker springs open and someone's holdall falls heavily to the aisle with a tinkling of glass. A bulky stewardess in a uniform two sizes too small and a fixed, painted smile rushes up to retrieve it and makes a joke to the passengers sitting nearby, probably about the waste of vodka. Roy turns away and watches with disinterest the vibrating rivets along a section of the starboard wing. This is Aeroflot, not known for its modern fleet, and after all the country is under communist control.

Exhausted by sadness, Roy allows himself to be rocked into a deep sleep by the shaking plane as it drops suddenly, recovers and drops again, so doesn't notice the heavy black clouds gathering around or hear the thunderous crack of lightning that hits the cockpit. And he doesn't wake up again.

"They came down on the outskirts of Nyrany, just outside Plzen," John said quietly. "No one survived. You didn't know about it, of course, because you... well..." He sat back again, his eyes still on mine but without a trace of blame, just love reaching out to hold me as I sat rigid with shock and remorse, utterly unable to think.

There was silence around us. The orioles looked away. A slight shuffle by my feet made me look down to see Iggy lying there. His nose was wet. There was a click as Jamie lit another cigarette. I recoiled from the grey smoke as it drifted across the table like a gathering storm.

"So... Roy is... no, sorry, I mean... well, where is he?"

"That's just it, lass," said Jamie. "And that's why, eh, John's here."

"Roy has no idea what happened," John took it up. "As far as he knows, life just carried on from before. He was in a bad way at first, on the streets. We managed to get him back on track, well, more or less. There's a few of us. Still, it's hard for us to reach him. But you can."

My plan just got tweaked.

Φ

"You see, Evička, however hard we try… there's only so much, eh, we can do. But you, lass…" Jamie leaned forward and held out a hand to me with palm up, "you are closer to him. No, it doesn't seem like it right now, eh, in this place. Yet you two have touched the deepest part within one another."

"And that awareness," added John, "will always be unbroken."

To buy myself a moment, I went inside the cabin to make tea. It seemed the right thing to do for one's visitors, however pointless. They sipped it politely as silence descended around us. That is to say, no one made any outward sign of forming words yet the whole clearing was a battleground of thoughts, mostly mine, shouting over one another and jostling to be first in line.

"So," I finally gave in, "where is he?" The Franciscan shrugged as though this were obvious.

"Roy is in his own world, where he believes himself to be. It is, if you like, a state of mind. Like you being here, Eva — it's more or less what you expected, isn't it? I mean, the vehicles, the hospital, nature, a place to live…"

"There's been a few things I didn't expect," I objected wryly.

"None of us know everything that's in our minds," John smiled. "But look, none of this is that unusual. I'd say most people think they're in one world when really they're in an entirely different one."

"Or even, eh, more than one," Jamie added, as if from personal experience.

Unsurprisingly, my head was spinning at this point and its management team sent frantic signals out to every available worker, instructing them to search through dusty boxes of archives for a helpful memory or two. 'Got one!' the basement neurons called out.

"I remember Roy telling me once that his people believed —"

"His people?" The instant challenge was from John and I immediately understood that this was another of those... differences... that I hadn't, indeed, understood. His mind had been more open than mine, so why had he not been able to...?

"Grief, Eva. The deepest grief overcomes the clearest reason."

"I see that now," I continued, chastised. "I was thinking about some of the people he knew — like that Marian woman, and the church he went to."

"The church he had been to," Jamie corrected me again, "years before. Roy explores all kinds of ideas, takes them in, leaves them behind, always, eh, moving on. He is always searching — and one cannot ask more of anyone. You knew that about him, lass. And that's why you came so close. Yet at the most, eh, important moment..."

"I guess I just forgot." My eyes became moist and the pain raced through my head again. I hadn't been feeling it so much lately.

"Indeed. But now you remember. And you have rediscovered that feeling, at the lake."

"The one that isn't there." John smiled again, wanting to lighten the mood. "What you're thinking of, I suppose, are the books of so-called afterlife evidence, like the one by Freddie Myers. Seven ethereal spheres that people hop from one to another once they've passed the exams until atonement with God. All blindly accepted as the new gospel."

"That's the one, yes. It all sounds... sounded reasonable."

"It's not a matter of reason, though, is it?" Jamie countered. My attention was spinning from one to the other like a tennis umpire and with the same fixed concentration. Crash courses in metaphysics by a tag team of Franciscan and Presbyterian don't come along often. "Does it seem, eh, reasonable that the Almighty Creator of the infinite universe and beyond would be content with a mere seven spheres?"

"Aha!" I jumped in triumphantly. "So there is a Creator, then." Jamie snorted impatiently.

"Jamie is merely pointing out," said John, calmly, "that people believe what they want to believe. They see what they expect to see. Even Freddie. But even the greatest minds only see so far. No one — Jamie and I included — has the slightest idea just how vast their minds are."

This was at once liberating and intensely depressing. What chance do any of us have if all the great teachers have got it wrong or, at least, have only got part of it?

"Teachers have the worst job in the world," John laughed. "Can you teach a fish to climb trees? Or nuclear physics to a five year-old child? You can only give your student a little more than what they already know and hope they will want more. For example, everyone knows that human life is full of suffering so you get their attention by trying to show them a way of being liberated from that — letting go of false beliefs about being separate from everyone else, thinking we're all just physical bodies and we can only be happy if some thing we want comes to us sometime in the future. But that's not easy to grasp so there's the dharma, the natural way to live, the noble path of moral thoughts and actions, mindfulness and meditation. People can see that may lead to less suffering, at least, even jnana, enlightenment."

"Hang on," I objected, "isn't that Buddhism?" He just smiled again.

"It's all the same, Evička."

"I see." I didn't, of course. "Well, I seem to be very far from liberation myself, then. If that's even possible."

"Perhaps not so far, lass. If you can, eh, keep alive the love you feel."

This last simple sentence was the most heavily loaded either of them had spoken. It was my cue, an invitation to tweak my seedling even more. All right, the original plan had been to find a way off this island, pleasant though it was — and José Duartes seemed to offer that possibility — and find a more expansive place to live among other like-minded souls with adventures to be had and a nice home with creature comforts including a bathroom where the soap didn't get eaten by rats.

Yes, the not-lake had given pause for thought. A lot of it. Now that I had remembered so much of what had gone before, of where I'd come from, I realised that I had learned so much from Roy and that eventually I could find a way of making good the hurt I'd caused, not just to him, to my parents and Aleš. And goodness knows how many more. In my new world, I would change and grow and nothing would ever be the same as it was. What was it Paul had said once, sounding very wise and mysterious? 'No one ever steps in the same river twice.'

"Heraclitus," said Jamie. "All things change and yet all things are, eh, unified by the logos. Light needs the dark. Heat needs the cold. All things, all people, all beings are, eh, interdependent."

"And to love," murmured John, "is to be aware of union."

He wasn't letting go, the invitation was being repeated. My mission — should I choose to accept it — was now to find Roy and then... what?

"Free him from his grief."

"And, just by the way, eh, free yourself too, lass," added Jamie.

You know how it is, when your brain's been torn this way and that so you hardly know who or where you are anymore and you're not actually thinking, that's the moment when a sign comes, a synchronicity that demands to be noticed and be allowed to tear up any plans you had for the rest of your life. When there's a crack in your brain and a ray of light gets through. In this case, it actually was a vision.

Something made me shift in my chair — perhaps Iggy had stretched out on my feet — and shake off the stillness that all these words had held me in. The slightest of movements caught my eye and I turned towards the archway at the entrance to my home. Beyond the gate, a mist had risen up again and as it swirled around a figure slowly emerged, very still and far away yet fixing me with a deep sadness. Roy's mother.

"Mrs Cart—"

But my words broke the spell and she was gone, swallowed up back within her own world. She hadn't said anything. She didn't need to.

Once they had left, promising never to be far away, I sat for a while and smoked a couple of cigarettes from the pack that Jamie had left on the table. He hadn't even looked at the picture card inside so I took it out, meaning to keep it for him. It was Robert Falcon Scott, the Royal Navy officer who led expeditions to explore the uncharted frozen Antarctic worlds. It seemed appropriate right now.

Eventually, I knew I had to move so I went back into the cabin to clear up. There wasn't much to do. The wardrobe and kitchen cupboards were practically bare, clothes, packets and utensils having apparently decided for themselves that they were no longer needed. My favourite book, *Brigáda v Mateřské Škole*, was still there, though, along with my gymnastics medals and Králi, my dear rabbit doll. These were part of me, from kindergarten to woman, and couldn't leave.

Perhaps because decisions were now beyond being considered, I slept deeply and peacefully and didn't remember any dreams when I awoke. After coffee — it knew it was still needed — and a few deep breaths, I then set off for a final tour of my island, first heading to what I called east and following the coastline down and across the barren ground to the barrier of thick, tangled and very thorny brambles. Of course, the huge, dark-skinned shadow guard instantly appeared, but this time we just smiled at each other and I went on my way.

To the south-west, I soon found the white cedar and neem woodland with its own rather smaller guardian, Tabby. We skipped through the winding paths to the steep ridge with its mossy stepping stones and I more or less floated down to the lovely shingle and black sand beach, Tabby impassively watching me settle myself on the heavy black boulder from the safety of the treeline. The pale blue water gently breathed in and out and, yes, there was the pelican again, drifting this way and that on the thermals and keeping an eye on me.

The same presence I had felt before was beside me again, with a distant echo of guitar music, but this time there was only a dull ache in my head. I cleared it by swimming for a while in soft, warm water that was actually there, then said goodbye to my private beach — there would surely be others — and allowed Tabby to lead me back along the winding path up to the top of the small hill.

The tiny church no longer appeared neglected, the thick dust that had covered the pews now wiped away and the mahogany pulpit repaired. I didn't need to ask myself who might have done this, I was just happy to see the sanctuary table covered with a rich purple brocade cloth and vases of white orchids. Light streamed through the stained-glass window above, its missing panels replaced, illuminating the image of a vast, beautiful landscape. At the forefront were the greys, magentas and greens of rocks and forest that spoke of the island itself and which then moved through lilacs and pale blues, out across other lands linked by arches, caves and paths, ever lighter and lighter into the distance to an almost blinding focal point at the top.

I clearly had a long way to go.

In the peace of this place, the Franciscan's final words came back to me.

"The first necessity," he'd said, "is having the courage to face life. It's only when we take risks, open ourselves to annihilation, that we find our true indestructible nature, reveal the depths of who we really are."

Φ

At first meeting, Ian is not so much dour as downright sullen. Scottish and ageless, with sun-hardened features and the body of a barrel, he appears the least engaging of characters. Young pupils and their teachers live in daily abject fear of him.

This is all an act, as carefully cultivated as the tumbling foliage, cascades of yellow forsythia and purple rhododendron that are his trademark throughout the grounds of Lakeside College. It ensures that his work remains undamaged by litter and stray footballs and the gardens offer youngsters some appreciation, however subliminal, of the ineffable beauty of life.

Ian loves this place, especially at times like this when the arched windows of the Great Chapel catch the last crimson streaks of a summer sunset and shadows pick out the cracked render of the West Block. These imposing buildings are the reconstruction of a sixteenth century Augustinian priory with just the right sense of history and tradition, along with the pretentious name, to persuade the great and wealthy to send their less than academic offspring. Here they will be force-fed through the entrance exams of even more expensive and exclusive secondary schools.

A few hours earlier, the place was a maelstrom of high-pitched voices, swirling energy and rushing feet wearing ever deeper valleys in the stone stairways. And a few miles away, the streets of Guildford are filling up with noise. But here all is quiet and Ian patrols his territory with keen eyes and one hand hovering over a .22 Webley Mk1 air pistol. Most of the local vermin, though, have learned to stay clear.

There's just one thing out of place. Across the tennis courts shrinking into gathering darkness and beneath the canopy of the Corsican pine, swaying in the gentle breeze, the door to the swimming pool is slightly open. The building is dark, silver patches of twilight on the still water, but it's not empty. Exactly in the middle, as though carefully placed by a mathematician, is a floating Vitruvian man, arms and legs outstretched, head staring up to the glass roof, athletic and naked.

"Are ye deed, then?"

Startled out of his meditation, Roy gulps down a mouthful of water and turns towards the voice.

"Oh, it's you, Ian. Good, uh, evening. I didn't think anyone was about."

"I'm allus about, laddie."

Roy swims slowly across to the steps where he's left his towel and pulls himself out.

"Aah, bowfin'. Ye dinna want t'let Gillian see that."

Roy grins and pads to the changing room where he wipes himself down while Ian settles on a wooden bench to chat. An odd friendship has begun between the two diametrically opposite characters in the week since Roy arrived. There's a mutual respect, by the young for the beauty and order the other creates and by the ageless for this fledgling's worldliness. None of the other staff have done a proper day's work between them.

And it's only human nature that people who know all the local gossip love nothing better than newcomers asking them to share it. Roy already knows most of his new colleagues' very personal secret habits, stored away in the brain's ammunition drawer just in case.

He has presented himself on Monday to Steven Wellesley, Head of Maths, to find out what's required of him. This is virtually nothing since there's less than a fortnight of term left and many of the parents have already taken their children away, two months not being long enough for a summer holiday. The man handed him a few sheets of paper, run off on a Gestetner and smudged with purple ink; one has the names, and nothing else, of the children in his classes and the other has minimal and almost indecipherable notes on the syllabus and disciplinary policy.

Steven Wellesley is a long, thin, wet streak of a man with combed-over hair and pencil moustache, wearing a stained white linen suit that hangs loosely as though it can't wait to be removed. He is not welcoming, with a habit of closing his eyes when he talks, the words slipping lazily out sideways.

"The job's easy enough," he drawled. "Most of the little buggers can't tell one end of compasses from the other. You get the odd one out, of course, like your Chink."

"Beg your pardon?" said Roy, taken aback. A bony finger pointed down the list of names. "Oh, Xiao Li. Is she good, then?"

"She'll keep you on your toes. Father's something in computers. Pointless things. But she's years ahead of the others, no idea why she's here. Still, we just do what we can. On the Day of Judgement, no doubt Solomon will reward the faithful Hercules with a bird in the hand, eh?"

Roy decided there was no point trying to unmix the metaphors of a man who speaks out of the corner of his mouth and took himself back to the flat in Clandon Road to prepare his lessons for the week.

"Y'all settled in then, laddie?" asks Ian as Roy ties his shoelaces.

"Thanks, yes. It's a decent place, plenty of room. Furniture's a bit… minimal, but it'll do for me. Quiet area but close enough to the town. Oh, I meant to ask, Ian — all that art equipment in the spare room… and the paintings. Is someone going to collect them?"

"Thought ye may like a new, eh, hobby." Ian smiles, a rare sight. "Nay next o' kin, yon poor gadgie. Do as ye want."

"The poor chap, er, snuffed himself, you said?"

"Aye, seems so. Strange boy yon Neil, allus, eh, somewhere else in his heed. Not really here. Tried talkin' to 'im, jus' said they uz comin' fer 'im."

"They?"

"Aye."

"Don't think the place is haunted, do you?"

The flat does have atmosphere. The air is very still, expectant, and when Roy sits at the desk with his textbooks he can almost feel… a presence. Whatever it is, it's not unfriendly and it's somehow not human, and after the strangeness of the last few months it doesn't trouble him. He's become used to people who disappear and presences that aren't really here.

If there are neighbours on the ground floor below, he's seen no sign of them. He feels at peace. There is that large, circular dark red stain on the spare room carpet, of course. But it could just be paint. Some large canvases are stacked against one wall and may offer clues to Neil's talent and state of mind.

Two of them are quite impressive. One shows a still lake fringed by mahogany trees within a mountain crater, a beach of black stones in the foreground. On a solitary lilac flowering shrub sits a butterfly. It seems to have the letter E within a yellow circle on each of its black, silky wings. The other painting is much darker, closing in on the oval-shaped mouth of a cave where a black wolf with pale golden eyes sits on guard.

A light shudder, like a very distant memory, passes through Roy as the oils take effect and a cold chill passes through the room. As soon as he can, he decides, he will hang John Cotton's two portraits together in the lounge.

He takes his first classes on Tuesday and, much as Wellesley predicted, realises that he may as well tear up his lesson plans. The squares of Pythagoras remain a Greek legend although the class laps up the story of how the great man met his gory end at the hands of Cylon in revenge for being excluded from the Brotherhood. Children understand how this feels, not being allowed to join gangs. Roy is going to have to use blood and myth to get their attention.

That's not the problem in the afternoon, though, when he meets Xiao Li's class for the first time. As the others stare blankly at their desks or out of the window, Li's attention is fixed unswervingly — and unnervingly — on his face throughout. And at the end of the lesson, without apparently having moved at all, she comes forward, bows slightly, and presents him with a perfect solution in beautiful script to his question about Gambrel roof design. Moreover, she's used trigonometric rules years ahead of the syllabus. He is indeed going to be on his toes.

Xiao Li is nine years old, a small, slim child with elfin face and wide eyes. Her long, fine black hair is tied in a ponytail with a neat ribbon. It will take Roy a while to realise that the colour of the ribbon changes daily according to the rainbow spectrum, red for Mondays and so on. She is an outlier and the other children pretty much ignore her, perhaps fearful of her intelligence.

It's Friday before Roy gets to meet the headmaster. Having delivered his speech on the pre-eminence of honesty to morning Assembly for the umpteenth time, Gerald Sangster MA JP sweeps with as much dignity as he can manage, gown flying in his wake, from the Great Chapel and into his study. In one deft and practised movement, hood and gown are hung on the ornate oak coat stand and with great relief he is into the private washroom behind the Japanese screen in the corner. Headmasters have fairly normal biological weaknesses yet should not be expected to share others' facilities. There's a tentative knock on the door.

"Go away," he calls over his shoulder, the tension in his face beginning to ease.

"But, sir," a tiny voice answers, "it's my birthday." The daily ritual of shaking hands with children on their birthdays and telling them how much they've grown since last year is supposed to reassure them that they're valued members of the community.

"Can't you come back on Monday?" He really needs a cigarette.

"It won't be my birthday then."

This is inescapable logic so with resignation Sangster gathers himself in gown and stern expression before opening the door. At first he thinks the boy has gone away until he lowers his gaze. Good heavens, they get smaller every year. His heart melts slightly as limp fingers are extended.

"Well, congratulations... um... you must be..." The children would be more reassured of their value if their teachers remembered their names. He shuffles papers on his desk before giving up and lifting the telephone.

"Aubrey Garner," comes Gillian Diamond's professional voice, "eleven years old, father has the tacky men's outfitters in Leatherhead but has promised a hundred pounds to the Appeal. And the new Maths teacher is waiting for you."

"Yes, Aubrey, sorry about that — an urgent message. Happy birthday. My, you have, er, grown. I trust you appreciated my Assembly?"

"It was pretty standard, sir. But I don't think many people would entirely agree with you. My father says he'd never sell anything without white lies, sir. And if you do need a new suit, sir, I'm sure—"

"Quite, I'll bear it in mind. You'd better cut along to first period now."

"It's only History, sir, and we've done the Normans to death already. Did you know—"

"All the same." Sangster gets up and holds the door open. The boy is replaced immediately by the much larger and more impressive figure of a young man.

"Roy Carter, sir. Pleased to meet you." He is waved to the high-backed Visitor's Chair beside the desk. "I'm very grateful for this opportunity. It was kind of you to get in touch with Professor Meeks and suggest—"

"Who's Meeks? Never heard of the chap. Aren't you from the agency? Never mind, Wellesley says you've got a good degree and seem to know what you're doing. Look, Cartwright, it's a pretty simple job here. You set the children a good example and get them through the bloody exams, all right?"

Five minutes later, Sangster can sit back in his chair and calmly contemplate the evening's governors meeting. The Appeal is not going well and, with time running out before retirement, he's determined that the new Sports Hall will be his legacy. Some creative accountancy may be needed. For his part, Roy wanders out into the sunshine, somewhat bemused yet still determined, yes, to set a good example. Whatever that means. After all he's experienced, this is a fresh start, an opportunity for a good future, a career, friendships and a peaceful home. Normality.

Perhaps he should realise by now that nothing about his relationships with people, with homes and even with time is normal.

"Good arse, eh?"

"Beg your pardon?"

"Yon lassie." Ian has appeared quietly from nowhere and nods towards the tennis court where the PE teacher is doing her best to persuade ten-year-olds that the idea is to hit balls over the net.

"Oh, sorry, I was miles away. Yes, I suppose so. Russian, isn't she?"

"Aye. Miss Lena Volkova. Daddy's somethin' at the embassy in London. Culture, ye ken. Nae, ye canna trust they Ruskies. Still, good arse."

It will be another week before Roy meets Lena and life turns upside down again. Meanwhile, he spends some hours in the library researching the shady history of mathematicians, as gory as possible, and writing new lesson plans while at the same time refreshing his own knowledge so that he can stay a step or two ahead of Xiao Li. In between, he gets to know the streets of Guildford, buys a few coloured throws for the tired furniture in the flat and stocks up the cupboards. He'll soon have to think about replacing his ageing Ford, too, its engine spluttering more each morning.

In the last lesson of the term, he sets the children a holiday project, to make something creative using Pythagoras' theorem. Surely that's not asking too much? As they file out, muttering about cruelty and their rights, Xiao Li hangs back and shyly approaches him with a small piece of paper.

"Thank you, sir," she says politely. "And this is for you."

Roy watches her leave and smiles. She's a special girl and he has to do his best for her. Only then does he look down at the paper where she has written a simple row of numbers.

4681220

He has no idea what they mean. A code? She is challenging him to find out.

There is a tradition among teachers at the end of the school year to go out, get drunk and exchange rude stories about senior staff. Extra entertainment is being provided by Russell, a young Geography teacher getting married next week to his childhood sweetheart, who's securely fixed in the old stocks on the village green facing The Case Is Altered. His beer has been placed on a bar stool in front of him, reached by a long straw, and the others sit scattered on the grass nearby.

"Last weekend of freedom," Tony taunts him, ironically.

"I don't know that freedom's all it's cracked up to be," Russell observes glumly. A Geordie down south, he often finds life a bit serious. And there aren't many laughs in regional rainfall averages. "I mean, is any of us really free?"

"That's up to you, mate." Tony lights another cigarette from the last one and draws deeply. In his thirties and a Games coach, he's a picture of strength on the outside with a less healthy inner attitude towards women. "All these frustrated housewives within reach and your Jen three hundred miles away, and what do you do? Monday to Friday prepare lessons — come on, who does that? — and come the weekend you're on a train out of King's Cross. I bet you don't even get to watch the Magpies."

"I don't like football."

"Proves my point." He hadn't made one but the others are used to his way of thinking. You didn't have to dig far below the surface of his conversation to find the dirty water table.

"Surely you're free if you want to be," Roy tries to be sympathetic but Russell shakes his wrists in response. "We can all make choices."

"And it's Jen's choice to stay in Newcastle." Tony can't help making things worse. "Just like a woman to imprison a chap by giving him complete freedom. It's tactics, see? Filling you with doubt so you never know the truth."

"And when did truth ever matter to a man?"

Lena Volkova's voice is deep and rich with barely a trace of accent, and her measured tone makes others turn round and listen. This is a woman who naturally gets her own way. Mid-twenties, she is very attractive with a Scandinavian look about her, long blonde hair and high cheekbones and a trained, athletic body.

"You're talking out of your jockstrap, Tony. Lay off the man and get him another drink." Tony meekly does as he's told. "All that matters is love, Russell," she turns to him with a wide smile and feeds him a couple of crisps like a chimp at the zoo. "Two souls meeting and being happy."

"You believe that, do you?" asks Roy, a shadow passing across his eyes as the headache returns briefly. There's something happening here. A small, long-forgotten surge of energy has flashed between him and Lena. "About souls, I mean. Two halves making a whole? Perfect union?"

"Nothing's perfect, Roy." She gives him a long, very cool look and raises an eyebrow.

"Jen's not perfect," mutters Russell. Tony's got to him and he's considering his options. "Don't get me wrong, she's lovely.

In her way. It's just... well, her hair's always a mess and she does keep interrupting."

"Maybe the perfect woman's just round the corner," another voice joins the sabotage.

"That's just Descartes' fault," Roy laughs.

"You what?"

"'I can conceive of God therefore He exists', sort of thing."

"But plenty of people do believe marriage is something... holy," Lena continues. "Yes, Roy, a communion of souls."

Tony has returned and this really seems to get up his nose.

"That's just commie rubbish," he growls. "People fooling themselves, can't accept we're all just animals and life's crap so it has to have some higher purpose with rewards in the hereafter. Very convenient, can't be disproved."

"Haud yer wheesht, laddie. Ye've never loved, then?" Ian's voice takes everyone by surprise. He's arrived silently and is standing behind them, a glass of single malt in hand. Roy smiles, he's allus about.

"One love's as good as another," shrugs Tony, inspecting the surface of his beer closely. Even he is not going to challenge Ian. "It lasts a few years or an hour."

"Ah ken what you mean, most marriages are pure shan, anythin' for a quiet life, eh? But there's summat else, laddie, that feelin' deep down that ye's allus goin' to belong to yer lassie, whatever life throws at yous." He speaks softly, in a tone no one has ever heard from him before and a hush descends as each face turns to him. No one knows anything of Ian's back story but presumably he has one, far longer than any of theirs, and obviously heartfelt. He steps forward to release Russell then sits down beside them.

"So we're back to half-men running around looking for a bit of soul that fits, are we? Happy ever after." Tony lights another cigarette.

"Nae, laddie, ye canna fraction the soul. We're all soul. An' love is touchin' the soul in another, deep down."

"And when two people do that... communion," murmurs Lena. She seems to be glancing at Roy.

"Aye, lassie."

"It's irrational," says Russell, rubbing his wrists to get the feeling back.

"It's absurd," mutters Tony.

"Aye, it is, an' thank God for tha'. What's the point o' life if ol' farts like me could explain it, eh? Love is soul, tha's all, nothin' tae do wi' perfect fits or messy hair or sweaty feet—"

"I never said she had sw—"

"—or simultaneous orgasms." That shuts everyone up.

As light fades, the rest of the group drift away one by one, having poured the last of their drinks over Russell's head to wish him good luck, leaving Roy and Lena alone. He hasn't drunk much — somehow Adam's voice is always in his ear when he has to drive — but she is clearly mellow and a little unsteady on her feet.

"Give me a lift?" she asks with a warm smile, leaning against him for support.

The night is still warm and they wander slowly, arm in arm, back towards the school along the narrow country lane beneath a clear sky. Away from the city's light pollution, this canopy of stars will always make one feel small.

"Big bear," she says, pointing up.

"Beg your pardon?"

"And there, the Pleiades. They're watching us, you know."

"Are they? I wonder what they'd make of what Ian said, then."

"I'm sure they'd agree with him. When we love someone, we touch a power beyond ourselves. It's nothing to do with who or what we are or whether we have messy hair." She tosses her head back so that her own soft hair brushes his face and her girlish laugh races through his brain, sending neurons scurrying for cover and waking up long-dormant electrochemistry. Is he really feeling this? After everything?

They squeeze awkwardly through the gap in the hedge and Roy turns towards the carpark but she pulls him away.

"I want to swim."

"But…"

"Come on, Roy. We all know you come here when you think everyone's gone home. And you keep a towel in the changing room, don't you?"

"But…"

Across the tennis courts shrinking into the darkness and beneath the Corsican pine, the door to the swimming pool is slightly open. The building is dark and quiet, silver patches of moonlight on the still water. Ian smiles to himself as he patrols his territory with keen eyes and one hand hovering over his pistol. Under cover of a large, sweeping willow, Inspector Jones stands beside a large black saloon car without number plates in the lane beyond the hedge and lifts the Army issue Mk 1 infrared night vision binoculars to his eyes, cursing himself for not bringing a camera.

It is a fact that, given the right circumstances, a woman can make a man do whatever she wants. Lena takes Roy's hand and leads him, uncomplaining, through the door. She hangs her short, fawn leather jacket and bag on a hook before, completely unselfconsciously, unfastening two buttons and letting her dress slip to the ground followed in one practised movement by her underwear. She is very beautiful, slim and muscled, and she is smiling coyly.

"Come on, Roy."

"But…"

She dives, cutting the surface smoothly. Her head, strong shoulders and small, perfect breasts break the water and the last of his resistance. Within a minute their bodies are clinging together, indivisible, so that he can no longer tell or care which limbs are his. No longer alone, he is waking up at last. And then she breaks free, laughs again and crawls powerfully to the far end of the pool and back and forth, inviting him to follow and allow the water to wash away the shadows, the guilt and the grief.

In the changing room they allow the feelings to flow and settle, hand in hand under the warm shower, without saying a word and then she stands calmly with arms outstretched, allowing him to dry every part of her body gently with his bath towel. When he's finished and turns away, she draws him back and takes the towel from him.

"But..."

"Shhh." She wipes him down very slowly, finally discarding the towel and using her dress to caress his penis and trembling legs. They get dressed and stand close together again for five minutes, hand in hand and brow to brow, breathing each other's breath, in awe of the beauty of it all.

"Is this what Ian—"

"Shhh. Let's go home."

It's hard to let go but they have to get into the car. As soon as the doors close they wrap together again until she, the one in control, draws back to allow him to start the engine. It bursts into life first time and she rests her head back onto his shoulder, one hand on his thigh, as he drives slowly back to Guildford, fighting to focus his eyes on the road. A black saloon car driven by a gorilla follows at a safe distance.

At Clandon Road they climb the stairs three-legged and only once they are inside does she let go and wander around the flat inspecting his spartan bachelor life. It probably does, as they say, need a woman's touch. She frowns at the red stain on the spare room carpet and shudders slightly as she turns one of the canvases away from the wall to look at it.

"Neil was pretty good, wasn't he?" Roy says, coming up behind her. The still lake seems to shimmer in the moonlight filtering through the window and a light breeze rustles the lilac flowers of the shrub. "Oh, I'm sure there was a butterfly..."

"I don't like it," she whispers, replacing the canvas. "It's a threat."

The atmosphere is changing so they return to the lounge where she turns off the light, lets her damp dress fall to the carpet, and pulls him down beside her on the small sofa with its new Indian print throw. She takes out a small bottle of Stolichnaya from her bag and they share it in utter silence, her head on his chest, as a soft shawl of tiredness finally creeps over them.

"Where do we go from here?" Roy whispers.

Without a word, in answer she levers herself up and takes his hand, leading him to the bedroom. He moves to draw the curtains but she stops him.

"Let the world see us."

But Jones has seen enough and given up for tonight, already heading fast up the A3 to London and his own rather more palatial bachelor flat in Chelsea. The vision is clearly imprinted on his mind so he'll write up the report in the morning, suggesting that a watch be kept on Aeroflot manifests.

Lena undresses herself and then Roy, since he's standing unmoving and unable to take his eyes off the gift she is offering him. With the sheets pulled to the floor, they lie together face to face, breathing one another again, fingers of one hand lightly tracing the other's body.

"Did anyone ever tell you... you look even better without clothes?"

When he enters her, she cries quietly but holds him tightly and draws him deeper. An energy that he'd begun to doubt now resurfaces and flows up through his body, opening and spinning each chakra. His heart stops for a fraction of a second then restarts with a new rhythm. Passing through the third eye, the flow sets off a throb at his left temple again.

They lie back with her head on his shoulder, one arm across his chest, and he wonders why a dark sense of foreboding is edging into his mind.

There's a thud from the next room.

As she sleeps, he eases himself out of bed and covers her with the sheets before stepping quietly out of the room with adrenaline pumping. The portrait of the Franciscan monk has fallen from its wall mounting to the floor, illuminated by moonlight through the uncurtained windows. As a cloud passes, its shadow seems to bring the face to life with a gentle smile.

This should be the happiest of times, the end of so much loss and the beginning of peace, with a security he's never had. So why does it feel like someone else, somewhere, has other ideas?

Finally overtaken by exhaustion, the last couple of weeks trip over each other in his dream in their search for memory cells. And then he's inside Neil's painting, the black stones rippling beneath his feet as he looks out over the still lake. He turns to the bush to see its flowers detach themselves and become a cloud of butterflies, Pseudophilotes vicrama with lilac wings fringed in white, black spots at their edges, four and six, then another four and six. They flutter away as one, leading him along Leninská Cesta to Prague and into the square, Václavské Náměstí, where they settle on the Bohemian saint astride his dark grey horse, transforming into Erebia aethiops. There are bright red-orange splashes at the edges of their wings now and all their eyes are turned on him, black circles with white spots, one alone then two together.

He turns away, feeling threatened, and pushes his way through a crowd of students, past a small kiosk where a long line of women queue for German biscuits and then pausing outside the Jalta Hotel where a distant piano can be heard playing the theme of Blaník from *Smetana's Má Vlast*. But the butterflies, Papilio machaon now, have followed to encircle his head and it's the twelve cream piano key splashes at the centre of their wings that are being played by an invisible musician. At the edges of the wings are small white semicircles, a group of four then eight. A man of medium height wearing a light raincoat despite the sunshine stands nearby.

"Perfect, isn't it?" he says.

He turns to Roy and his face is the grinning skull of Polyploca ridens, the death's head moth, his raincoat its dusty wings that spread out and harden into shining metal as he rises up, up to become a Tupolev Tu-128 intercept fighter that rakes the square with gunfire.

Over breakfast, a smiling Lena asks him why he's so distracted and he tells her about the dream, every detail still vivid.

"I have no idea how I knew the names of the butterflies," he says. "But I did solve one problem. Four, six, eight, twelve and twenty are the number of faces of Plato's perfect solids."

"Nothing's perfect, Roy," she says.

Φ

"Everyone on the true path," Jamie had said, "needs someone who will faithfully help them to endure hardships and pass through them. You are fortunate to have a good guide. Carlos... I mean, José is a good man. Sorry, I forget where I am sometimes."

Naturally, when I returned to the cabin José was waiting for me. Beside him sat the most beautiful black wolf, sleek and muscled, with old, light golden eyes.

"Meet Cody," said José. "He my guide. He know the ways, keep us safe. Say hello to Miss Eva." The wolf pointedly ignored me, keenly watching the nose of Iggy who was peering around the corner of the cabin. "You'se ready, then? We got a way to go. The others waiting us."

I had no idea who the others may be but José was not in a chatty mood. He was more solid to me now, dressed as before but with a thick woollen green gilet covered in pockets and carrying a battered leather satchel on his back. There were more feathers in his hatband, yellow, red and black, and tucked securely alongside was a serious-looking knife with an ivory handle and a long, curved blade.

Before leaving, I had to say a final goodbye to my home. And a girl can't set off on an important trip without checking her hair and clothes. I hadn't bothered with the mirror since I arrived but I was glad to see that the wound on my head had virtually healed, leaving just a faint scar to remind me of my other self, and my hair, still short, had grown back around it. I then found that my fawn jacket, pale blue jeans and black ankle boots had laid themselves out on the bed, obviously feeling needed.

When I came out and shut the door for the last time, there was a scuttling of small feet and I looked down into Iggy's plaintive eyes.

"I's coming with you," he said. But he changed his mind when Cody rose, stretched and ambled over to stand nose to nose with him.

We set off at pace with Cody loping effortlessly ahead, pausing every now and then to check we were keeping up, and had soon crossed the mountainside heading north-east. A small nervous shadow crossed my mind as I realised we were going to the wild part of the island where I had felt ill at ease before. Perhaps facing one's fear was what this journey was all about, though. As we followed the deep gulley uphill I became aware of Ashly's presence too, floating among the trees and staying nearby, then we descended through the thickly wooded valley to the head of the vertical cliffs that looked down on that hostile, rocky shore where waves crashed with a hellish roar, driving a salty wind upwards to sting our faces. It would be so easy to jump...

Suddenly, Cody turned off to one side and entered a narrow, stony path that I hadn't seen before. It wound its way down from one side to the other like a fairground switchback between overarching mahogany trees that clung tenaciously to the rock and all but cut out the light. I had learned to move effortlessly on this island but this was testing my balance and vision, and I fell behind a little, feeling unsafe for the first time, as the other two skipped on. They were waiting for me at the bottom, José smiling encouragingly, Cody glaring pityingly.

"You all right, Miss Eva?" my guide asked kindly. "We nearly there." It was hard to hear his words above the angry noise of the waves just a few metres away but then Cody turned again, inland and around a promontory to a small clearing of black sand where, magically, the sounds of the water became a whisper on the cool breeze.

I gasped. Ahead of us stood the dark opening of the most extraordinary cave, about two metres high, an oval edged with rock carved by the ages in the shape of labia.

"We call it o útero," José said reverentially and needlessly. "Is vagina da deusa... what you say, the goddess."

"What... what's her name?" I stammered.

"Many name," he shrugged. "Most say Hecate, a mãe... the mother. She guard door to new world."

At the entrance, Cody laid himself flat to the ground as though in reverence and then led us through musty tunnels of damp rock just high enough for us to be able to walk upright. My mind flashed back to the underground of the forbidden area of the island where I'd come across the elders but this felt very different, somehow darker and even more secretive, if that were possible. However, as the light grew — or my eyes adjusted to it — and a long bend in the tunnel opened out into a large, high chamber, the first figures I saw were indeed John and Jamie.

I burst out laughing. This was clearly not the proper thing to do in this most sacred of places and a sea of faces turned to me with dark frowns, but I simply couldn't help it. Jamie was wearing long khaki shorts, a green vest that showed off strong shoulders and sinewy arms and open-toed sandals with white socks, whilst the monk's sandy habit had been replaced by torn blue jeans, a Hawaiian shirt and white trainers.

"What?" hissed Jamie. "He said casual dress. Be, eh, comfortable."

With a hand over my mouth and shaking shoulders, I took in the others already waiting for us. There were two men I hadn't seen before, shimmering indistinctly like the first time I'd met José yet clearly of the same tribe as him and dressed pretty much the same in vibrant colours, decorated with feathers and strings of beads and animal teeth. I couldn't help noticing that each one carried a long knife too, tucked into waistbands, and the light glinting off these quickly changed my mood.

José introduced me to Rosa, his partner and "a sacerdotisa" — the priestess. There was nothing shimmering about her. She was, shall we say, rather solid and well rounded yet with the most beautiful clear-skinned face and the deepest brown eyes I'd ever seen, framed by long, jet-black hair in braids tied with silver ribbons. In contrast to the others, she wore a simple white robe with a thin, colourful band at the waist and, on her head, a garland of leaves interspersed with tiny white flowers. An imposing woman, she stepped forward to take both my hands in hers and gave me a sweet smile that made my heart jump.

"Bem-vindo, criança."

"She say welcome," José translated. "The others—" he waved a hand towards the shimmers "—my friends. Here keep you safe, Eva."

The group spread out to the sides of the cavern, small lights twinkling around each one from crystals in the rock, and I gasped again. At the far end of the chamber stood the statue of the goddess. Well, that suggests the figure was man-made but no, she was hewn from rock by the ages, by the salt winds and by the waterfall that framed her in light as it rushed silently from somewhere above us. Yet there was no mistaking the serene face, the slight smile, the hair that flowed over her shoulders and small breasts and the swollen belly. She seemed to be sitting within the stone within the pool of water gathered where her feet would be. Someone had already placed a flaming torch just to her right and one of those knives to her left.

"Now we give our offerings," John murmured next to me.

One by one, the other seven stepped forward and laid something on the ground in front of the figure — fruits and flowers, an egg and some small cakes — and even Ashly managed to manifest some herbs. The sheer incongruity of a Franciscan monk and a Presbyterian minister offering gifts to a pagan goddess somehow didn't even cross my mind. Then all eyes turned to me.

I panicked. No one had warned me about this and I didn't...

"Check your pockets, lass," whispered Jamie.

My hand searched through my jacket and settled on something soft and round. A mushroom. It had a broad red cap with yellow-white warts and I had no idea whatever how it had got there.

"Amanita. Perfeita, criança," smiled Rosa, gesturing for me to take it forward. "Temos treze presentes."

"Thirteen gifts," Jamie translated this time. "Well done, lass." I no longer questioned how it was that my friends were apparently multilingual. It was all a matter, as José would say, of thinkings.

The mention of gifts made me suddenly remember the Scott picture card I had kept for him so I fished it out of an inside pocket and passed it over, to be rewarded with a broad smile and nod of thanks.

The group gathered together again and one by one we headed to the far end of the chamber where, hidden by the goddess, another low tunnel could now be seen. To enter it, though, we would have to pass through the strangely quiet torrent of sparkling water from above. As guest of honour, so to speak, they all waited for me to go first.

"This is to purify us," murmured Jamie as I hesitated. And as I began to undo the buttons of my jacket he chuckled. "No need for that. You'll not catch your death, lass."

This tunnel was very dark and I had to bend over with hands outstretched to the walls to find my way forward. Gradually, after a couple of turns, a faint flickering light up ahead made things easier and I emerged into a final vast cave. Rosa and the others had clearly been here ahead of us to prepare the... whatever was coming. There were flaming torches placed on the walls and a wide ring of eight colourfully embroidered, thick cushions at the centre around a firepit over which was hung a black cooking bowl with steam gently rising from it into the incense-laden air. Each of us took a seat, Jamie and John either side of me, and Cody laid himself at the entrance facing back the way we'd come, watching the tunnel attentively.

In the silence that now fell, my gaze was drawn up towards the domed roof of the cave, astonished to see not rock but a beautiful tangle of thick, gnarled roots, presumably belonging to the forest of trees above ground. They interlinked and spread out across the walls, becoming ever finer, and were all connected one to another by a network of microscopically thin, white filaments more intricate than any spider's web. Ashly noticed my wide eyes.

"You see, Eva?" he whispered. "This is how we know each other. We are all one."

Then the music began, softly and melodic, José and his companions taking up verses of their canções sagradas, at times from one another in turn and then together, accompanied by gentle fingers on gourds covered by taut animal skin and decorated with coloured ribbons. The sounds rose and fell and echoed from the chamber walls, filling every part of me, as one song then overlaid another in a choir. Jamie and John had joined in with a deep undertone duet too.

"Abide with me, fast falls the eventide,
as darkness deepens, Lord, with me abide.
When other helpers fail and comforts flee,
help of the helpless, oh, abide with me.
Swift to its close ebbs out life's little day..."

And, involuntarily, I found myself contributing, whilst knowing that, somewhere, the merciful would hear and understand.

"Hospodine, pomiluj ny,
Jezu Kriste, pomiluj ny,
ty Spase všeho míra,
spasiž ny, I uslyšiž hlasy nášě..."

As the music slowly died away, it was replaced by a low guttural growl from Cody and I looked across to see him with hackles raised and open, snarling mouth revealing some serious teeth. There was a swirl of white robe in the tunnel and then peace descended again. John leaned over to me.

"Elder," he said simply. "They're not keen on this sort of thing."

"Or many other things," observed Jamie with a touch of bitterness.

"Good job we have Cody, then," I muttered.

"You have us, too, lass. We're all here to keep you safe, help you, eh, on your way."

Perhaps to confirm that and seal in the energy that had grown, José and Rosa stood up now and began to move slowly around the group in opposite directions, singing almost inaudibly and waving small glowing bundles of wild sage and juniper sticks.

Despite the brief interruption, the atmosphere was hypnotic and all-embracing and it seemed to me that I had almost left the island already, indeed that somehow I had always been living in this cave. And as the shamans passed behind me, flames of the torches cast flickering shadows of their heads on the opposite wall. First came... a bird I had never seen before, with a large, rounded head and long curved beak, its plumage flying out behind... and then, in the opposite direction, a small group of dancing elves with many arms and hands entwined with each other... In the heady scent and warmth of the fire, it was becoming difficult to know just what was real. But I dare not voice this thought in case I was the only one. And from somewhere far away came a memory of someone telling me that we all only see what we want to see...

At length, José took his seat again and Rosa came to kneel in front of me with that sweet smile. It was fortunate that this relaxed me because she then gently unwound the rope from her waist, which turned out to be a slender coral snake about a metre long. Admittedly it was rather beautiful, red and black with bright yellow bands, but I appreciated this beauty less as it wound itself around her arm and lazily stretched out to inspect me with its bulbous head and small round nose. It definitely didn't seem to like what it found because it then gave off a loud, rapid popping noise before retreating to Rosa's shoulders. She laughed and said something that John translated for me.

"Not to worry, Eva, that was actually its tail. Looks the same as its head, a defence mechanism."

"You can't mean it's scared of me," I muttered.

Rosa fixed me with her dark eyes and began to speak fast, which John again translated.

"She's explaining what this is all about and what's going to happen," he began. "Basically, she's brewing some tea for you."

"Not like any tea I've ever had," sniffed Jamie, leaning over the pot.

"They call it cipó, their word for the forest vines they use. Some call it hoasca."

"What sort of, er, vines?" I asked suspiciously.

"Well, if you want to know, they're Banisteriopsis caapi and Psychotria viridis. They complement each other so that the DMT is activated."

"What's DM—"

"Don't worry about it. Oh, she's saying there's another ingredient, too, her own special recipe. Look..."

With a flourish and another smile, Rosa reached up to pluck some stems from her headdress and toss them into the pot. There was an instant puff of green steam with a fetid smell that made us all recoil, even Ashly.

"Aaah, that's one bowfin' bree. Rank!" Jamie coughed, instinctively reverting to vernacular.

"They've been preparing this for quite a while," John continued, his eyes still streaming. "Has to be done in a particular way, saying prayers over each leaf... cleaning the vines... breaking them down with wooden mallets... José brought everything over ahead of us... She says they've taken a lot of trouble and..."

"Go on."

"Um, she hopes you're worth it."

"I see. Well, I hope so too. Brother John, if she doesn't mind me asking... er, what's the point of it?" I mean, I'd gone along with all of this so far in the belief — the expectation — that José was going to help me leave the island and find... another place. And I trusted my friends to wave me off. I hardly thought it was going to involve a tea party. John said a few words and Rosa's eyebrows almost disappeared into the leafy garland. Then she began again, as patiently as she could.

"So... these plants have a kind of spirit. What?" She was gesticulating to John with a wagging finger. "Sorry, no, the plant is a spirit. It shows us what we need to know about ourselves... and what must be healed from the past—"

"Ye shall know the truth and the truth shall set ye free. Gospel of John, eight thirt—"

"All right, Jamie. And it shows you how to move forward to... a new place. She says the plant is kind and only wants what's best for you, although..."

"Go on."

"...you, er, may not like all of that."

"I see." I didn't, but that wasn't unusual of course.

"But she says you're not to worry. You'll be quite safe — that's why we're all here — and a new guide will probably come to help you along."

"Probably?"

"Yes. That's all."

Rosa had finished speaking and turned back to see whether her, um, tea had boiled sufficiently. As I tried to digest all this information, a sudden thought struck me.

"Brother John, in all of that — thanks, by the way — you kept saying 'you' and not 'we' or 'us'. So aren't you going to—"

"Good heavens, no. We couldn't possibly. No, this is all for you, my dear. We're just here for, ah, moral support. And to hold your hand when you're sick, of course."

"What?!"

Up to this point, Ashly had been sitting opposite me and uncharacteristically quiet. He rose now, drifted around the circle, and his soft mist enveloped me in the warm embrace of nature.

Φ

Rosa was satisfied that the cipó was ready and she poured some into a small, intricately carved laurel cup. The figure of a snake wound itself round the thick stem and seemed to squirm in my hand as I took it. The songs began again quietly in the background while Rosa herself spoke rapidly — perhaps a prayer — then took my head in her hands and kissed my forehead before gesturing that I should sample her recipe.

It was pretty foul. I did my best to drink it down, urged by my friends' smiling encouragement, and... nothing happened. I put the cup down, only to see it immediately refilled, and looked around at the expectant faces. Should I apologise to them for, I don't know, being immune?

And just as I opened my mouth, it hit me.

To be fair, from this point I wasn't really aware of what happened but most of it came back to me later in frighteningly clear visions. The first thing, though, was the tremors. Jamie and Brother John took my hands as I began to shake a little but the real quake was inside. Leafcutter ants pour out of their huge underground nests in their thousands, heading for some unfortunate myrtle or acacia that the scouts have identified to be stripped. Then they stream back in a red river torrent, each carrying several times its own weight, to feed the host fungus. Inside me, tiny red beings with hairy feet and wild eyes were biting their way painfully along my entire nervous system, queueing up to chomp on my hippocampus and tear off fragments of memory before disappearing into a black hole at the top of my head. Heaven knows what they were feeding them to.

I couldn't help myself cry out in pain, though I barely had a chance because then the flushes started... can someone please explain how a flush can be both hot and cold at the same time?

My body shook with shivers as sweat poured down my face — which at least hid my tears — and I lost control of my limbs, the spirit of the vine taking over and doing its will with me. What it wanted to do next, to make sure I'd properly noticed it, was send a few g-forces through me so that, like a trainee fighter pilot banking sharply to close on the enemy, my chest felt it was being crushed by stampeding rhinos as every last cubic centimetre of air escaped my lungs.

It was probably fortunate that the chorus grew louder now, filling the cathedral chamber, because it would have drowned out the sound of my retching into a bowl that Rosa kindly held out. I have no idea, nor do I care, what it was lovingly carved from. And I probably didn't thank her for pressing the cup to my lips again and forcing the awful brew down.

I think I lost consciousness although it was that strange kind of hypnagogic hovering between worlds, vaguely aware of figures moving and murmuring around me while another me wanders along a shadowed, stony path overhung by dense foliage towards, of course, an archway with a low wooden gate. I flick open the latch without thinking and find Petr, my father, waiting for me.

"Eva," he says sternly, "don't suck your finger. That's for babies…" He follows up with several more don'ts and stops and mustn'ts, a dark angel towering over me with hand raised in warning.

"He only wants to protect you," reasons my mother, Amálie, entering stage left. "There are bad people in this country and they mustn't notice you. You have to be timid. You have to do as you're told."

Somehow this isn't working for me.

"I'll stop if you don't tell me to," seems a perfectly logical response. By the age of five I am already versed in the stubborn ways of all Czechs, who cannot be criticised and who learn resistance. So I continue to suck my finger all the way to Charles

University, where it is replaced by cigarettes that I lick the ends of before lighting, telling the noisy people who gather in a tight circle around me demanding answers that this softens the coarse, dark Bulgarian tobacco. And then the cigarette smoke becomes a light mist that swirls around me, like when I arrived on... some island or other... and it follows me everywhere I go now so that I only see grainy snapshots of what's happening.

What's the other thing I mustn't do now? Oh yes, sex. It's after Mr Parker's lecture on clause analysis that I swing out of the Carolinum doors in high spirits and along Na Příkopě towards the square, walking straight into Josef. He's a journalist on *Rudé Právo*, darkly handsome and athletic with long fair hair, determined to make a name for himself with bold stories. Apparently I'm one of them. We're in his untidy studio flat and barely through the door when he pulls off my jacket and rips my dress in his haste, pushing me back onto an unmade bed that still smells of someone else as he pulls down my underwear and forces himself inside me with a hand over my mouth, not even noticing my lithe, perfect body toned by years of gymnastics.

"You're beautiful... I love you..." he grunts.

"What you hear someone speak is not necessarily what they have actually said," asserts Mr Parker, looming up at the side of the bed and holding out my dress hanging from his little finger. "I did tell you, silly girl. Only got yourself to blame."

"I'm sorry, sir," I mutter, curling into a foetus as a yellow, jabbing cloud of shame envelops me, leaving ugly bruises on my breasts and thighs.

But the cloud dissolves and on the ceiling I can see slow moving patterns of moonlight reflecting from a turning Welsh tide and I feel like a child again, in awe of Roy's gentle strength and the way my skin melts into his. He is lying on the bed almost asleep with the sheets pulled back and as I sit on the edge to watch his breath my every thought dissolves and the world slips quietly away to nothing. His being is joining with mine in non-being. One eye opens and I say, "You're the only man I've known who looks better without clothes."

"What about me, though?" demands a rough voice with a Scottish accent and I turn to watch wide-eyed as the naked figure of Jamie nailed to a cross slowly rises in mid-air just outside the hotel window. There's blood streaming from his wounds and broken ribs sticking out and he's laughing hysterically. "That's right, well barry, eh, lass? Ah dinnae ken what y'see in yon gadgie."

So I gather a sheet around me and open the window to remonstrate with him but the students from the Strahovska hostel rush through insisting that I join their march. We're carrying nothing more offensive than lighted candles and history textbooks as we cross the bridge and move towards Staré Město. There's a cold night wind and the sky is lit by tracer fire and the glow of shells hitting their targets on the outskirts, and we get no further than Jilska where grotesquely masked pocket money toy soldiers are lined up across the road, waiting to be picked up and dropped when their naïve young owner has saved up for a tank or two. But within seconds, the unimaginable is in full flood, childhood plans splintering with weapon butts on skulls, eyes streaming with gas as reality runs riot. More soldiers appear, marching on stiff legs from the direction of the river to cut off our retreat. There are candles strewn absurdly across the street, some still flickering weakly, among crying and moaning bodies that can't get up. I recognise Pavel Dušek, one of the students in my English class, and realise he will never get up. His sightless eyes stare up at me pityingly.

"You'll never be safe, Eva," he says quietly. "Keep your head down. When this is over, in the final release, who will pick up my pieces?"

So I turn to run but a storm is breaking out and I can't see the way to get back to anything I think I know, leaving behind everything that I've believed in, everything I've learned, because this path is winding away out of sight and I'm just searching the shadows for footholds until at last I think I've made it but this door is unfamiliar...

It belongs to a large black saloon car without number plates that pulls up beside me as I stand frozen in terror and a tall, fair-haired man in dark suit, white shirt and sober blue tie gets out to face me.

"Miss Nováková? Please come with us." The driver is a leering gorilla with a thick neck and short arms and broad shoulder jammed against the side window. The man holds open the rear door for me. "Keep your head down," he says as he flashes his identification. "I'm Inspector Peter Jones. Her Majesty's Government. We just need to ask you a few questions, such as are you a communist and who's Roy and what are you doing in Salford and exactly when and where is the invasion going to begin and will we ever be safe... safe... safe...?"

His voice reaches a screeching crescendo as he turns into a hooded monk but no, it's not Brother John because the habit is black and when he shakes off the cowl there's just a grinning skull with a stream of red ants pouring out of an eye socket and down under the cloth. The gorilla laughs.

"Ha, those fools know nothing," laughs Leonid Mikhailovich Sokolov, checking the corridor outside the Emigration Office and turning back inside to lock the door. In the harsh yellow glow of a cheap desk lamp he opens a bottle of Stolichnaya and fills two small glasses. I watch in cool fascination from my chair, this fat middle-aged slug, as he pushes a glass towards me, loosens his tie with the other hand and comes round the desk transforming into a huge, stooping beast on two legs with black hair and horns pointing backwards and white stripe down the middle of his face. He looms over me.

"Do you really have to do this?" he screams.

"Yes," I reply calmly, withdrawing all sense of feeling back down deep within, "if it's the only way I can get out."

And after all, I have discovered one benefit to this hell-hole. While Sokolov was in his secretary's office making sure she was leaving for the day, I've found the Tokarev TT-33 semi-automatic pistol in an unlocked drawer of his desk. It's now in my burgundy leather shoulder bag and I'm pretty sure I can work out how to use it...

...and now I'm putting the bag down on the hotel towel as a young man approaches across the beach. He looks nice and my heart is jumping and there are waves of gratitude flooding through me for his courage in lying about needing a cigarette and when he smiles ruefully all the pain I've ever known dissolves in a silent lake within the crater of a mountain...

...and of course fire begins to shoot up from the water, spewing burning rocks above us so I take out the pistol and level it at him.

"You should've stuck to what you know," I say.

And he's racing away, scrambling up the glowing scree and I follow across bare valleys and snow-packed Hradec Králové mountainsides as darkness falls and a biting wind brings tears to my eyes.

"You will never be safe," I shout, bringing up the pistol and taking sight. He stops and turns to face me, a small, black-haired chamois with horns pointing backwards and a white stripe on its soft, beautiful face.

I squeeze the trigger.

Φ

"We hardly know anything about each other," Roy smiles, stirring the scrambled eggs.

"Let's go to Leningrad, then," she says. "You'll meet my Babushka, she knows everything about me. My mother died when I was little so Babushka brought me up."

"What about your father?"

"The life of a Party official is... demanding. I moved to Moscow with him later but Leningrad will always be home."

They are hungry this morning and eat in silence, watching each other between mouthfuls with wide eyes and smiles. Roy doesn't tell her that the painting had fallen down. He doesn't know yet how she'll respond to his strangeness and wants to hold fast to last evening's beauty, still hardly believing that this lovely creature could want him and give herself to him. And somehow she already looks different this morning. There's a glow.

"It'll take some organising, though," he says over his shoulder as he washes up. "I'll have to apply for a visa and to be honest money's a bit short. I haven't been paid ye—" She comes up quietly behind him and puts her arms round his waist, pulling him closer.

"What's the point of having a father in the government if he can't organise things?" she murmurs, a cheek pressed to his.

"Ah, I thought he was a cultural attaché?"

"That's one of his jobs."

Her hands move up and begin to undo his shirt buttons, exploring inside before turning their attention to his belt. Plates are left in the bowl. As he turns, she is kneeling in front of him and sliding his shorts down.

"Don't move."

When they wake up again on the bed, they are wrapped in one another's arms and the gods' dice have well and truly been cast. Roy stares at the late morning sunlight flooding through the window, still mesmerised by the speed with which his life moves from one scene to the next, the past already stored in a cupboard behind the backdrop. Who's writing this script and why does it keep getting revised? It doesn't matter. He is happy for the first time since the doors opened.

"Hurry up and get dressed," Lena calls from the bathroom. "There's shopping to do."

He does as he's told. She makes a phone call, talking rapidly in a serious, low voice before bursting out laughing, then they're walking briskly into Guildford, hand in hand and arms swinging. They don't notice the large black saloon car driving very slowly at a safe distance behind them, holding up the traffic on London Road. Along the High Street, she stops outside Harveys.

"The most important clothes we'll need," she says, "are jeans. Three pairs each. Blue denim. One for the journey and the others will need to look worn before we get there."

"What? I've never worn jeans. Except on the building site."

"You do now. And of course you'll need some other trousers to wear while we're there and coming back, something that matches your jacket."

Mystified, he trails around the store behind her like a puppy as she picks out this and that — two of his jeans are even too small for him — and an hour later is even more surprised when they get to the desk and she pulls out a wad of notes. She silences his protest by kissing him on the lips.

Early in the morning three days later, a large manilla envelope arrives by courier. It contains two airline tickets and a document in Cyrillic script on the headed notepaper of the Russian Embassy.

"That's your visa," she says. "Well, sort of. It'll get you anywhere you want to go."

"Anywhere?"

She giggles and unties the cord of his dressing gown, wrapping it around his neck to lead him back to bed.

"And now," she whispers, "it's time for me to teach you some Russian." Of the half dozen phrases he learns today, possibly only one may be used in polite company.

The Ilyushin Il-62 lumbers through the afternoon sunshine and, as it flops like a tired goose into Shosseynaya Airport, Roy finally opens his eyes. Lena is looking at him worriedly and he realises he's gripping her hand tightly.

"You should've told me you were nervous of flying."

"I'm not. Or I didn't think I was. Sorry, something just came over… aaah." He puts a hand to his temple. "It's nothing, I get these headaches sometimes."

"How often?"

"They come and go. The last couple of years. It's nothing."

"Years? That's not nothing, Roy. We'll have you checked out as soon as we get back. My father has this brilliant doctor in Harley Street."

"I'm sure he has."

The plane is barely a quarter full. It taxis up towards an old diesel bus and the handful of tourists and returning émigrés jostle for their luggage and queue patiently in front of the attendant who has one hand on the door and a forced smile on her hard face. She doesn't want to be here and is already counting the minutes until her outbound flight.

In this last whirlwind week or so, Roy has wondered several times about Lena's background and how it is, despite international politics, she appears so free and self-confident. At Passport Control, he gets his answer and it becomes clear just who is writing this part of the script. The officer spends a good two minutes studying his face and the passport, back and forth, eyes narrowing and lips tightening.

"What is purpose of you visit?"

"Tourist."

"You have no visa here."

When he hands over the document the man's face visibly pales. He passes it back as though his fingers are burning and waves Roy through without stamping the passport. Nothing to prove he's been here. A similar scene unfolds at Customs. Every personal item is removed from his suitcase and inspected carefully, eyes lighting up as they discover the new Kodak 110 Instamatic camera. It's about to find its way beneath the desk when Lena, with an amused smile, leans forward and whispers a few words. The man hurriedly stands alert and even repacks Roy's suitcase for him, to the blank astonishment of other tourists nearby who are struggling to find all their belongings strewn along the counter.

Notwithstanding documents and fathers, Roy is obliged to stay on his own at Intourist's Hotel Astoria on St Isaac's Square. This is not a great hardship, the place having welcomed the imperial family, the aristocracy and Lenin himself in the past, although these days it is less than welcoming to Westerners. Somehow Roy was not bothered at all by the sight of armed soldiers throughout the airport, turning to watch the pair as they wandered through hand in hand. All this seemed familiar and he felt safe with her. But the hotel staff emit a special kind of cold aura that suggests they are merely waiting for one wrong move.

Even the dull cream walls of his corridor feel as though they want to close in. The floor concierge is a middle-aged, shapeless woman with thin hair tied back tightly and a mask of total disinterest. She wears a large metal ring on her belt carrying twenty or so keys and she opens his door without a word. The room is functional with tired wallpaper and minimal furniture, a single central lightbulb and a cracked window streaked with dust that overlooks a small yard. Even Mrs Graidy cared for her rooms better than this.

He unpacks his clothes into the small wardrobe and chest of drawers and sits on the hard bed, all recent excited happiness draining away as he looks around. There must be hidden bugs. Should he check behind the pictures? Would he know what he was looking for? There's a low buzz coming from the telephone on the bedside table and he picks up the receiver to listen.

"Da?"

"Oh... um, could I have some coffee, please?"

"Restoran zakryt."

He is hungry and feels very alone and the pain has returned, but there's nothing for it but to write off the evening and look forward to tomorrow when Lena will come for him. He must put himself in her hands. After all, he doesn't seem to have made many decisions for himself in quite a while.

His sleep is fitful and disturbed in the early hours by another dark dream. This time he is within Neil's other painting approaching the oval-shaped mouth of a cave where a black wolf with pale golden eyes lies on guard, watching him intently. There are other shadowy figures nearby and one of them levels a small handgun at him as the wolf gets to its feet and begins to snarl, red saliva dripping from its long, bared teeth. He awakes with heart jumping, sure he can hear someone trying his door handle...

In the morning he pulls on the small backpack stuffed with jeans and, before leaving the room, takes a hair from his comb and sticks it with spittle across the lock of his suitcase like he once saw someone do in a film. It drops off in the draught as he goes out. He has to help himself to a cold breakfast of bread, cheese and pickle because they stopped serving five minutes ago, although with elaborate gestures he manages to get some coffee.

The August sunshine is flaring off the cathedral's golden dome as brightly as her smile when they meet in the square.

"I had some naïve idea," he says, stepping back from their embrace, "that tourists would be welcome. The hotel staff aren't at all friendly."

"You're welcome if you have dollars."

"Do you think my room's bugged?"

"Are you important?" she laughs.

"I suppose not. Look, are there any cafés?" he asks tentatively. "I need some more coffee to settle my... my stomach." She smiles and takes his hand, leading him to a kiosk at the shaded end of the square. It's ferociously strong and sweet but does its job, and after a second cup he's relaxed enough to realise what's been bothering him.

"There must be a couple of hundred people in the square, but it's so bloody quiet."

"It's normal these days," she shrugs, leaning back against a stone wall. Yet she also feels uncomfortable. The city she loves is seeping back into her blood but it can never be the same now that her home — and her heart — are in the gentle green fields, colourful shops and a bedroom in England. "Look around, Roy," she continues. "How many men can you see wearing light grey raincoats?" There's at least half a dozen, all standing still in pairs with bland faces.

"Good heavens, you're right. Do you think it's going to rai— Oh, I see what you mean."

She wants to show off her city so they begin with the extraordinarily beautiful cathedral. Although it's now a museum, its reverential peace, a world away from outside, calms his nerves and he stands for five minutes fascinated by the mathematics of Foucault's pendulum. When they leave, one pair of light grey raincoats detaches itself from a doorway and follows at a respectable distance.

"They're not very good at it," she laughs as Roy glances over his shoulder. "Come on, I'll show you." She takes his arm and quickens their pace, turning right then left three times and emerging onto Nevsky Prospekt just behind the two men. They're like a comedy double act, one tall with military bearing, the other short and dumpy. Lena whispers something to them as they pass and they both grin sheepishly, dropping back.

They cross the Moyka River and she introduces him to Dom Knigi, her favourite bookshop, where he dutifully buys State-published translations of Pushkin and Dostoevsky. With dollars. Lunch is frugal and similar to breakfast, vegetarianism not having reached these parts, and then it's back to the Palace Square, where other revolutions have started. The triumphal arch wants to draw Roy through and give himself up to this new life. But last night's dream, and the wolf at the entrance, holds him back.

Tired of walking now, they take the Metro from Dvortsovaya and head away from the city centre, Lena visibly excited to be on their way to see her grandmother. After an hour and two changes of line, they emerge in the cool of late afternoon and begin to thread their way through streets of identical grey, high-rise blocks. A brief memory of Birmingham flits through Roy's mind but in truth he has absolutely no idea where he is anymore.

Lena stops triumphantly at block number 108. The lift isn't working and Roy can barely stand by the time they reach the eighth floor.

It's a full minute before they hear the shuffle of feet, the sliding of bolts and the turn of the lock. Babushka is short and stocky with grey hair in a bun. She supports herself with a walking stick and wears a long black dress, a red cardigan, and a kind smile beneath sharp, twinkling eyes. As they follow her slowly back to the cramped sitting and dining room, Roy sees that there is just one small bedroom and even smaller kitchen and bathroom. The two women sit together whilst he is bidden to stand, shifting uneasily from foot to foot, and be inspected. Finally, in a weak, throaty voice, Babushka gives her verdict.

"She says you'll do," Lena translates, "but your hair is too long."

He smiles with relief and gladly accepts the glass of vodka offered. For the next hour he has that unsettling experience of listening to others' animated conversation although not understanding a word yet feeling sure that most of it is about him. From time to time the old lady smiles at him and bids Lena translate some embarrassing story or other about her childhood, which at least makes him feel welcome.

"It must be difficult for you, living here," he offers in return. "I mean, you can't get out easily."

"Oh, that's not a problem," Lena answers for her. "Babushka has a toyboy who does her shopping for her. Ivan Ilyich. He's seventy-two and lives on the floor below."

He can't imagine this proud lady's life, confined for decades in a tiny apartment with just her memories. And now he's taking away the last of her family. Yet she is unbowed and her mind is still sharp. And she is a very good cook. Refusing all attempts to help, she takes herself to the kitchen while Lena lays the solid oak table and returns with a huge pie full of cabbage, potato and boiled egg, topped with a thick, sweet and perfectly crisped pastry. It is perhaps the best meal Roy can ever remember having tasted. A bottle of Abrau-Durso champagne is also produced, as the vodka glasses are refilled.

"Well…," he murmurs, sitting back contentedly as Babushka serves him a second helping, "someone's going to have to carry me back to the hotel. And in the morning…"

"It's an old Russian custom," Lena laughs. "If you have champagne and vodka together — the good ones — there's no hangover."

This hospitality has not come cheap, though, and the answer comes with a quiet knock twice on the door half an hour later. Lena gets up immediately, taking the two backpacks with her.

"My friend, Kolya," she explains when she returns empty-handed. "He'll sell the jeans and I'll give the money to Babushka. He'll get about a hundred and fifty roubles."

"Gosh, that's a decent—"

"For each pair."

Over the next few days, Roy decides there's no point trying to understand how this economy works. The most basic essentials are ridiculously cheap, everything else is beyond the reach of the likes of Babushka. Whilst tourists eagerly throng the dollar shops on Nevsky Prospekt for souvenirs, there are long queues outside suburban groceries. Lena pauses outside one of them to translate the wry humour of a handwritten sign in the window.

"We have no butter today. But the five-year plan is working perfectly because we have no jam either."

On the other hand, high culture is freely available. They spend the best part of a day in the Hermitage. Lena knows it well and acts as guide, giving Roy an intense course in art history. As groups of American, Japanese and French tourists gather and move on, they are both drawn to the Madonna Litta and study it for several minutes, Roy absorbing the mathematical proportions typical of da Vinci while Lena seems withdrawn, discomfited, one hand to her own breast.

Next day, Kolya takes it upon himself to check whether Roy is worthy of his friend. The plan unfolds at a Finnish sauna where long periods of intense heat are interspersed by liberal vodkas, mutual beatings with birch sticks and laughing banter that Roy understands not a word of. He limps into Lena's arms afterwards, raw and aching yet having apparently passed the test.

One evening, she insists on taking him to the Kirov Ballet at the Mariinsky Theatre, although the beauty of the swans fails to inspire him.

"You were asleep!" she accuses as they sit around Babushka's table on their last evening. He is happy to find another cabbage pie there.

"Just resting my eyes," he protests. "Sorry, it's not really my thing. Although I did notice that half the audience were wearing jeans. Surely it's traditional to dress up for the ballet?"

"At our prices, they were dressed up," she shrugs.

Babushka is quieter than usual, her face drawn, eyes downcast. She must be sad that they're leaving tomorrow. But there's something else. When they've cleared the table and washed up, she beckons Lena to stand close to her then reaches out a frail, slightly trembling hand to touch her granddaughter's stomach. And when Lena then sits and reaches for the vodka, she speaks sharply to stop her.

"Nyet. Ty beremenna, moya devochka. Vosem' nedel'."

A deep silence fills the room.

Ф

When I woke up the cave was empty, just a few charred sticks remaining in the firepit with wisps of smoke rising up to the web of roots high above. The beings, the cooking pot, the torches had all gone although a faint glow of daylight now filtered through the entrance. I moaned as the last waves of pain drained away save for a persistent light throbbing in my head where someone was trying to get in to steal my story from me.

I lay unmoving for a while with my head on the rocky ground, one eye level with the surface watching a tiny movement a short distance away. It paused, scurried closer, waited with sharp eyes fixed on me and then came into focus, a small gecko with iridescent green scales and a red stripe along its back. It studied me closely then, satisfied, ran along my arm up to my face where its tongue touched my skin gently before it jumped down to bury itself in my jacket pocket.

Slowly pushing myself up to a sitting position, I found that I was not alone after all. The small, black-haired chamois with a white stripe lay nearby watching me calmly with kind eyes, waiting for my next move. Eventually I stood shakily and took a moment to inspect myself. Yes, it was me, pretty much in one piece. I knew there had been some kind of ceremony here but the memories would only come later; for now there were just lingering shadows lit up by flashes of emotion. Little by little they all settled back down and... I realised that I was feeling strong, refreshed. And light.

Whatever had confronted me, I had come through the other side.

Shammy — you know I'm not very imaginative in naming animals — trotted to the entrance of the cave and turned to look at me, inviting me to follow. I scrambled through on my knees and the sight that awaited me would have taken every breath away.

The first thing to notice was that this was not after all the same cave where I had drunk Rosa's foul brew, although it had the same kind of oval and rocky labial entrance. No forest or raging waves nearby. Rather, I was high up on a snowy mountainside reminding me of Sněžka on the Silesian Ridge, overlooking an apparently infinite vista of expansive interconnected islands that swirled and flowed and danced in the soft light. Those closer undulated with wooded hills and valleys in which a few small dwellings were scattered, reflecting a distant pale golden sun around which two white moons were suspended. Far away could be seen arched bridges linking one island to another, becoming ever lighter and lighter so that little detail could be made out.

Down below, not far from my mountain, there were small movements of people or animals near the rivers that fed into calm seas, fringed in azure and deepening to cobalt, surrounding the lands. And the centrepiece of it all, just before my eyes lost focus, was a huge city of white, oddly-shaped buildings with angles and domes and towers, spread out beside wide boulevards and green spaces and full of movement, presumably of people.

Yet everything was moving, like an Emily Carr painting with the ethereal strokes of William Blake. This was, indeed, another place. And what was to be my place in it?

In answer, Shammy nudged my leg and began to lead me along a steep and winding, narrow pathway of icy stones, past great black boulders streaked with silver seams, down and around until we emerged onto a wider track that circled the mountain. She stopped and looked back at me with a cute sort of smile, before turning a corner.

"Ahoj Evička, máš tady!"

The young man stood with arms outstretched and the widest smile. He had tousled blond hair, a short beard, and was wearing blue denim jeans and a red T-shirt with the image of a burnt-out Soviet T-55 tank on it. He looked somehow familiar, yet... then it suddenly came to me. I had seen his photograph. Everyone had seen his photograph. Tomáš Holub had been shot by a Russian soldier for handing out flyers protesting the invasion.

"Tomáš! How good to see you. Why are you... I mean, where are... what's happening...?"

He laughed and came forward to kiss my cheek, then inspected the side of my head.

"You look good, Eva, considering everything. All healed and ready to move on. Let's go." He took my hand and we set off down the track at pace and only now did I notice the beautiful white arctic fox trotting along by his feet, its thick fur tail brushing the ground as its plaintive face looked up at me curiously. "Ah, this is Marek. He's a fighter but a big softie, really."

"Oh, right. And this is, er, Shammy. Sorry, yes I know..."

"And I suppose the little one peeping out of your jacket pocket is Gecky?"

"No, of course not. That's Iggy."

The track spiralled all the way down the mountain, the snowmelt becoming crystal streams that raced on ahead, and we threaded our way through the tall grasses of a valley before climbing again. Tomáš didn't say much except that he was taking me to "our home" where I would meet "the others" and prepare "the plan". This raised various questions.

"We're not going to the city, then?"

"Heavens, no. Awful place, soulless. Well, that's not strictly true, of course, but it's just full of people accepting what they have and doing what they're told."

"And you're... we're not like that?"

"Never. We're what you might call the resistance."

"Outlaws?"

"I prefer outliers. We do things our own way. And, okay, we do things we're not supposed to." He grinned. "You know exactly what that's like, don't you?"

Rounding yet another promontory, I stopped in amazement at the sight of the house. It seemed to be made entirely of some kind of mirror glass so I couldn't see inside, and was dodecahedral, every wall a regular pentagon with seamless edges although, like everything else in this new world, there was slight movement throughout as though the very building was breathing. A vision of some kind of perfection. It stood on a broad ledge just out of sight of the city far below and was built into the mountain so that whilst the entrance was light and airy the back parts were shaded and cool.

Inside was much more spacious than I had imagined and was furnished with comfortable chairs, low tables and wide, pine-coloured desks. There were glass steps to an upper level with beds to the darker rear of the building. Near the entrance, a young man who looked somehow familiar sat on a sofa bent over an acoustic guitar, singing quietly.

"Yesterday is an eagle,
diving down, tearing at today.
Tomorrow is a ghost,
almost alive yet so far away.
Time is like my song,
it's here and then it's gone.
Then it's gone."

He put the guitar down beside him and looked up. I gasped. "Paul?"

"This is Pavel Dušek," said Tomáš, leading me over to introduce us. "You must remember him — he was on the Jilska bridge with you when the students were attacked."

"Oh, yes… of course. Sorry Pavel, you reminded me of…"

"In this place, there are always reminders," he observed softly.

Tomáš took my hand again and we turned towards the far end of the room, half in shadow.

"And this—"

Sitting at a large glass desk was the most beautiful young man I had ever seen. He was quite tall, extremely slim, hairless and with extraordinary, strange features that reminded me of that time by the lake when I had wished to be a different sort of human. Ears and nose were small and almost flat to the head, eyes were large, wide and gleaming lilac. He wore a long, pale green tunic.

"—is Maia. She's from… well, another place. She's our scientist."

"Hmm, not really," she smiled self-deprecatingly as she nodded a welcome to me. I think I managed to hide my embarrassment.

It was certainly no kind of science that I had ever seen before. She seemed to be studying a shifting pattern of coloured lights in mid-air above the desk and manipulating them with slight waves of her long, thin fingers. On the back of her chair sat a magnificent falcon, dark grey with white breast and leg feathers and a black beak splashed with yellow, absolutely still and impassive yet clearly also watching the images intently.

"So, welcome to our humble hideout," said Tomáš, "and to the Fearless Five."

"Thank you. Um, there's only four of us, though."

"Sara will be along. She's just busy... elsewhere... at the moment."

He suggested that I may like to rest, given the rather extreme recent events and surprises, and as I opened my mouth to protest the exhaustion overcame me. He led me upstairs where a soft, comfortable bed awaited me and I was asleep before my body touched the sheets. A deep and dreamless rest, for how long I have no idea.

When I awoke, someone had taken off my jacket and hung it over a chair on top of which Iggy sat watching me. Shammy lay beside the bed but got quickly to her feet as mine touched the floor. Maia and her falcon were still in exactly the same positions although the hovering images had enlarged to cover the whole desk. There was no sign of the others so I wandered outside to the ledge. It took a while to adjust my balance with the continuous slight movement — like finding one's sea legs — but my body soon synchronised and I felt lighter and at home. The atmosphere here was pleasantly warm and unchanging and nor had the distant sun or its moons moved from where I first saw them.

"Feeling better?" asked Tomáš, appearing from nowhere.

"Mmm, yes thanks. Refreshed. I was just wondering, Tomáš... I mean, everything is moving here and yet nothing moves." I pointed towards the sun. "So how do you keep track of time?"

"It's here and then it's gone," Pavel's voice sang from around the corner of the mountainside. We wandered round to sit with him, our legs overhanging the edge. He was looking through large, powerful binoculars towards the city in the distance. "It's like a collection of long elastic strings," he added, as if this made any sense. "All depends on where you are in your mind." I didn't comment, having nothing intelligent to say. "For example," he continued, handing the binoculars to me, "how long do you think has passed on Earth — I mean, our place — since...?"

"Surprisingly," I answered, "I have no idea. I suppose you're going to tell me that the Berlin Wall has come down and the Soviet Union has collapsed?"

"That's right. Although the Russians are up to their old tricks again."

I couldn't tell whether or not he was joking so I put the binoculars to my eyes and studied the city. It was a Cubist glazier's paradise with street upon street of neat houses, all with their own neat, green gardens, spread out in arcs around a centre of grander buildings. Some of these were shaped like our house whilst others were multi-sided with icosahedral or hemispherical domes, all silvery as they reflected the sunlight. Further away on the outskirts of the city were several pyramids, some triangular and a few like in the pictures I had seen of Giza in Egypt with their golden caps. And everywhere there were people going busily this way and that along the streets and in and out of buildings.

"There's libraries and theatres and art galleries and colleges and all sorts," Pavel waved a hand at them dismissively. "And everyone sees what they expect to see. Do you want to visit, Eva? We'll take you if you like."

I shook my head. It was not for me. But my mind was still troubled by what he'd said earlier.

"So... does Roy know about the Wall and all that? What's his, er, time?"

"Well, that's rather the whole point of why you're here, Evička," said Tomáš, "of why we're here. No, he's in his own personal place, kind of moving from one scene to another like an actor, although he doesn't realise it. And like a play, or a novel, where one thing doesn't have to follow logically from another, time stretches and squeezes around him but it all seems perfectly natural."

"How do you know so much about him... I mean, where he is?"

"Well, Jamie has told us everything we need—"

"What? Jamie's been here too?"

"Of course. He pops in regularly to update us. Nice chap. Though it takes ages to clear the cigarette smoke."

"And you can actually see what Roy's doing?"

"That's Maia's job. With the lights, you know? It's a sort of..."

"Interface," suggested Pavel, shrugging. "Think of binoculars that let you see whatever you want to see. Maia's much better at that sort of thing than us. But she'll train you so you know what you're doing when..." His voice trailed off as though he'd said too much.

"When what, Pavel?"

"We know about your plan, Evička," Tomáš took over.

"I'm not sure I do," I muttered.

"It's there in your heart. And that's why Jamie has got us together, to make it happen. You do want to help Roy, don't you? Put things right?"

He took my hand again to reassure me — it only helped a little — and promised that Maia was kind and patient and a good teacher.

My lessons began almost immediately and I soon came to doubt the second of those qualities. Certainly, Maia genuinely cared for me and knew what she was talking about, but her high, sing-song voice could become pretty strident when she thought I wasn't working hard enough. It was fair enough. This was the greatest struggle I had ever faced, no longer against soldiers carrying Kalashnikovs but against my own ego.

First she took me to her glass desk and asked me what I could see in the hovering images. There were just thousands upon thousands of tiny, flashing coloured dots without any pattern or meaning.

"We shall use this to measure your progress," she began. "Now, you must let go of everything you have experienced in the past. I don't mean forget things — you couldn't do that and in any case they have made you who you are. I mean you must break all attachments to them — rational, emotional, psychic — to make you clean and new."

This involved a strict regime of exercises and periods of enforced rest, when she would sit beside my bed and encourage me to recall the seminal experiences, especially those flooding my mind during the cave ceremony. Then she would gently touch my brow and I would fall instantly into a deep sleep where I relived the visions and felt them healed, restoring harmony.

No sooner did I awake than she was beside me again, leading me down to a quiet area beneath the rock at the back of the house where she taught me the breathing technique.

"Breathing is not the same as it used to be, of course," she said, "yet you do have an etheric body with energy centres. A different sort of energy. And the proportions of this building enhance your awareness of them." I had to visualise a pure white light above my head and slowly draw it down inside, past the base to the back of my knees and the soles of my feet, to a count of nine, and then reverse the process by, as it were, breathing out.

"This is called the Longest Breath," she went on. "It's basically what the Buddha taught his followers."

"Buddha? But surely he was...?"

"The great teachers are everywhere," she shrugged.

I had to do this twelve times, then repeat the cycle for shorter breaths of six, three and one, before reversing the whole set and ending with twelve slow, deep breaths. The numbers were important, apparently. Over and over again she made me practise, stifling all protest with a flash of those lilac eyes, and very, very gradually I discovered that she was right — as mischievous thoughts flitted through my mind I became able to let them pass and disappear on their way. I became quieter and could feel the spin and flow of energy within.

"You're coming along," she admitted, almost grudgingly, after a while. "Now there are three more stages to the exercise."

"Aaaargh!"

Mind you, even I could see that I was coming along. The points of light above Maia's desk were not quite as random as before and I was beginning to pick out vague shapes with flashes connecting them. They were still unrecognisable but I felt encouraged, even more so when Sara arrived. She was a young, dark-skinned girl with her long, black hair in… yes, I recognised her immediately.

"Hello, Miss, you found your way, then," she said. "Said you would." I smiled in delight and went to hug her but she pulled away. "Nah, I's not ready yet, have to settle in."

"Oh, sorry."

"'S not your fault. An' Maia's doin' a good job on you. You'se changed."

"She's right," agreed Tomáš, coming in behind her. "Your body is lighter, more fluid. You're on the way."

To where? I still wasn't aware of the whole plan and Tomáš just repeated that it was need-to-know and I had to heal first.

I wanted to chat with Sara and ask how she kept turning up in different places and what her part was in all this but she went straight to the stairs, saying that she needed to rest and "come back up". Tomáš answered my question instead.

"Sara's special," he said with unmistakable awe. "She comes and goes, this place and that, wherever she's needed."

"So what did she mean by coming back up?"

"Ah, that's my cue," interjected Maia, getting up from her desk and leading me outside to a shaded area of the ledge where we sat with our backs to the rock. I hadn't been out for a while and everything looked and felt rather different. For one thing, as I leaned back my body melted slightly into the surface as though the mountain was embracing me. The landscape, too, was flowing even more so that the outlines of trees and dwellings and figures below were less defined and more at one. There was an ineffable sense of peace.

"How much Maths do you know?" Maia surprised me. Seeing my expression, she went on, "Look, I'll keep it easy."

"Yes, please."

"Every world, every state of consciousness, if you like, has its own fundamental energy vibration. Let's call it a power. Suppose yours is two times ten to the power four and Jamie's at two point five times ten to the power eight. Obviously, this is a huge simplification—"

"Obviously."

"—so if Jamie wants to contact you he has to bring down his power and hope that you can bring yours up a bit, so you meet somewhere in the middle."

"Okay. I think."

"That's what Sara does and she's very good at it. Maybe a child has less inhibitions about what's possible. But she can pretty much go wherever she wants and that's good for you."

"Um, why?"

"Well, obviously," the voice became strident as she began to lose patience with this dull pupil, "she's been keeping an eye on you, hasn't she? And she's been keeping an eye on Roy."

"Aah. Wow. That's clever."

"So now you have to learn to do the same."

"Oh. Why?"

There was a long, exasperated silence.

"Because you're going over to his world."

I gulped. So this was my plan, was it? Yes, I'd sort-of had the idea that I would somehow get through to him and make him know... how I felt... how sorry I was... But I hadn't articulated it fully and now saw that this wouldn't be enough: the endgame of my own logic was to put myself right there.

Saying "sorry" isn't enough.

We have to do it.

The exercise, out there on the ledge, was actually simple enough in principle. I just had to train my mind to understand powers and how to change them so that when it came to doing it for real — no one would tell me what that meant — I would accept the idea as natural.

Along with my breathing, I had to visualise a number that Maia gave me — a decimal point followed by lots of noughts then one, six, one, eight, nought, three. With each breath cycle I had to move the decimal point one place right to make the number bigger. It's harder than it sounds and I kept losing track and having to start over. Then the process was reversed. And just when I thought I'd mastered it, with many efforts, Maia would turn up and add a lot more noughts in.

There were, of course, moments when the ego, floundering weakly yet refusing to give in, piped up in a thin voice to object. Why was I doing this? Why put myself through this struggle, being bullied by this strange woman? I never asked for this, did I? Life could be so much easier, more comfortable. Here I was in a nice world, much better than the island, and there was a nice city down there with nice buildings and probably nice people with nice things to do...

At these moments, Maia proved what a great teacher she really was. She'd know what I was feeling, take my hand, help me up and lead me to her desk where I'd sit beside her with the falcon gripping my shoulder gently as she almost imperceptibly waved her hands within the images as though to switch something on.

And I'd see Roy, vaguely at first and then ever more clearly each time. He's parking his car outside an ugly, concrete block of flats as a young girl approaches on the pavement with a shopping bag in each hand and a satchel on her back. She's of mixed race with... it's Sara! With wide eyes I look at the falcon.

The falcon looks at me. When I turn back, he's... what's this? He's on a building site in muddy shorts with a spade in his hand, watching a short, tubby man with silvering hair, wearing a light grey French linen suit, marching across a carpark towards... I recognise him, too. It's the university professor I met a couple of times. Meeks, was it?

"Very good," Maia smiled widely and I felt like a little girl being given a gold star. "Not long to go now."

As reward for my progress, I was allowed 'time off' from exercises and Tomáš took me exploring the surrounding countryside, accompanied by Shammy and Marek who were becoming close friends. Whilst there wasn't much point in getting to know this new island, since I wasn't going to stay, it would still be good to know what was, as it were, available. We crossed to the other side of our mountain, keeping well away from the city and its satellite villages and climbed a higher peak where hundreds of birds nested and overlooked an extraordinarily beautiful landscape of flowing forests and calm valley fields grazed by every animal I could think of. In the distance, a silvery shoreline was lapped by cyan waters between us and the next landmass, connected by a narrow, incredibly long white bridge with no visible means of support.

"There," he said as we sat on a ridge to take it all in, "is that how you expected paradise to look?" This was a trap, of course, and I considered it carefully.

"I guess it's what most people expect," I tried.

"Right. And that's why the city is there too. But this is nothing." I followed his gaze as he lifted his head to the far distant, almost invisible islands of light. "I come here while you're working," he went on, "to remind myself what's possible."

"So why are you here, Tomáš? Why do you stay?"

He turned to me with a deeply penetrating look into my soul.

"For you, Evička. We've been brought together by... others... to make this thing happen. We know you, we're part of your story. We're your tribe. Everybody needs their personal tribe, however small. We're holding the space for you, keeping you safe. Pavel plays his music to cleanse the energy in our home. Marek and I stand guard and keep others away while—"

"Others?"

"There will always be those who want to interfere, to invade, to steal others' minds. Even here."

Despite all reason, I felt tears running down my cheeks as I realised, with a surge of gratitude that made my whole being throb, the enormity of the sacrifice that so many others had been making for me. He put an arm round me and let me cry for a while.

"You're doing the same, Evička. For him. We do it because we know what love is. At least, we have a small idea. Now, sit very still for a moment, close your eyes and just listen."

"To what?"

"Listen."

I did as I was told and now instinctively began the breathing. I heard the light breeze around us and the buzz of insects, then the murmuring of trees and running waters and the quiet cries of animals below... until they all passed by and faded away to absolute silence... except for a soft, gentle rhythmic pulse. The heartbeat of soul. It was calling me away but I wasn't ready yet, so I opened my eyes and looked dumbly at Tomáš.

"As long as you can hear that," he said, "you'll be safe."

We made our way back slowly and left the animals to play in the snow while I went up to rest and Tomáš resumed his patrol.

Maia had more exercises for me and I soon realised Tomáš' ulterior motive for our exploration because the most difficult challenge yet was to be utterly still within that silence he had shown me, at any moment and in any circumstance. As I practised, moulded into the rock, one or other of them would appear trying to interrupt and distract me. Pavel wanted to know what I thought of his latest song. Tomáš told me about some hiking city dweller who had strayed too close. Even Shammy got in on the act to nuzzle my face.

Yet all that I had learned so far had changed me. I was in the moment, at a different level. Even my body was becoming translucent. So there came a point when Maia called me in again to watch the lights.

"Your turn now." She sat back in her chair and nodded towards her desk so I reached forward tentatively with one hand and copied what I'd seen her do. To my surprise, the images clarified instantly in sharp colour. "Good," she said, "you're almost like one of our kind now." I think that was meant as a compliment.

Roy is sitting on the grass with beer in hand, surrounded by several other people, and a glum-faced young man is fixed into some old-fashioned stocks. I can't hear their voices yet but there's clearly an animated discussion going on. An attractive blonde woman says something to Roy and I see — and feel — a flash of energy pass between them.

"By the way," I sat back and turned to Maia, "how is Roy going to, well, raise his power towards mine?"

"Why do you assume he's the one who has to raise their power?" she grinned. I felt suitably chastised. "But yes, you're right. It's simple really. Love."

She nodded towards the images again and I felt, as it were, a lump in my throat. He is with the blonde woman again, this time in a dark swimming pool with moonlight dancing on the surface, their bodies clinging together, indivisible.

"Oh."

And now they stand together naked in a changing room and her arms are outstretched as she calmly allows him to dry every part of her body gently with his towel.

"Oh."

"It's all right, Eva," Maia said quietly, taking my hand to reassure me. "This is just earthly love. Temporary."

"I see." I didn't really but I was trying to. "Who is she?"

"Her name's Lena Volkova."

"Oh." There was another very long pause while I tried to process all this, unable to drag my eyes from the scene. "And... where exactly do I fit in?"

Maia leaned forward and with a wave of her hand zoomed in on the picture so all we could see was Lena's bare abdomen, taut and muscled and moist.

"In there. You're going to be born again."

Some forgotten feeling, thought long-abandoned, slowly emerged from its shadowy hiding place and began to creep menacingly throughout my whole being. It wasn't fear. Oddly, the idea of a new incarnation didn't trouble me at all, having recently had two of them already. No, it was much stronger than fear and it invaded every part of me and claimed me for itself.

"A fucking Russian? I mean... a fucking Russian? You have to be joking. No! No!"

And that outburst set back my training almost to the beginning.

The tribe united. They understood, and with amazing patience put me back together. The plan was now clear and I had my own tweak that they might or might not have known about. Either way, they were there for me.

So it was that we all quietly made our way back along the track and up the mountain to the cave.

Ф

Cody was waiting for us at the entrance and when he saw me he came forward to lie at my feet for a moment before padding back to resume guard. Pavel and Tomáš took up positions either side of him, the one with his guitar and the other holding what looked uncommonly like a small Beretta pistol. Jamie was pacing up and down outside with a cigarette and was clearly very relieved to see us.

"Ah, at last. Good. I just wondered if you were going to, eh, change your mind."

"Of course not, Jamie. It will always be unbroken. Is Brother John here too?"

"Nay, lassie. He's in... the other place."

Shammy and Marek wandered off to patrol the area with Maia's falcon hovering overhead. I again felt humble that so many souls were united in protecting me.

Sara went in first. I'd been told that she was coming with me and would be nearby, although of course I wouldn't see her. I hesitated — there would be no going back and I would be leaving behind everything and everyone I had found — but Maia put an arm around me and smiled, leading me through. We were met with the most welcoming sight.

"Olá, meus amigos!" said José with a broad, toothy smile. He wore the same bright clothes, feathers and shells as before, and Rosa was by his side. I was glad to see there was no fire or cooking pot. The cave was indeed bare save for several candles whose light danced around the web of white filaments linking the gnarled roots above. As I looked up, the whole place seemed alive and shifting and breathing. On cue, Ashly floated out of the shadows to hover nearby.

"Hello, Evička. I told you we fuckin' everywhere are."

We sat with reverent heads bowed in a wide circle on the ground and I began to let go of all that I'd learned and become. Soon we heard the soft tones of Pavel's song outside.

"When I was a river
the mountains couldn't hold me.
I ran through rocks and valleys,
escaping to the open seas.

And every undercurrent
sounded just the same
and every tributary
was singing with your name..."

The others quietly took up the song, each in their own words indecipherable to me yet somehow all blending into one, Jamie's ecclesiastical bass counterbalanced by Maia's strange staccato alto rhythms, with José and Rosa echoing one another's primaeval sounds in the middle of it all. Binding everything together was Ashly's deep hum.

I felt wholly at peace. This wasn't going to be easy but I was ready and, yes, it was all I wanted to do. To put things right. To be at one. To take up the song again where it had been so foolishly interrupted. At length, the music faded away to linger around the rocky walls and I felt again that gentle pulse of the soul's heartbeat in the silence.

"You've done well, Evička," murmured Jamie. "Very well. I'm sure everything will be... eh, just fine." I noticed a slight frown crease his brow.

"You don't sound very sure," I smiled.

"No, no, it's... fine. It's just that we, eh, haven't actually..."

"You're saying that you haven't done this before?"

"Not... as such. It's a big thing, this, you know."

"And you thought this was a good moment to tell me, did you?"

"He mean anything doesn't by it," breathed Ashly, slipping into his old scansion and glaring at Jamie, insofar as a wisp can glare. "Men of the cloth always worrying are."

Beside me, Maia reached out her hand to mine and smiled the sweet smile of teacher to favourite pupil.

"We's okay, Miss," piped up Sara. "'S easy once we gets going."

Once all was calm again, we got going.

Maia had gone through every detail with me several times. It was clearly something she was as familiar with as Sara, this world-hopping. I took off my clothes and laid them neatly on the ground — sorry Králi, you can't come this time — with Iggy looking somewhat forlornly at me from the top of the pile, then laid myself down in the centre of the circle in the position I'd been taught. Rosa covered me with a thin, soft white shawl.

I began the breathing as Pavel took up the song again, softly, distantly.

"When I was the wind
I thought I was so free,
I ran through every country
and nothing could ever stop me.
Then, when the storms were over
and the sky returned to blue,
I listened to my breathing
and every breath was you..."

My friends again joined in the music, more quietly yet somehow more intensely, inviting new sounds to enter the space — from where? — that almost overwhelmed me, the deep, guttural voices of Gregorian chant overlaid with ... what's that? Tchaikovsky's *First Piano Concerto*? This should be chaotic yet somehow it all melded into a beautiful tsunami that flooded through me and washed me as, through half-open eyes, I saw the atmosphere crack and splinter like a broken window into tiny fragments reflecting a blinding light in which my body was dissolving.

And just when I couldn't bear it anymore, everything gradually calmed down leaving me not knowing who I was becoming and the last things I saw were my friends' faces alive with love before they faded away as the very cave began to move and breathe to a different, slower rhythm.

161.803

16.1803

1.61803

Becoming smaller.

But it was not me becoming smaller, it was my world. The rocky walls crept closer and white strands of the web above reached lazily down, carefully taking hold of my limbs as the roots released a warm moisture to enfold me.

Silence.

Greater silence.

Then it began. I could feel him nearby. I could feel him and almost reach out to him.

The gentle pulse of the soul slowed down to a different, regular beat.

The heartbeat of my mother.

Φ

He watches the wing rivets rattle as the plane heaves itself into the bright morning sky and turns west. With a tremor at his temple, he reaches for her hand but she pulls away. At the height of summer, the world has suddenly become very cold.

Leaving his hotel room this morning, the concierge has roughly pushed him back inside and, with a ferocious glare, made him wait while she checks the wardrobe, drawers, bathroom and even under the bed. Satisfied, she then holds out a hand for his tip. Feeling alone and fearful again, he gives her five dollars, is rewarded with a thin, toothless grimace, and gets out as fast as he can. But Lena is still not speaking.

They're well across the Baltic before she relents.

"She said I'm pregnant."

"What? Oh... that's a surprise. Still, it's wonder—"

"Eight weeks."

"No... that's not possible. Is it?"

"No, Roy, it isn't," she replies sharply, glaring at him. Seeing his crestfallen face, she softens and takes his hand. "But she's never wrong. She has these... special gifts. Everyone goes to her."

"She must be wrong this time." He is trying to be reassuring, but dark clouds are gathering and the barometer is falling fast. Everything is changing again, almost before peace has had a chance to set in. "She does seem to be a remarkable woman, though."

"She is. She's lived through so much hardship. Suffering. Lost so many. Yet she was always kind and patient with me — I wasn't an easy child... upryamyy... what's the word? Yes, headstrong."

"I can imagine." He grins and squeezes her hand.

"And she's always calm. She accepts whatever comes — calls it 'the art of living'."

"Last evening..." He pauses because this could open up a wound. Before they left, the two women had cried and held one another for several minutes. "She talked to you for quite a while... and she kept looking at me... but you didn't translate."

The flight attendant stoops beside them, trying to smile through a face thickly made up, and offers coffee and pryaniki spiced biscuits which Roy gladly accepts. Lena asks for water, met with raised eyebrows. They're over Denmark before she feels able to continue.

"She said we have to remember that we're not separate beings. We think we're two individuals—" she touches her stomach, "—or maybe three, but that's an illusion. We share our lives with everything that exists. We are part of others' lives and they are part of ours. And the ones we have lost live on in us."

She can't help a tear escaping and somehow Roy feels it on his own cheek too. There's a long pause as Lena tries to find the right words, fighting off the clear and vivid recent memories of a swimming pool changing room and her lover's bed, where they had each been in awe of the other's beauty and lost in the brief eternity of orgasm.

"She says we are not these bodies. We are... waves on the surface of an ocean. And how long we live is not important..." The tears are flowing now. "All that matters is how we live. Not tied down by thoughts of the future. Enjoy the life we have every day for as long—" That's enough, and she buries her head on his shoulder, sobbing. The attendant pauses nearby, then goes on her way.

This trip was meant to be joyful, an opportunity for Roy to know her, but already they both know more than perhaps they wished for.

She busies herself with moving her life into the Clandon Road flat, which is an improvement to its warmth and comfort, while he studies textbooks, writes lesson plans for the autumn and visits second-hand car dealers only to worry even more about money. The old Ford is on its last legs but he cannot ask for Lena's help.

She makes him an appointment for a scan at a private hospital in north London and visits a GP in Guildford — not wanting her father to know anything yet — for a scan of her own. Eleven weeks, perhaps. It's not possible.

Despite his rediscovered resilience of the last couple of years, Roy now begins to flounder. Whatever little control of life he's had is a thing of the past, with any decision out of his hands. Tall waves are approaching, he's lost the oars and there's no life jacket. And it's not as if he has a model loving family behind him to fall back on, one that teaches how to swim under water.

He's doing his best to stay calm, to be supportive, but with every passing day he knows less what to say or do for the best. Lena has changed, her vibrant personality submerged, withdrawn into shadows so that he cannot even tell what worries her. She is certainly not excited about the baby within.

He senses that she is somehow afraid. And she is no longer interested in sex.

Little more than a month ago they had been locked in one another's arms, their minds equally overflowing with hopes and desires for the future. But Babushka has said they must let go of such thoughts, enjoy the life they have for as long… Lena is not enjoying her life. She has been brought up with her grandmother's love and the security of her father's status in a regime where life is planned in detail. A child is not part of the plan.

As the holidays draw to a close, Roy tries again. He prepares a picnic, ignores her protests, and drives them out to Frensham Little Pond in the Surrey hills. There are linnets hopping between the trees and grebes at home among the tall reeds. As they set out the blanket, there's the orange flash of a grayling gliding down in a long loop to land on nearby purple heather, disappearing from view as it folds its wings, as disguised as human fears.

Yet the beauty of nature, and the carefully chosen favourite cream cake, begin to warm Lena's heart a little.

"I'm sorry," she says quietly, allowing him to take her hand, "I know I'm being… difficult. I just can't get Babushka's words out of my mind." He waits. "She said how long we live is not important. It makes me wonder whether…"

He tries to tell her that she will be well cared for. But when a tiny brown studded lizard with a black stripe along its back takes an interest in their sandwiches, she recoils in horror and the mood is lost. They head back to the car and don't even notice the early evening nightjar's churring song.

There's nothing he can do about this threat she feels and he becomes consumed by the thought that she will leave, return to where she once felt safe.

It's something of a relief when the new term begins and there are other things to focus on. Roy looks forward to his first lesson back with Xiao Li's class, quietly pleased that he's solved her numbers challenge although still mystified by her purpose. What will the children have made of the task he set them? Disappointingly, if not really surprisingly, half of them have forgotten all about it whilst others have simply drawn pictures of yachts with triangular hulls and sails. One lad has at least added in a right-angled shark's fin. Finally, all eyes turn towards Xiao Li, knowing with resignation that she will have outdone them all again.

From a large box beneath her desk she carefully produces two square-based pyramids made out of thick white card, each with one face missing.

"What's that got to do with Pythugus?" scoffs shark-boy.

In response, the girl then takes two triangular cards from the box and shows that they fit exactly inside the pyramids. Roy realises that the dimensions must be significant and urges her to explain while he draws the images on the chalk board. In a quiet, shy voice she tells them that one model is a scale copy of the Great Pyramid at Giza whilst the other has different proportions but the same volume.

"But why have you made two, Li?"

From the box she retrieves two small pots full of earth and two dried broad beans. The class watch open-mouthed, not sure whether to laugh, as she plants the seeds, waters them equally with a syringe, and places the pots inside the pyramids.

"Put them somewhere safe, please, sir," she whispers, "where no one can touch them. I'll water them every lesson and we'll see what happens." As Roy stands on a chair and carefully puts the models on top of a cupboard near the window, a loud chattering breaks out as the other children confirm their opinion that Xiao Li is very weird and probably not human. Roy smiles reassuringly to her, knowing that she is teaching them all something. He vaguely remembers reading about a Czech scientist, Karel Drbal, who claimed that pyramids had some sort of special properties. Well, this young girl is at least distracting his mind.

"Ah dinnae ken much about mathematics," observes Ian, appearing from nowhere at Roy's side as he watches Lena with the older girls on the outdoor netball court, "but yon lassie's, eh, well into her second trimester. You's a sly dog, then."

"It doesn't make sense, mate."

"Irrational, ye could say?"

"Indeed. But the most important numbers are."

"Still, good arse." Then, as he moves away, "Sangster's not happy, laddie."

Indeed he isn't and he calls Roy in to point out that when he said teachers have to set an example to the pupils he didn't mean... Fortunately, his own grasp of arithmetic isn't as good as Ian's. But Lena is showing now and the rest of the staff are gossiping, which is not good for a headmaster. Added to this are the rumours of some kind of witchcraft going on in the young man's classroom...

At each lesson, Roy carefully takes down the models so that Xiao Li can water the pots, always the same amount each, and after two weeks a small cheer goes up as the bean plants also begin to show. In another fortnight it's evident that the one in the Giza pyramid is taller and stronger than the other one, and it's soon outgrowing its home to the genuine astonishment of the class. With a kind voice, Roy persuades Li to come out to the front and tell them what's going on. Instead, she simply takes the chalk from his hand and writes on the board.

$$[2(14/22)]^2 = \Phi$$

Roy draws the pyramid again, showing that its height is 14 cm and length 22 cm and explaining that Φ is a mysterious number with no fixed value.

"That's daft, sir. How can a number have no value?" says shark-boy.

"It's called irrational."

"And how does it make beans grow?"

So that's the next couple of weeks' lessons planned. It's about time the children learned what Roy himself has had painfully to recognise.

Many of life's big questions have no answer.

As the children leave the room later, muttering new kinds of questions about Xiao Li, she hangs back and approaches him again, taking the chalk.

"But if we use the ratio 34:21," she writes it up, "the error is only 0.06 per cent."

He is faced with yet another mystery when his scan results come back.

"Is your father sure he's a good doctor?" he asks Lena over an Indian takeaway as he rereads the report.

"The best in London."

"Well, it says here that all my symptoms suggest a brain tumour—"

"What?" She puts her fork down as fear again brings tears to her eyes.

"—but they can't find any trace of it."

"Oh. Then we'll just have to get a second opin— aaaah, baby's just kicked me so hard."

She needs to know that I can't stand spicy food.

Φ

Vladimir Davidovich tells his driver to pull up behind the black saloon just so Jones knows that he knows, and strides purposefully up the stairs to the first floor. He's a self-possessed man who rarely betrays emotion yet even he is taken aback to see his daughter dishevelled, unkempt and very pregnant. They talk quietly and urgently for half an hour while Roy makes tea and then hovers in the hallway, listening for anger. Luckily, Vladimir Davidovich can do arithmetic and, though Lena can't explain herself, agrees not to have Roy killed.

As he walks back down the driveway, he is watched carefully by a quite handsome fox with a white tip on its tail.

Roy creeps back in, sitting beside Lena to comfort her. I hadn't understood what the other man said but I sensed that the mood was dark, the words aggressive. Now, however, I can feel Roy very close and his words are soft and caring. My heart leaps and I can't help myself kicking the sac. He puts his hand to her abdomen and his touch only makes me happier.

"He's angry," she says, "but whatever people think of him he's a caring man. Well, he cares about me. He says that when the baby's born we have to go back to Moscow."

"What? He can't do—"

"You don't understand, Roy. My father can pretty much do whatever he wants."

There are many things he doesn't understand. Things that are happening too fast. Things that are irrational. It's true that in this last year or two he has learned to be untroubled by aberrance, but the present is on a different scale. He's doing his best to support and reassure Lena while trying to hold down his job — she's left the school so he has to provide for them both. The atmosphere at school, the gossip and innuendo, are getting oppressive. He's getting exhausted.

And it's not as though he can rest at home, with Lena withdrawn and the looming threat of losing her and the child hanging over him. Moreover, there's definitely a presence in the flat now — no, presences. In every room, from waking to sleep, what little he has, he is watched. No, it's not a ghost. It's not Neil. In fact it feels... gentle, friendly, more than that as though some... beings... are looking out for them.

But it's no less unnerving for that.

I so wish I could do more to let him know that everything will be fine, that it's all part of the plan, but I'm just a little half-formed thing inside another woman. Still, I remember what it's like for people to struggle, caught up in all the everyday worries and unable to see the bigger picture, to see that there's a purpose to it all. All I can do for now is practise moving my limbs around and respond to their voices and the music she plays — why is it always Rachmaninov? — to let them know I'm fine. My eyes should be opening soon, too, so then I'll be more in control.

"I'd like to call her Anastasia," says Lena one evening.

"Oh... yes, that's a nice name. Are you sure it's a girl?"

"Yes, she's a girl, Roy. Babushka said."

I quite like my name, even though nobody's ever going to use it.

On the last day before half-term, the car engine splutters and merely produces black smoke from the exhaust. Vladimir Davidovich has made it clear he's not going to help them financially. It's a matter of personal responsibility: in other words, when you're in a mess you have to get yourself out of it. Are all fathers the same?

Roy runs for the bus but is still late, the excuse Steven Wellesley needs to call him in for a dressing down. He enjoys this part of the job, reminding him that he has some power over others, although words tend to lose their force when they slip out of the side of the mouth beneath closed eyes. He sits at his office desk, the white linen suit still waiting to be cleaned, and makes Roy stand on the other side.

"I stuck my neck out for you, son," he begins, incomprehensibly since he had no part at all in Roy's appointment. "Told Sangster you knew what you were doing. But you're distracted, half asleep and—" as Roy opens his mouth to protest he holds up a hand to stop him, having no interest in relationships with women,

"—and this phi stuff you're teaching isn't even in the syllabus. I mean, growing beans in your classroom. The department's a laughing stock."

"Have you seen what happened, Steven? The plant in the Giza pyramid was five times—"

"It's impossible. So it didn't happen. In any case, it's got nothing to do with Maths."

"Well, actually..."

The blood is rising, more in defence of Xiao Li than of himself, and Roy sits uninvited opposite Wellesley and fixes him with a cool, angry stare. He then goes on to point out that the experiment caught his classes' imagination so that he was able to introduce trigonometry, followed by triangular numbers and other sequences, followed by quadratic equations (since there's one that defines phi), followed by irrational numbers — all aided by the new HP-35 pocket calculators that Xiao Li's father has supplied to the school. Moreover, most of these previously failing pupils are now ahead of the syllabus and have scored good grades in the recent test.

"All the same," Wellesley drawls, waving a hand to dismiss him, "don't be late again."

Still seething, Roy wanders out into the grounds and heads for the wooden bench on the far side of the lake. Staring into the unmoving water, he slowly calms down as he feels it drawing him in as though he were a drop of water in the unknowable.

There is silence.

More silence.

The day seems to be standing still, the air full of expectancy, as a distant memory of a beach and a girl edges apologetically into his mind and asks to be reinstated. She is doing gymnastics, oblivious to the effect she has on him. She is lovely. Why is Eva returning now, of all times? He is drawn inexorably towards her, approaching nervously, asking whether she has a spare cigarette... oh, how stupid is that?

"Will ye have a cigarette, then, laddie?" Ian has quietly appeared from nowhere to sit beside him, offering an open packet.

"Oh... hello, Ian," Roy starts back to the present. "I didn't know you smoked."

"Nay, I dinna. Call it a social service."

"I was trying to give up," Roy grins, lighting up.

"Nay, laddie. You'll never give up." Ian always seems to mean more than he actually says.

The simple friendship, along with the queue of returning happy memories, helps to get him through the day. The uplifted feelings dissipate, though, as he waits at the bus stop in the evening and a black saloon car without number plates draws up beside him.

"Can we give you a lift home, Roy?" says Jones, opening the rear door and flashing an ID card. It's not an invitation. "We need to have a talk anyway."

He'd thought this was a thing of the past, at the height of the Soviet invasion when Eva was given such a hard time, interrogated about her contacts. Now it was his turn. Good grief, why can't they just be left alone?

"You seem to have a, shall we say, special relationship with the other side of the Curtain," Jones begins. He sits beside Roy in the back of the car as it meanders the long way round through the leafy lanes of Surrey. Roy settles himself into the padded leather, realising that Eva herself must have sat in this very place. Everything about their past is flooding back into his mind now, just as a new life is supposed to be beginning. He watches the hedgerows pass by, turned grey by the shaded windows, and feels the morning's anger begin to rise again. Why is the world so full of stupid people with their own agendas who know nothing about what's really going on in others' lives?

Heaven save us from people who know the truth.

"Yes, I have had two special relationships," he mutters, "and you seem intent on ruining them both." In the rear-view mirror he sees the gorilla grinning through yellowing teeth. The man is indeed very large, with a neck twice as thick as his, so it's probably best not to annoy him or his master. "Look, Mr Jones—"

"Inspector, if you don't mind."

"Whoever. I'm just an ordinary chap whose life got messed up by..." he wants to say 'people like you', "...politicians and their armies. They cause nothing but pain. I know nothing about politics — I'm just trying to put my life back together again."

"You really don't know what's going on, do you?" Jones looks at him with narrowed eyes.

"Frankly, no."

"Have you never realised that you're not in control of any of this? That other people are pulling your strings?"

"Well, it does feel like that sometimes, I guess. But I'm still making my own decisions."

"Hmm, is that so? Tell me, if you don't mind, how did you and Miss Volkova... um, get together? Was that your decision?"

Roy is momentarily stunned. This is a good question. When two people discover love, decision-making is rather off the menu. But perhaps this isn't what Jones meant as he doesn't appear to be the sort who engages in the numinous or metaphysical.

"And whose decision was it to go to Leningrad, on the other side? First the Czechs, now the Russians. You surely see that this is... of interest."

"I... um, I was a tourist."

"That's what George Blake said. And Kim Philby. And—"

"Look, this is silly. I'm nobody. Could you just take me home now, please? My girlfriend is pregnant and I need—"

"And do you know how difficult it is to get a visa these days? Yet you managed it in less than a week." He sits forward, thrusting his chin towards Roy in direct challenge. "You do know who Lena's father is, don't you?"

"Sort of."

"Well, he's the sort of man you don't want for a father-in-law, believe me, son. You'll let them go if you know what's good for you."

Roy has no idea anymore what's good for him. But he's given some encouragement when they finally pull up in Clandon Road. Jones reaches into his jacket pocket for his wallet and takes out a hundred pounds in new notes which he presses into his hand.

"Get the car fixed, son. You'll need it."

Lena is standing by the window watching this and even at this distance I can sense that man. A shadow crosses my eyes and I have to fight back the old memories, telling myself they don't matter anymore, it's all in the past and soon we can move on. I'm just rather sad that Roy is having to go through it. And I wish I could shake my mother out of her depression, because I can't help feeling it and that's bringing me down too. So I kick hard, twice.

"Who was that man?" Lena asks at last as they're finishing another silent dinner. "I've seen the car in the road."

"A spook," he almost spits the word. "Same as the grey raincoats in Leningrad only a better suit. I just wish they'd all leave us in peace. I mean, we're not interesting."

"You don't think I'm interesting?"

It's the first time he's seen her smile in weeks and they both reach a hand across the table to hold on to whatever this is. They leave the plates where they are and sit together in the lounge, watching the mid-October twilight descend around the ash tree at the entrance to the driveway. She wants to talk, to explain what's thrown her life into such disarray. She knows she's hurting him. But she's not even sure what it is. She doesn't seem able to make her own decisions anymore. He waits patiently.

"I know that... some women do get perinatal depression," she begins hesitantly. "The body's changing, hormones, chemicals..." Yes, I can vouch for that all right. "And this life now isn't exactly how we thought it would be." Maybe you didn't, mother, but there's a bigger picture than you. Don't you get that? She squeezes his hand and rests her head on his shoulder. "But I do love you, Roy." Oh, give me strength. Kick. "What I can't shake off is the feeling... no, conviction... that this baby... that Anastasia hates me."

Ah, well that's my fault, then, and I should probably do something about it. She's not stupid, this one. It's true that the old me had certain... prejudices, let's be honest, and I had to do some retraining. Maia was very strict about that. And I thought it had all been healed, back there on our mountain. But perhaps it's not so easy to be reborn after all. Clearly, traces of the past are still coming through and I'll need to face up to them when we... in due course. I'm sorry. It's not that I wish Lena any ill, as such, not personally. Yes, I'm a changeling, I'm not the child she thought she was going to have. And it's not her fault she has no idea of my consciousness — doctors just haven't caught up yet. But it will all come good eventually, in one world or another...

Still, for now I should go a bit easier on her. After all, I may be little but I've got all my fingers and toes and things and I'm nearly ready. And I do have the luxury of being able to go to sleep pretty much whenever I want. Who wouldn't like that? My dreams are lovely too, revisiting the island and my little cabin with its soap-munching rat and dear Iggy and the time my eyes opened in a cave deep underground where I met Jamie and Brother John... and I can still talk to them whenever I want. They seem nearby anyway. I have the advantage of knowing all this.

And knowing what's coming.

He lifts her head gently with one hand and kisses her, then she lets him slowly undo the buttons of her blouse and fold the silky material back over her strong shoulders before leaning forward to kiss each swelling breast gently.

Oh well.

After half-term, Roy decides it's time to take learning to another dimension.

"So, how did Li make sure her pyramids had the same volume?" he begins, drawing the shape on the blackboard and writing the formula next to it. "Calculators out, everyone."

They like these new toys that make life so much easier and hardly notice the new skills they're developing. A few children are just going along for the ride but there's a good response to the weekend's homework, calculating volumes of cupboards, tins of baked beans, dogs' kennels and the like.

Xiao Li, of course, is taking it a step further and places a small, spherical globe of the Earth on her desk. Roy passes from desk to desk, praising the simplest efforts, and pauses beside Li, intrigued by the sketch she has made of concentric circles. He smiles and encourages her to explain while he copies it on the board. She is more confident now though her voice is still quiet.

"Suppose there was another sphere around the Earth," she begins, with a collective raising of eyebrows behind her. "If it has, say, twice the volume, what would its radius be? And what if there was another one around that, then another one, and so on?"

He writes up the formula and demonstrates that the second radius is the cube root of two times that of the Earth, inviting the class to work out the next result. While half of them look blankly out of the window, watching Ian deadheading the autumn flowers, the rest manage to discover the sequence. Cube root of four, cube root of eight, cube root of sixteen... all powers of two.

"Sir, what on Earth's the flippin' point?" asks shark-boy. There's some general sniggering but Roy simply asks Li to tell him.

"Well... I suppose... we go up in powers," she shrugs. "And come back to earth in roots." There's a collective groan.

As he drives home this evening, Roy realises that this young girl has been planning all his lessons from the start. But it's not quite that she's telling him something... more that she's preparing him...

Back at the flat, while Lena sleeps, he takes a piece of paper and writes everything down, to figure out what he needs to know. Just maybe Inspector Peter Jones was right and he hasn't always made his own decisions. The thought takes him back instantly to the darkest day, waking up on a cold bench in Platt Fields with a young girl staring at him. What did she say? Whatever you decide is whatever you have to decide at the time. Not good or bad, just is.

And after that, everywhere he's been people have tried to tell him what to think and believe, how they get by in this world. Yes, sometimes it's been annoying, especially in that well-meaning way friends have. But others have cared for him. Professor Meeks believed in him and never gave up. And his short-lived friend Ashley had offered the greatest lesson of all.

The first necessity is having the courage to face life. Only when we open ourselves to annihilation do we reveal the true depths of who we are.

Yet it's the children who have really told him how it is. The girls, including Xiao Li, in their ways. And now... it's a baby.

Φ

At the end of the autumn term there is a tradition for pupils to bring in gifts for their teachers and, as the last lesson draws to a close, Roy's desk has all but disappeared beneath bottles of wine, boxes of chocolates and Christmas cards from parents thanking him for his extraordinary ability in getting their dull offspring to learn some Maths. As the cheerful chatter of the class recedes down the corridor, Xiao Li has hung back.

He watches her kindly, yet aware of a shadow flickering through his mind, the fear that a double-edged sword is about to appear. She hands him a large box.

"I thought you'd have enough bottles," she grins, "and Chinese wine isn't very good, anyway. This is for you to remember me by."

She has made a dodecahedron out of thick card, painted silver, the edges glued perfectly, and there's a hinged doorway in one of the faces. He opens it to find a white sweet in the shape of a small melon.

"It's Zaotang," she says, "malt candy. In the Little Year — what you call Yuletide — we offer it to the god Zao Shen so he will bless our homes."

"This is beautiful, Li, thank you." He turns the shape in his hands and feels a light flow of strange energy through his fingers. This is his prize for solving her puzzle but, once again, it means something more… Then he suddenly realises what she's said and opens his mouth to ask, but she's ahead of him.

"I may be going away for the New Year," she says quietly. "But I'm sure I'll see you again." And then she turns and is gone before he can say any more.

Yule is the festival of rebirth. The darkness has reached its peak and, when the longest night comes to an end, the holly surrenders to the oak and, it is said, the goddess gives birth to the Sun. As the child grows, the days become lighter, there is new hope for the future and all things that have been hidden will begin to be known.

I am ready now and begin to move myself into position, stretching my limbs and reaching my fingernails out to the edges of my warm little home. I'll be glad to leave. I can't say it's been comfortable but then it is what it is. And there's a new journey ahead. My mother is already exhausted — well, I wasn't on her agenda a few months ago and she really has no idea what's happening, poor thing. Still, needs must.

I wish I could let Roy know that it's all going to be fine, despite everything. I've tried to reach out to him but that's only made his headaches worse — they're pretty continuous now. Still, if we knew what was coming we'd only start making decisions, trying to be in control, people being what they are, instead of letting nature take its course.

But Roy does know that something momentous is building. If events themselves have not been clues enough, there is his dream during the night of December 20th.

He bursts with relief out of the Astoria's doors, straight into the arms of two burly men in grey raincoats who virtually carry him to a large black van waiting nearby. Looking back over his shoulder, he sees Lena in the centre of St Isaac's Square, watching impassively.

"Where are we going?" he demands, in rising panic.

"Big House," one man grins through crude dental metalwork.

They drive at speed along the Moyka Embankment and past the Field of Mars, arriving at a nondescript office building where he is frogmarched through endless corridors to a windowless room where a huge guard rips his shirt off and beats him with birch twigs. Sheer terror is taking hold, knowing that there is worse to come.

And now he is in a vast cathedral-like courtroom, bound in stocks before a judge wearing a Vladimir Davidovich mask who sits beneath an icon of Christ's transfiguration. To one side is a jury, a stony-faced Ray Carter alongside Meeks, Duartes, Wellesley… The judge starts to read out the charge of treason in a comical sing-song voice but suddenly Ian springs forward to untie him and drag him away along the nave to the heavy wooden doors.

"Run, laddie," he shouts, taking out the .22 Webley, "I'll hold 'em off. Just follow the waters. The waters."

With heart bursting and sweat pouring from him, he runs back beside the Moyka, follows a canal south then along the Fontanka, turning right on Rhizskiy Prospekt to the port where a Royal Navy frigate flying the white ensign is casting off. He stops, exhausted. Pounding feet are closing in behind. At the stern of the ship, Peter Jones in a white uniform throws a rope ladder down and urges him forward. But his feet are leaden, his head throbbing, and he knows there's nothing to be done. It is decided. As the ship slips away into open water, he turns into the arms of grey raincoats.

Next day, tension has gripped the flat. Lena is not talking, she refuses breakfast, she looks haunted, dazed. Nothing he tries is getting through to her so finally, in early evening, he heads into town where he props up the bar of The Seven Stars and drinks Bourbon to dull the dream still reverberating in his mind.

When he steps outside, he is approached by a small, well-rounded woman with a beautiful clear-skinned face and deep brown eyes beneath jet-black hair tied in braids with silver ribbons. She is wearing a long, colourful robe and a black bowler-type hat with a sapphire blue feather tucked into its band.

"Você precisa disso, meu amigo," she says, thrusting a large sprig of mistletoe into his hand. "It live between Heaven and Earth. It protect you."

He reaches in his pocket for some coins but she's already gone.

And now he hears the cry. He runs.

∞

In the beginning, there is nothing. It is the strangest thing imaginable, to be aware of nothing. There are no surroundings, nothing above, beside or below. Even we are not here. Yet there is no fear or pain, because we are... not. And it is beautiful. Nothing has real beauty.

Inexorably slowly, we become aware of self as we move from nothing into something. There is even a sense of loss at having to leave nothing behind. Still, we are beginning to be, even though we have no form and there is total darkness and silence.

Gradually becoming accustomed to whatever place this is, an outline of our bodies emerges and we sense, though we still cannot see, incredibly thin filaments like strands of a spider's web, too numerous to count, streaming out from these bodies. And although we still have no touch, I know that our hands are clasped together — and I shall never let go.

The darkness begins to lift and I watch curiously as the threads begin to detach themselves and float away, dissipating. There are other forms now, too, like the vague shadows of trees and beasts in a valley below a mountain beyond which the morning sun is about to rise, and the silence gives way to the soft murmurings of a gentle breeze carrying far distant sounds...

We are in a new world, prompting memories of the old.

This is what I believe happened.

Enraged by the sight of early moonlight reflecting from the binoculars in the black car outside, Lena rushes to the stairs to have it out with Jones. Upset and confused, she loses her footing. It really is as easy as that.

Roy arrives home breathlessly to find her barely conscious inside the front door in a pool of waters. There is a large red stain on the carpet. It's not paint. Kneeling over her is a man dressed in black.

"I heard her fall and cry out, Roy."

"Oh... I, um, I didn't know anyone lived down here."

"I keep myself to myself. Look, I'm a doctor. Lena's had an AFE — an embolism. She's losing blood and her heart's failing. And the baby's coming... like, now."

"I'll call an ambulance." He starts up the stairs but the man calls after him.

"I've tried. There's a pile-up on the bypass and all the emergency services have gone there. It will be quicker if you drive to St Luke's. Get some blankets."

I get myself out, the man cuts the cord and lays me in Lena's arms, all wrapped up, then helps Roy put us along the rear seat of the Ford while telling him the back streets to take. She's still bleeding but that can't be helped.

He sets off, spitting gravel, and doesn't think to ask how the man knows their names. Left, then right on York Road. It's dark now and the rain's been heavy, the car sliding as he turns down Onslow Street and into the long, straight Farnham Road. He's driving as best he can but exhaustion, dreams, whisky and the full beam headlights of the black saloon close behind are clouding his vision, all judgement failing.

He takes the turn back north onto the A3 far too fast and simply doesn't see the 35-tonne Volvo Titan truck.

We move forward, drifting without intention, and the shadows move around us too, some fading away whilst others loom up before us like great beasts inspecting these interlopers to their kingdom. Yes, a few even seem intelligent, peering intently at us, and I recognise some of them — the censorious monk and the straggly dog, the Templar knight with one arm and the woman in ragged clothes who leers scornfully in our faces... archetypes of the small mind that are no threat, nothing to fear.

We leave this place behind as though passing through a stage play into a new scene where the set hasn't yet been assembled, the rigs are unconnected and the players not yet called. But this scene does not have the peace, the beauty, of the nothing and for a moment I miss its darkness and silence. Still, we each now have a self of sorts with ill-formed and shifting bodies, almost transparent, just a kind of luminous energy. And with a body, however unfamiliar, one cannot help feeling fear, a loss of control that hasn't mattered before because it seemed meaningless. It's important now because I know he is still dazed, confused and in pain, so I move my arm around his shoulders, careful not to lose contact, in reassurance.

I reach out my other hand in front of us, my fingers at last finding that spidery, gossamer film that dissolves to the touch only to reform and envelop us in a gentle, moist embrace as we continue to move. And now again comes the thought that perhaps we aren't moving forward after all, since we have not willed it, but are entirely still as this new world comes to meet us. It is intelligent, it has a purpose, and this mist is indeed claiming us, enfolding us on all sides, becoming ever more dense.

Now I remember — we must give ourselves up to it.

Far, far ahead, there is that small light and the mist is beginning to glow with the pure white of newly fallen snow, becoming softer, gently moist and decidedly colder until it grows and grows, etched with silver and pale yellow, billowing into cumulus passing before a morning sun. We need to reach that light, yet even I am becoming exhausted by everything, by the nothing, by not being and then becoming, by the increasing effort of thought and of trying not to think.

Hold tight, Roy, this is where we let go.

Ah, this moment, if it is a moment, is beautful beyond description, like settling back into the softest imaginable mattress at the end of a hard day, and continuing to fall and to fall and to fall…

Φ

In transcendent moments, the mind lets go of reason and the self lets go of any sense of body, so we feel nothing but the unutterable joy of freedom from everything we've cared about before. All the extraordinary challenges that weighed us down for so long, all the anxieties that held us back from living fully, are now utterly unimportant. I sense his hand squeeze mine gently and turn to see a soft smile and a slight nod of the head. He may not understand yet, and he is still clearly in pain, but he knows what's happening and that he's safe.

We fall slowly and peacefully through the cumulus until very gradually it begins to thin out. Having been here before, I observe all that is happening to us dispassionately, knowing that when this new world has us fully within its grasp there will be no harsh and abrupt rocky landing. And yes, I know that we are free and we are greater than we have ever been.

We simply emerge onto relatively solid ground and with some feeling in our lower bodies there is a sense of beginning to learn how to walk again. We can still barely see our own hands in front of us, enveloped as we are in that soft, moist white mist we had entered before. But it is not so cold or dense and there ahead of us is still that light, much brighter now and clawing its way through the swirls of vapour as though parting one net curtain after another.

Almost involuntarily, I began to pick up the pace and encourage him forward, knowing that there will be some kind of path ahead, a path that's indistinct yet well-trodden. And with a small leap of joy I begin to feel something swirl around our feet like long grasses or perhaps small animals playing with these strange, lumbering invaders of their territory. All the while, the mist is thinning out and the light is becoming warmer as our senses begin to return, if still just out of reach. But nothing is certain yet, so better just to

∞

trust that life knows what it's doing and let things take their course.

I've heard it said that a bright path can seem dim, that going forward can seem like retreat and what once was easy becomes hard. No talent ever seems enough. But then, the greatest form has no shape.

The path is hidden and has no name.

And perhaps I haven't understood the plan fully, or I wasn't given all the details, because I definitely haven't expected what happens now. There is the sickening realisation that at the end of the day, as it were, we are all on our own and make our own choices, responsible only to ourselves. It hits me like a bolt to the head, clouding the mind that a moment ago had felt so clear and light with tendrils of fear I thought overcome long ago.

His grip loosens and he begins to draw away from me, holding back and, as his own senses return, looking around urgently.

Now I see her too. In the distance, still enshrouded by the soft white mist yet gradually emerging into her own light, is Lena. Even from afar I can sense her distress, her pain and utter solitude, having no idea where she is or why — and I can sense that he feels it too, his own grief still raw. It pulls him towards her, forcing his way through tall, stinging grasses and curtains of swirling cloud, because now he knows that he can help her to let go. I have shown him how.

There is nothing I can do. Because everything I have done has been to allow him to be free. I just didn't realise that meant...

Feeling numb, I walk on unsteadily for what seems timeless ages, stumbling over stones and hillocks, my eyes adjusting as colours emerge from the mist to welcome me and then retreat, seeing that I feel no pleasure. The beach is still a surprise, though. The soft sand glistens silver and yields to my steps leaving traces of water in their prints. And not far away is the faint but unmistakable sound of gently lapping waves.

I know where I am now. The dreamlike journey is coming to an end and I am arriving in a real place. And with this arrival, however reassuring, I suddenly feel incredibly tired. I have used every kind of strength I possess to get here, across islands and through transformations, and all shreds of comprehension I have nurtured now disappear, confusion flooding through me as though the dam of resilience has been breached by some great and terrible storm.

I must keep going, I can still escape the onslaught and destruction if I just put one foot in front of the other, one arm forward then the other, scanning the way and allowing primaeval instinct to move me along that beach. I am past caring whether this is the right direction. Stumbling, sinking in, pausing to fight off tears. And as my eyes clear I see the two figures far in the distance, stumbling together but almost at the shoreline.

The small craft with stubby wings sits a little way ahead, waves of light reflecting from the water and flowing over its silvery body. And there's the angel in a white trouser suit and red high-heeled shoes. As I limp closer, she smiles her beautiful welcome.

"It's good to see you again," she says, "though I seem to have been waiting ages." The door opens silently and she helps me inside, wrapping a blanket around me and locking a belt in place. "There may be a bit of turbulence."

She must see the question in my eyes because she puts a soft hand on my shoulder to calm me.

"Don't worry, you'll see him again soon. Now—" more business-like, "—where shall we go this time?"

Φ

ROUNDFIRE
BOOKS

FICTION

Put simply, we publish great stories. Whether it's literary or popular, a gentle tale or a pulsating thriller, the connecting theme in all Roundfire fiction titles is that once you pick them up you won't want to put them down.
If you have enjoyed this book, why not tell other readers by posting a review on your preferred book site.

Recent Bestsellers from Roundfire are:

The Bookseller's Sonnets
Andi Rosenthal
The Bookseller's Sonnets intertwines three love stories with a
tale of religious identity and mystery spanning five hundred
years and three countries.
Paperback: 978-1-84694-342-3 ebook: 978-184694-626-4

Birds of the Nile
An Egyptian Adventure
N.E. David
Ex-diplomat Michael Blake wanted a quiet birding trip up the
Nile – he wasn't expecting a revolution.
Paperback: 978-1-78279-158-4 ebook: 978-1-78279-157-7

Blood Profit$
The Lithium Conspiracy
J. Victor Tomaszek, James N. Patrick, Sr.
The blood of the many for the profits of the few... *Blood Profit$*
will take you into the cigar-smoke-filled room where American
policy and laws are really made.
Paperback: 978-1-78279-483-7 ebook: 978-1-78279-277-2

The Burden
A Family Saga
N.E. David
Frank will do anything to keep his mother and father
apart. But he's carrying baggage – and it might just weigh
him down ...
Paperback: 978-1-78279-936-8 ebook: 978-1-78279-937-5

The Cause

Roderick Vincent

The second American Revolution will be a fire lit from an internal spark.

Paperback: 978-1-78279-763-0 ebook: 978-1-78279-762-3

Don't Drink and Fly

The Story of Bernice O'Hanlon: Part One

Cathie Devitt

Bernice is a witch living in Glasgow. She loses her way in her life and wanders off the beaten track looking for the garden of enlightenment.

Paperback: 978-1-78279-016-7 ebook: 978-1-78279-015-0

Gag

Melissa Unger

One rainy afternoon in a Brooklyn diner, Peter Howland punctures an egg with his fork. Repulsed, Peter pushes the plate away and never eats again.

Paperback: 978-1-78279-564-3 ebook: 978-1-78279-563-6

The Master Yeshua

The Undiscovered Gospel of Joseph

Joyce Luck

Jesus is not who you think he is. The year is 75 CE. Joseph ben Jude is frail and ailing, but he has a prophecy to fulfil ...

Paperback: 978-1-78279-974-0 ebook: 978-1-78279-975-7

On the Far Side, There's a Boy
Paula Coston

Martine Haslett, a thirty-something 1980s woman, plays hard on the fringes of the London drag club scene until one night which prompts her to sign up to a charity. She writes to a young Sri Lankan boy, with consequences far and long.
Paperback: 978-1-78279-574-2 ebook: 978-1-78279-573-5

Tuareg
Alberto Vazquez-Figueroa

With over 5 million copies sold worldwide, *Tuareg* is a classic adventure story from best-selling author Alberto Vazquez-Figueroa, about honour, revenge and a clash of cultures.
Paperback: 978-1-84694-192-4

Readers of ebooks can buy or view any of these bestsellers by clicking on the live link in the title. Most titles are published in paperback and as an ebook. Paperbacks are available in traditional bookshops. Both print and ebook formats are available online.

Find more titles and sign up to our readers' newsletter, visit: www.collectiveinkbooks.com/fiction